FULL OF IT

FULL OF IT

Wendy French

A Tom Doherty Associates Book
New York

This is a work of fiction. All of the characters, organizations, and events portrayed in this novel are either products of the author's imagination or are used fictitiously.

FULL OF IT

A Forge Book
Published by Tom Doherty Associates, LLC
175 Fifth Avenue
New York, NY 10010

www.tor-forge.com

Forge® is a registered trademark of Tom Doherty Associates, LLC.

Library of Congress Cataloging-in-Publication Data

French, Wendy.
    Full of it / Wendy French.—1st ed.
        p. cm.
    "A Tom Doherty Associates book."
    ISBN-13: 978-0-7653-1377-5
    ISBN-10: 0-7653-1377-4
      1. Divorced women—Fiction.   2. Chick lit.   I. Title.
    PS3606.R468F86 2007
    813'.6—dc22

                                            2007008204

First Edition: July 2007

Printed in the United States of America

0 9 8 7 6 5 4 3 2 1

For Ryan Griffiths, Jennifer Goodall, Paul Halvorson, and Lisa Haas, dear friends who are full of a lot of things, but mainly mischief

ACKNOWLEDGMENTS

As always, I'd like to thank my intrepid agent, Sally Harding, who never fails to lift my spirits, and my editor, Paul Stevens, who has shown tremendous patience with me on the ridiculously long and bumpy road to the completion of this book.

I'd also like to thank my parents, Sally and Stuart McDonald, who always come through in the crunch.

And finally, Kris "Pity!" Hammond, who is still giving me grief for the oversight in the last book.

FULL OF IT

One

I HAVE A big mouth.

This doesn't mean that my face should grace the pages of Guinness, eyes bulging wildly as I strain to stretch my lips around thirty-one asparagus spears or the splintered end of a two-by-four.

It doesn't mean I have thick, juicy lips, or a wide grin, packed with an enamel army of pristine white teeth.

My big mouth isn't a physical characteristic, *it's a character flaw.*

It's my very own San Andreas fault, geographically positioned an equal distance from both my pointy chin and pointier nose. It may not tremble, and it may not crack, but it is *always* on the brink of doing major damage to myself and the people around me.

I've cursed it and been cursed *for* it since day one, but that's never stopped me from saying things without thinking, and throughout my twenty-six years, my tendency to blurt has continually landed me on the wrong side of a spanking, a cold shoulder, and everything in between.

"You forgot," Rachel groaned.

I'd just returned to our shared desk after running a lunch hour gauntlet that included U.S. Bank, Walgreens, Hollywood Video, and a high-speed pursuit of sustenance at a McDonald's drive-through.

"I can't *believe* you forgot," she said, then flipped her thick blonde braid over her shoulder, trained her striking blue eyes on me, and begged, "*Please* tell me you didn't forget."

"The coffee?" I asked, dropping my knapsack beneath the desk and slipping out of my navy peacoat. "No," I assured her, "I didn't forget."

"Thank *god*," she grinned, exposing the slightly overlapping tooth most men in the office found strangely intoxicating. This I knew because a traitor to their team—a surly claims adjuster called Keith—had told me about "the list." My best friend, Rachel (and her snaggletooth), had ranked number one until Sue Parsons in Accounting got a boob job and suddenly shot from seventeen to the top spot.

And me? I didn't know if I was even *on* the list and, to be honest, I wasn't sure whether it would be more humiliating to be a hit or a miss.

What if Randy Johnson, the creepy little troll in Claims, wanted to have sex with me?

Even worse: what if he didn't?

"So, where is it?" Rachel asked, peering over my shoulder at the swirling mass of paperwork covering my desk. I needed a proper filing system, though a shredder sounded much more appetizing.

"I didn't get any," I told her, shuddering at the sight of the Johnson file. That one could wait.

Indefinitely.

"What?" Rachel asked, and I looked up to see the crease of a worry line marring her otherwise flawless forehead. "But you just said—"

"That I didn't *forget*, Rach. The fact is, I didn't have time."

"No time, huh?" She leaned toward me and sniffed. "Is that a chickenesque McScent you're wearing?"

I averted my gaze and murmured, "McPossibly."

"Lauren." Her tone was as stern as my ninth grade P.E. teacher's, and I half expected her to demand I do laps of the building.

"Okay," I said, raising my hands in surrender. "Yes, I grabbed lunch."

"That's not lunch, it's toxic waste," she said, making no effort to hide her disdain.

"Yup, with a side of fries."

She grumbled about caffeine deprivation and I waited for the high-speed technology of my PC to join me in the present moment. I absently stared at the handleless ceramic mug I'd cleverly converted into a desktop pen corral, jam-packed with ballpoints, pencils, and even a pair of scissors. While my computer grunted and beeped its way back to life, I daydreamed about storming the office supply market with a new product line guaranteed to buy me early retirement: *Office Transformers.*

As usual, in mere seconds, the idea shifted away from the bright glow of brilliance to the shadowed caves of stupidity.

Ingenious, Lauren. Surely you are the only person on the planet with a broken mug full of pens.

Stick to Insurance, at least it's a paycheck.

"I was going to have a mocha latte," Rachel said, pointing at the wide, clear surface of her half of the desk. "Right *here.*" She paused for a moment. "With *cinnamon.*" She rested her delicately rounded chin in her perfect palms and stared despondently at the shriveled spider fern on my desk.

For crying out loud, it was coffee, not a heart transplant.

"Put it toward your student loan," I told her, typing my password.

"Excuse me?"

"Or your Visa bill." I shrugged, frowning as the system rejected me. I hit the Caps Lock button and gave it another go, this time successfully.

Rachel asked, "Are you referring to the *four bucks* that you—"

"Saved on your behalf?" I finished for her, then turned to meet a surprisingly angry gaze. *What was her problem?* "Hey, four bucks a pop adds up and—"

She raised a hand to stop me. "Lauren, I don't think you should be getting into *my* money situation." She continued to glare at me, for no apparent reason.

"*Lack* of money situation, you mean," I said, wiggling in my chair. I could tell that someone had "borrowed" it in my absence, sabotaging all of my ergonomic efforts. I immediately began lifting levers and turning dials to tweak it back into my ideal setting, muttering under my breath.

"The mouth," Rachel murmured, as she tucked a small stack of papers into a yellow folder and deposited it in her out-box, which was as full as my in.

"What?" I asked, finally settling comfortably in my chair and sipping borderline icy orange spice tea from a chipped Oregon Museum of Science and Industry mug.

"Your *mouth*," she repeated, lightly glossed lips pursed in disapproval.

"What?" I asked again, totally lost. "I didn't say anything."

Did I?

I replayed the conversation in my head, looking for objectionable lowlights. There were none that I could recall.

While I was mulling over her sour mood, a couple of adjusters came through the front door on their return from lunch and gave us their usual cursory nods.

"Assholes," I muttered.

"Sorry?" the shorter guy asked, as he straightened his tie.

"Oh, nothing," I stammered. "I was just talking to myself."

"Okay," he said, skeptically. "Well, you have a good day." The comment and a bonus leer were directed solely at Rachel, who was oblivious to her power over the male population.

"Oh my god, Lauren," she groaned when the two men had left us alone, "you should wear one of those collars that silences barking dogs." She shook her head and a couple of golden hairs broke loose from her braid with the movement, picking up added shine from the fluorescent lights above us.

"Nice, Rachel. Thanks a lot."

Not that a shock collar wouldn't have saved me from time to time.

"Just a quick blast to the vocal cords," Rachel continued, with a sharp laugh.

"Yeah, great idea," I said, rolling my eyes. "So, how would the collar differentiate between the things I should and shouldn't say?"

She leaned toward me conspiratorially and whispered, "Laur, ninety percent of what you say is a mistake, and the rest is questionable, at best."

"Okay," I said, waving at Candace the half-wit as she walked by on her way to the break room, wearing enough bangles and bracelets to sound like half a dozen wind chimes in a freaking tornado. I turned back to Rachel, growing exasperated, and asked, "What exactly did I *say*?"

"I can see the packaging now," she said, laughing again. "They'd call it *Blurt Alert*. Gavin could design the logo, but the marketing campaign? That would be *all you*."

"Hey," I said, perhaps a couple of decibels too loudly, considering Kevin and Scott were passing our desk on the way to their weekly meeting with Knutsen. "Are you or are you not living under a mounting pile of debt?"

Scott snickered, but kept walking.

"Lauren!" Rachel gasped. "I already told you—"

"All about it," I said. "That credit card is your constant companion, Rach, and—"

"Hey! Back off, Peterson," she said, rising from her chair and grabbing an empty Aquafina bottle from her desk. She moved toward the break room to fill it.

"What did I *say*?" I asked, utterly bewildered.

"Let's just end the discussion before I say something I regret, too," she snapped, over her shoulder.

"But I *don't* regret anything I said," I called after her. All I'd done was state the facts, for crying out loud.

She turned to shoot me an unwarranted dirty look and said, "I am walking away, Lauren."

Yeesh. My best friend, the emotional mystery.

Grateful for the momentary break from her crappy mood, I decided to tackle my backlog of paperwork. I pulled a pile of folders, painstakingly labeled by someone who clearly cared far more than I did, toward me. But rather than attacking the pile, I simply stared at it, wishing it would miraculously disappear, much like the four hundred thousand dollars that landed our former vice president in a prison cell substantially larger than my work space, though less comfortable, I was sure.

When Rachel returned with a full bottle of water and the same attitude, made apparent by her jerky movements, dour expression, and utter silence, I was still staring at the stack of files. Five minutes later, however, I'd moved on . . . to staring blankly at my surroundings.

My best guess was that whoever painted the west wall pale beige and its eastern counterpart a slightly darker beige (which would have gone unnoticed by anyone who hadn't spent countless hours transfixed by boredom, as I had) was guided by the firm hand of an actuary, who had somehow calculated the odds of a Knutsen employee being startled by the sight of a blue or yellow wall, tripping over their feet in wonder, and filing a worker's comp or medical insurance claim for their injuries, hitting Knutsen right in the pocketbook.

The only artwork displayed in the foyer was a small collection of black-and-white photographs, depicting pastoral scenes whose blandness was only upstaged by the cream vase to the left of my desk, filled with polyester-blend flowers in various shades of yawn.

I thought of the previous month's Bring Your Child to Work Day, when the building had been overrun with eager little faces, thrilled to be missing out on the mundane schedule of their elementary school programs, even for a day.

By the morning coffee break, those faces had lost some color, and by noon, the children were listless and wan. As I'd watched them exit the building after what had to have been the longest day of their young lives, I wondered how many would vow to pursue their dreams instead of a paycheck, and how many wished they'd just spent the damn day at school, where they wouldn't have had to watch their mothers slurping cheap, stale coffee and ignoring the flames of hell, licking the rubber soles of their Naturalizer shoes.

I sighed.

So what am I doing here?

Doesn't life have more in store for me than this?

Before I could wander any further into wondering, my phone rang.

"Knutsen Insurance, this is Lauren."

"Honey, it's Mom."

I could practically smell the SPF 30 through the receiver and I glanced at the framed photo of my folks next to my monitor with a smile.

They wore matching royal blue and green tropical print shirts in front of a fabulous sunset I would have thought was fake, had I not known they'd embarked on their retirement by moving from the Portland home where they'd raised me to *Florida* six months earlier.

So far, they'd survived three "adventures," which anyone else, including meteorologists or kindergarten students, would recognize as "hurricanes."

"Dad and I are at the airport," Mom continued.

"Already?" I asked, checking my watch.

"We're early for everything these days, hon. Doctor's appointments, the brunch buffet at the hotel down the street, and now, the airport. It's just as well we have the spare time, though. After we'd filled four tubs with our belts, watches, shoes, cosmetics, cell phones, and that pesky laptop, your father made a silly remark when he went through the X-ray, and now the Gestapo has stepped in for an impromptu interrogation and possible strip search. They have no sense of humor, whatsoever."

Good grief. What was Dad thinking? "Yeah, but in a post-9/11 atmosphere—"

"I know, I know," she sighed. "But does your father *really* look like he poses a threat to national security?"

"Nope." He looked like the accountant he'd been for more than thirty years.

"And tell me, do *I* look like a terrorist?"

"Well—" I hedged.

"They confiscated my deodorant, Lauren."

"Was it Secret?" I couldn't resist asking.

"It was Ban, Smarty-pants."

"And now it's Banned," I laughed.

"True enough. Personal hygiene be damned, I suppose. So, did you talk to your boss?" she asked, hopefully.

"I wished him a good morning when I came in." Mr. Knutsen had frowned in response, then glanced rather pointedly at his watch. I was ten minutes late, and as my heels clicked against the skidproof linoleum, I'd considered that if he was the whiz everyone claimed he was, he should have come up with some kind of tardiness insurance for me, so he could not only charge me an annual premium, but hit me with a deductible once a week.

Well, more like three times, actually.

"You know what I'm talking about," Mom said.

"Yes, and I won't be able to get the time off." The lie slipped through my lips before I'd given it a thought.

"He said that?"

"She wasn't immediate family, Mom," I said, hoping that would be explanation enough.

Of course, it wasn't.

"She was your *great-aunt*," my mother said, over the din of distant boarding announcements.

"Exactly. Not *immediate* family." I pulled the top file from my stack and glanced at the contents. *Car accident.* I set it aside, the first item in a brand new stack-to-be.

"Did he offer a partial day, at least?" Mom asked.

I slowly inhaled then released the breath, weighing the pros and cons of continuing down the path I was on.

"Look, I haven't even asked him," I admitted, with a sigh.

"You think I don't *know* that?" Mom chuckled, grimly. "Please make the effort, will you? It's important."

"Mom, I guarantee Aunt Ida's too busy either sprouting wings or trying to score a flame-retardant jumpsuit to give a rat's ass about whether I'm a no-show at the funeral."

My comment was greeted with chilly silence.

Oops.

When she finally did speak, there was an edge to her voice. "I meant that it's important to *me*," she said, quietly. "You and Ida may not have known each other well, but she was the last of her generation. My *mother's* generation."

"Mom, I—"

"I've got to check on your father," she said. "We'll see you at six, and Tim's flight gets in just after us."

"Tim's coming?" I sighed.

Just what I need.

"He's your *brother.*"

"So you say," I muttered.

"*Lauren,*" she warned.

"What? I just like to leave a little room for doubt, considering."

"Considering what?"

"That he's a total weenie."

It was her turn to sigh. "We'll see you in a few hours."

When I hung up the phone, Rachel tilted her head and gave me a quizzical look. "What's going on?"

"My Aunt Ida died," I told her.

She winced, and the anger she'd been misdirecting at me immediately faded away, replaced by sympathy. "Laur, you never even *mentioned* it."

"It happened a couple of days ago, and I guess it's sort of been sinking in," I told her. "My parents are flying in tonight."

"Aunt Ida . . ." Rachel murmured, blonde eyebrows furrowed. "Was she the one here in town?"

"Yup."

"I never met her." She paused. "What happened?"

I shrugged. "She just kind of dropped dead, I guess."

Rachel shook her head, braid swishing against the silk of her periwinkle blouse. "*Very* tactful, Laur."

"What? She was, like, a hundred years old."

"You're unbelievable," she sighed. "So when's the funeral?"

"Friday."

"Which means you've only got a couple of days to get your grief under control," she said, with the hint of a smirk.

"Do I detect a note of sarcasm?" I asked.

"A note? Actually, it's more of a symphony, Supersleuth."

I faked a chuckle and turned back to my paperwork, my heart sinking over Mom's insistence that I attend the main event.

I'd never been a fan of funerals, and always figured that when my time came I'd like people to have a party and share amusing anecdotes about me instead of sitting in a solemn church, listening to a minister's voice bouncing against the high ceilings as he spoke of me in soft, generic terms, as though I'd never kicked Ben McDowell in the nuts when I was eleven or taken out two park benches and an astonished squirrel on my driving test. I didn't want some heavily powdered spinster to adjust her huge, googly glasses and smile to herself as she caressed the keys of an organ, playing a song I didn't know, which had been deemed *appropriate,* when I would have chosen something more along the lines of Quiet Riot's "Cum on, Feel the Noize," just to get some toes tapping.

I'd always hated funerals, but I was feeling especially leery of this one.

"What's wrong?" Rachel asked.

"Nothing," I said, absently.

Ida had never married or had children.

She'd spent her entire life alone.

"Is it Daniel?"

"No," I told her, but in a way, it was.

I'd broken off our engagement a couple of months earlier, which had been a grueling and heartbreaking process I never wanted to repeat. *Ever.*

And, the truth was, I had mixed feelings about Ida's circumstances.

Sure, she'd undoubtedly been lonely, but her spinsterhood meant that *she'd* never had to field countless questions about what went wrong with her relationship, or wonder who was fueling the ever-productive rumor mill. Aunt Ida never had to split up the proceeds of an eight-year pairing, pausing only to negotiate who kept chipped plates or lidless Tupperware. *She* didn't have to bargain for which friendships she got to keep, or prove which CDs she'd owned before she'd moved in.

But most importantly, Aunt Ida didn't have to wonder whether there was a perfect partner out there, waiting for her.

Her life was over, while mine was spread out before me like a blank canvas. Hell, I wasn't even sure where to find paint.

While the apartment I'd shared with Rachel since the split seemed impossibly cramped, part of me envied the compact design of the casket I imagined Ida would be buried in, and the white satin pillow she'd rest her worry-free head upon.

"Lauren." Rachel laid a manicured hand on my arm. "What is it?"

"Nothing," I said, trying to shake it off. "I guess I'm just sad about Ida."

The truth was, I felt terrified I'd end up just like her and die alone.

"Did Knutsen give you the day off for the funeral?"

"I haven't asked," I told her.

"I'm sure he would."

Unfortunately, when I spoke to him ten minutes later, he did.

Two

I DROVE HOME from work to change my clothes and have a quick snack before retrieving my family from the airport, and by the time I'd showered and made myself somewhat presentable, I was running late.

Surprise.

I tossed the sweaters, fast food wrappers, and plastic Safeway bags that seemed to breed on my backseat into the trunk, quickly swept the questionable grit from my front passenger seat into the footwell and climbed inside for the half hour drive.

Traffic was appalling, as usual, and my CD player was on the fritz, so I had the radio tuned in to NRK. Sitting in a traffic jam, appeasing my gnawing hunger by picking at the top of a stale bran muffin I'd found in the glove compartment, a sudden downpour of rain pelting my windshield and an utterly foreign techno beat assaulting my senses, I felt not only tired, but *old*.

I glanced in the rearview mirror.

There was a new, uninvited crease between my eyebrows, and I had the sneaking suspicion it was permanent. I could see laugh lines—just like my mother's—at the corners of my green eyes and bracketing my thin lips.

I was twenty-six years old, and I'd plucked two grey hairs from my scalp that very morning.

Old.

Old and alone.

I arrived at the airport ten minutes late, which turned out to be early, thanks to a delay of some kind in Denver. My brother's flight was late too, so I killed time wandering through Powell's Books and admiring the wonders of the PDX food court. Eventually, I walked the teal carpet to the arrivals area and joined the masses of bored nontravelers waiting for friends, loved ones, and, as various handwritten signs could attest, complete strangers.

❧ Hurricanes aside, part of me was happy for Mom and Dad's new life in Florida, but most of me wished they hadn't moved away. Portland seemed . . . *emptier* without them. It wasn't just the Sunday dinners I missed, or the holidays. What I'd lost was the sensation of stepping through a door that had been open to me for an entire lifetime and into a family fold that was consistently warm and welcoming. No matter what happened out in the world, there was a safe place to go.

At least, there had been.

I'd only visited their condo once, and the pullout bed had been almost as disappointing as my parents' frantic schedule. They were happy as clams, enjoying table tennis one night and a guided ornithological walk the next. Water aerobics three mornings a week, and tai chi the other four. Everyone in their complex was involved in various "programs" and it turned out that if Mom and Dad happened to miss a bocce game because their daughter had flown thousands of miles to see them, they'd be ostracized.

It seemed my parents had bought a condo and sold their souls.

After several minutes, during which I watched lovers reunite and kids complain about being tired, hungry, or both, my mother appeared at the gate.

"There she is," Mom said, hustling through the crowd and pulling me into a tight embrace, enhanced by her powder blue velour tracksuit.

Sporty.

❧ "It's good to see you," I murmured into her neck. It was even better to *feel* her, as nothing on earth could compete with the soothing effects of a maternal hug.

She released me and I was able to admire the suntan I wouldn't have until the following August.

"You look well, honey. Healthy," she said, grinning.

"And it looks like Florida agrees with you."

"Well," she said, with a light peal of laughter, "we bicker a bit during the stormy season, but for the most part, we get along."

"Where's Dad?" I asked, scanning the endless stream of faces pouring past us.

"He got to talking with a museum curator on the plane and, well, you know how he is."

"*All too well.*"

Mom and I had been the same height since I was in eleventh grade, but she was suddenly shorter than me.

"What are you, shrinking?" I asked.

"I'm getting old, Laur. My bones are doing whatever they do during menopause. I'll probably be down to your shoulder by Christmas," she said, with a laugh.

"And you got a perm," I said, admiring her chestnut curls. "It looks great." And it did, but I couldn't imagine why anyone with straight hair would want to curl it. I patted my own wiry mass and figured we looked more related than ever.

"There we go," she said, waving at the man at least a head taller than anyone around him, as he forged his way toward us.

"Dad," I murmured, wrapping my arms around his windbreaker-clad torso.

He gave me a squeeze. "You look well."

"So do you."

He released me and adjusted his glasses before smoothing his thinning but still mostly sandy brown hair back into place with slender fingers. "It's the racquetball, I think. I just love how it gets my juices flowing."

Mom slung her purse over her shoulder and I grabbed her bag. "Let's get out of the way, here," she said, moving toward the lounge and continuing to talk as she walked. "We got a room at the Red Lion, figuring you'd be short on space. Tim will stay there too."

Dad added, "He had some kind of a business meeting in Seattle, and he arranged a stopover to attend the funeral. But don't worry, we'll all be out of your hair on Friday night."

I had no desire to share my parents with my big brother when the visit was going to be so short.

Leading us to three empty chairs in a room packed with weary masses, Mom slipped out of her jacket.

"Wow, that's some shirt," I said, slightly alarmed by the hippie nature of her purple tee, which was splattered with a baffling pattern of pale dots and lines.

"Batik," she said with a shrug. "Dad and I took a class."

A couple of seconds passed before my head wrapped around the idea. I turned to face the man I thought I knew.

"*You* have a batik T-shirt?" I asked, wondering if I would have recognized him if he'd arrived wearing it.

"No, no." He laughed, exposing an errant grain of pepper held hostage by his two front teeth.

"Good," I told him, relieved.

"Mine's a tank top."

As if I needed to entertain the image of my sixty-year-old father wandering around Florida in a batik wife-beater, black socks, and sandals.

"Isn't that . . . *something*," I said, my throat strangling the words on their way out.

He smiled again, with what I interpreted as pride over his artistic achievement, then something behind me caught his eye.

"Tim!" Dad called. "Over here!"

I turned to see my brother, looking both bigger and balder than when I'd seen him last, moving toward us in slow, measured steps, his unbridled enthusiasm on display, as usual. He extended a hand toward Dad, who laughed and pulled him into a hug, creasing his suit.

When he was free of the paternal grip, Tim straightened his tie and frowned as he glanced over his shoulder to make sure none of the people he'd never see again in this lifetime had seen him embrace his own father.

What a putz.

"Tim," I said, as I stepped toward him and offered a limp hug. He smelled like citrus and cigarettes. "Nice to see you," I lied.

"You too," he said, his lack of sincerity rivaling mine. He let go and looked me over from head to toe. "You look good, Lauren. *Well.*" Before I could respond, he looked over my shoulder and grinned, exposing square, horselike teeth. "*Mom.*"

At least he was genuinely happy to see one of us.

"So, Tim," I said, once he'd finished fawning over Mom, who giggled like a teenager at the attention. "Did you check any bags?"

"No, it's all in here," he said, pointing to a grey wheeled suitcase.

"Same as us," Dad said cheerfully, tilting his head toward the mammoth orange case at his feet. "So we're off and running, aren't we?"

IT TURNED OUT that Tim had rented a car, which he'd neglected to mention to any of us, so when Mom commented on the time change and her hankering for a teriyaki chicken sandwich, we split up for the drive to the Red Robin in town, which was not only right by their hotel, but somewhere we knew we could eat fairly quickly and comfortably.

Mom rode with me, and it was nice to have a few moments alone.

That is, until we started talking.

"So, things are working out at Rachel's place?" she asked, once I'd merged onto Highway 84.

"Yeah. She's rarely there, since she's dating this guy, Steven."

"You like him?"

"He's great," I told her. And he was. Rachel had managed to find a genuinely nice guy who took the time to write and mail her love letters from just a couple of miles away. He cooked her dinner at least twice a week and even packed her a lunch for work when she stayed overnight.

He tucked love notes in with her sandwich or salad.

"Have you thought about branching out a bit when you move on?" Mom asked. "I know Beaverton is home, but the suburbs aren't for young, single people. There's plenty more out there to experience."

"Branch out?" I murmured, tapping the brakes as a Jetta swooped in front of me, boasting a "Keep Portland weird" bumper sticker. "Well, I'm sure the city has more than its fair share of leafy limbs, but right now I kind of feel like clinging to the trunk, if you know what I mean."

I passed a lurching school bus packed with kids who must have been on their way to or from a field trip or outdoor camp and found myself longing for the simpler days of playgrounds and recess.

"I understand," Mom said, and silence filled the Toyota for a moment before she spoke again. "I don't know if this would be of interest, but Dad and I were looking at promotional materials for one of the cruise lines the other day and thinking of you."

I tried to make the connection and failed. "I'm not sure I follow."

"There are *singles* cruises for young people, hon."

"Mom," I warned, laying on my horn as the Jetta darted halfway out of my lane and back again.

"Just an idea," she said, raising her hands in surrender. "Something to think about."

All I could think about was Gopher from *The Love Boat,* whom I'd had a significant crush on in the fifth grade. And Doc, who found reasons to showcase his jump rope skills in an extraordinary number of episodes.

A singles cruise?

"I don't think I'm the cruising type, Mom."

"Dad and I just thought might be a good way to meet people," she continued.

"I *know* people," I reminded her, edging past the idiot driving the Jetta, who was naturally yammering on a cell phone. I hoped my "Hang up and drive" bumper sticker didn't escape their attention.

"*Honey,*" she sighed.

Here we go.

Again.

"Look, the concept of meeting someone or dating is terrifying, Mom. I think I've mentioned that *several* times already."

Several thousand times, actually.

"Well then, what if you meet someone you already know?"

"Meaning what?"

"Well, Don Nguyen's son is divorced . . . and training to be a chiropractor."

"And he's a good five years younger than me."

"Three or four years, at the most, Laur."

"Look, I don't have time to renew my babysitter's license right now."

She let the topic of dating lie for the remainder of the trip, and even managed to hold back on driving tips when I rocketed onto the Lloyd Center exit ramp at twice the posted speed limit.

"SO, WHAT HAPPENED?" Tim asked, when we'd all settled into our squeaky vinyl booth at the Red Robin on Northeast Grand. "To Ida, I mean."

"She *died*, Tim," I said, sarcastically.

He scowled at me. "Is it a crime to want the details?" He turned to Mom. "How did it happen?"

"She was at Safeway, and—"

"Which one?" I asked.

"Does it matter?" Tim snapped, smoothing his few hairs into place.

"Hey, you're the one who wanted details."

"It was the one by her house, on Sandy Boulevard," Mom explained. "They were having a big sale, and—"

"On what?" I asked, naturally curious.

"Good grief," Tim groaned. "Can we get to the point?"

I glared at him, still angry over countless childhood slights and fights. "Geez, it seems you're as short on patience as you are on hair," I snapped, eyeing his shiny pate.

"Lauren," Mom warned, before continuing, "It was a meat sale. Pork, I think. Anyway, she was pushing a cart instead of using the motorized vehicle her doctor had recommended."

"The Speed-Walker," I said. "Which has to be the dumbest product name on earth."

"Let her finish, Laur," Dad said, glancing up from his menu.

"There isn't much more to it," Mom said. "She collapsed in the meat department. One of the store managers knew CPR, so he tried to resuscitate her, but she was gone." She quietly snapped her fingers. "Like that."

"A shame," Dad said, gaze returning to the menu. "She was quite a character."

"It really makes you think, doesn't it?" Mom asked, then bit her lip.

"Yeah," I agreed. "I think I don't want to keel over in the meat department during a gigantic pork sale, if that's what you mean."

"Lauren!" she gasped. "What's gotten into you?"

"She's always been like this," Tim assured her, rolling his beady eyes. "Tactless."

"She's a straight shooter," Dad said, without looking up from the menu. "Nothing wrong with that."

"Unless she's aiming for vital organs," Tim said to me, then directed his attention toward Mom. "So, can we sue Safeway?"

"And *I'm* supposed to be the tactless one?" I asked, lifting my menu and allowing them continue the conversation without me.

As if dying alone wasn't bad enough, she'd passed away in a *grocery store*, with strangers gathered around her, gawking.

The thought made me queasy.

"Are you listening?" Mom asked, interrupting my runaway train of thought.

"Hmm?" I scanned the laminated menu in front of me, trying to think of anything but lying in a fetal position at the end of aisle seven.

Chicken or beef?

A burger loaded with mushrooms would probably do the trick.

"I *said*, that was very rude." Mom sounded annoyed.

"What?" I asked, taken aback.

"Your comment about Ida's demise. The keeling over business."

My gaze met hers. "Mom, you just told me that's what happened to her."

Dad cleared his throat before speaking. "I think she means that 'keeling over' is not an appropriate description of the event." He glanced back at his menu and asked no one in particular, "When they say *bottomless* fries, are they serious?"

"Yes," my brother Tim said, loosening a paisley tie that looked tight enough to decapitate him.

"As in *no limit*?" Dad asked, peering at his son through freshly polished glasses.

"Yes," Tim assured him.

"I can eat as many as I want?" His tone was incredulous.

"*Yes,*" Mom and I groaned, in unison.

Dad chuckled and shook his head in wonder. "How can they afford to do that?"

"Dad, we're talking fries, not fois gras," Tim sniffed, his inner snob surfacing.

"Been watching the Food Network again, huh?" I asked him. "Next you'll be telling us how marshmallows are made, or maybe educating us on the history of the Dorito."

"Lauren," Dad warned, taking over for Mom as the parental referee.

"What?" I raised my hands in self-defense. "I can't *wait* to hear more of Tim's wisdom."

There was a time when I'd actually looked up to the guy, but those days had ended when I realized he'd never see me as anything more than an immature pest.

I thought of the awkwardness of Tim resting an arm on my shoulder while I faked a smile for the annual Christmas photo Mom liked to send out of us looking like a perfectly well-adjusted family.

I glanced across the table at Mom and Dad, who truly were well-adjusted, and wished Tim and I could get along.

I then looked at my brother, who glared at me before letting his gaze sweep the restaurant and asking Mom, "Why are we here?"

"Good question," Dad murmured, still perusing his menu. "One for the ages, really. Why *are* we here?"

"For the bottomless fries?" I asked, chuckling to myself.

"*Mom,*" Tim said, pointedly staring at me, "you said on the phone that there were some issues to discuss, so why don't we discuss them?" He checked his watch.

"I didn't know there were *issues to discuss,*" I said, raising an eyebrow at Mom.

"Why would they tell you ahead of time, Laur?" Tim asked. "You'd just blab about it to one of your little friends, or make a stupid joke."

"That's not true," I told him.

Well, not entirely true, anyway. He made my blurting sound sort of vicious, which was never my intent, though occasionally it was an added benefit.

I stared across the table, noting that while his well-cut charcoal suit made him look mature and professional, no matter how hard he tried to portray himself as an adult, I still saw him as the seven-year-old boy who'd worn Superman underwear as a Halloween costume.

As I watched him squint at the salad section of the menu, an image filled my mind and I giggled to myself.

"What?" my brother asked, shooting me a suspicious look.

"Have you got *Underoos* on beneath that suit?"

"Have I *what?*" he choked.

"I said—"

"I heard you, Lauren," he snapped, checking over his shoulder to see if anyone else had.

"And?" I asked.

"And?" He paused to stare at me. "I'm not dignifying that with an answer."

"So you do!" I crowed.

He rose from the table, claiming a need for the restroom, and excused himself to wade through the crowd of yapping waiters and diners filling the restaurant.

"Lauren, you haven't seen each other for *months*," Mom said, resting a hand on top of mine.

I looked at the diamond anniversary band Dad had given her and idly wondered whether I'd have a *first* anniversary, let alone a *twentieth*.

I gazed into green eyes that matched my own, aside from the chocolate brown rims around her irises. "True, we don't see each other."

"He hasn't moved to Calcutta, honey," Mom said, a plea in her voice. "He's in the next state."

"Yeah, but that state is *Idaho*."

"Nothing wrong with Idaho," Dad murmured.

"You talk on the phone, don't you?" Mom asked me, hopefully.

"Every now and then."

Maybe once every six weeks, tops.

"But you correspond online." Her nod urged me to respond positively.

"Sure."

If updating me on his new e-mail address counted as "correspondence."

"I just don't understand you two." Mom sighed. "You used to be so close."

"Not really." I shrugged.

"Just try to get along," Dad said, resting his arm across the top of Mom's half of the booth in a gesture of solidarity.

When Tim returned, I was on my best behavior, and the four of us managed to place our orders in record time, aside from Dad verifying "the ins and outs of this French fry situation" with the waitress for a solid three minutes.

"So," Mom said, once our freshly agitated server had left the table, "the funeral is Friday."

"I'll be there," I sighed.

"There's a reception afterwards," she added.

"Hey, I can't stay in town forever," Tim said. "I'll need to get back to work."

"It'll be the weekend *and* you're self-employed," I reminded him, then promptly told Mom I wouldn't be able to make the reception.

"I think you owe it to Ida to go," she said, while I frantically tried to concoct an excuse.

"I don't *owe* her anything," I finally countered. "I barely knew her."

"Surely you have a fond memory or two," Mom prompted, hope in her voice.

"Uh . . ."

Aunt Ida.

She was always covered in cat fur, but never owned a cat. Her hands were cold. She used the word *honestly* too much. I sighed and wracked my tired brain, but no glowing tribute came to mind. The memories I had were vivid, of course, but the way Great Auntie Ida waited until her flypaper was absolutely packed with petrified bugs before she took it down wasn't something I recalled with tenderness. I'd marveled at the overburdened swatch of sticky brown paper hanging over the sink, space remaining for one or two average-sized victims, while Ida's patience filled the room.

I didn't know how I could put a positive spin on the scent of Vicks VapoRub that always emanated from the sharp and shiny peak of Ida's sternum, or her countless glistening jewels: clip-on earrings, not quite centered on her droopy lobes, jingling bracelet bangles and rings trapped below the bulging lumps of her arthritic knuckles.

Fond memories?

My jet-setting parents had taken a cheapie, all-inclusive trip to Reno for a long weekend when Tim was eight and I was a mouthy six-year-old with ponytails and poor etiquette. They'd left us, against our wills, in Ida's care.

During our visit, she only let us watch TV if we cracked walnuts at the same time, although what she needed them for, I never knew. Just like the ten gallon buckets we could never quite fill with blackberries from her stunted bush, or the endless rolls of multicolored yarn we rolled and unrolled on command, there were projects we knew not to question.

Ida and I had been seated on her couch one afternoon, watching Richard Dawson kiss the blushing female cheeks of a family from Madison, Wisconsin, when she said, "I *do* love the *Feud.*" She popped some sunflower seeds into her mouth. "That man is a dream."

I looked at Mr. Dawson's pale blue suit and the hound dog bags under his eyes before turning toward her and solemnly stating, "You're my weird aunt."

Instead of telling me off, like any other adult would have done, she cackled hard enough to spark a coughing fit, spat a mangled seed into her palm, and grinned. "You got that right," she said, winking, then turned her attention back to the screen.

When Sunday night arrived, and my parents' wood-paneled station wagon pulled into the driveway, Tim and I raced into Mom's arms, knowing freedom was ours. Sure, we would miss the big band music on her kitchen radio, and her homemade peanut butter cookies, but Aunt Ida herself? That was another story.

MOM DUG INTO her purse, rummaging around until she located two white envelopes, which she handed to us.

"It turns out she left something for each of you."

Tim and I exchanged guilty looks.

My dear brother smoothed his thinning hair back from his forehead, as though there would be a live camera directed at him as soon as he opened his mail, while I slid my thumb under the corner of my flap and slowly tore it open.

Unfolding two crisp, white, stapled pages, I began to read.

I was only halfway into the second paragraph, my jaw slack with shock and wonder, when my brother groaned, "What am I going to do with a bunch of 45s? Christ, I don't even have a record player."

I kept reading, the typed lines beginning to blur as reality set in.

I remembered saying good-bye to Ida as Tim and I left at the end of that long weekend. I could still smell the medicinal mint of her skin and feel the squeeze of her fingers against the soft flesh of my forearm before she let me go. I could see the smudge on her glasses, the loose button on her cotton housedress, and hear the sound of wind chimes made from shells.

As instructed by Mom, I'd given Ida a cursory kiss on her whiskered cheek, then wiped my mouth with the back of my hand (with neither flair nor subtlety) before scrambling into the car. I thought of the quick drive home, when I'd felt only a tiny twinge of guilt about the crayon drawing—featuring flypaper and a crazy woman—I'd propped on Aunt Ida's nightstand.

At the age of six, I'd left her a carefully colored insult.

Twenty years later, she'd left me her house.

Three

"I CAN'T BELIEVE it," I murmured, once I'd spilled the news of my inheritance to my astonished family.

"Neither can I," my parents said, in unison.

"Neither can *I*," Tim snapped, pushing his plate toward the center of the table in disgust.

My brain was spinning in a thousand directions at once. I hadn't expected *anything* from Ida, and even if I had, I wouldn't have imagined more than some costume jewelry or old photos.

A house?

A house!

"She left me the whole damn house?" I asked, softly.

"It's in *northeast* Portland," my brother was quick to remind me, with a sardonic smile.

Party pooper.

This was the guy who not only told me there was no Santa, but had taken a cut of the Tooth Fairy payoff whenever I'd tucked a canine or bicuspid under my pillow. This was the guy who acted as a human spoiler for every cinematic plot twist of the twentieth century, usually when I was on my way to the theater.

"Okay, so it's not on the west side, but—"

"It's *ancient*," he said, as though he'd been appointed the architecture authority of the Northwest.

I vaguely remembered the house as old but classic. "Wasn't it built in the twenties?" I asked Mom. She nodded.

"I'm not sure. Before the forties, anyway. It's a Craftsman."

"It had that beautiful stained glass around the front door. Remember?" Dad asked.

"Not really," I said, heart and mind still racing.

A house!

"It's probably decrepit by now," Tim warned, with a touch of glee.

"It'll still have *charm*," I replied. "It's got to be worth something."

"*Northeast Portland,* Lauren." Tim shook his head. "Not exactly the real estate jackpot."

"There are a lot of nice neighborhoods in Northeast," Mom told him. "Prices have been increasing for years. The East Side has all the character homes, anyway," she added, smiling at me.

"The real estate bubble is about to burst," Tim said, "unless it has already."

"Could you be a little more negative?" I asked, plunging a French fry into barbeque sauce and shoving it into my mouth.

He watched me chew and drew his plate back to his side of the table to attack his meal with renewed fervor.

So much for the drama of a lost appetite.

"I'm being realistic," Tim said. "For crying out loud, *someone* in this family has to be." He glanced at Mom, who had removed the bun from her chicken burger and created a makeshift wrapper out of lettuce. The moist leaves were no match for the globs of mayo and teriyaki sauce oozing forth to drip all over the tabletop, her lap, and her sleeve.

"What?" she asked, taking a bite. "What's wrong?"

"What are you doing?" I asked.

"Cutting back on carbs."

"One bun isn't going to kill you," Dad told her, patting her arm affectionately.

"No, I'm sticking to breadless living," Mom said, shaking her head.

Tim rubbed his forehead with thick fingers he'd inherited from Dad's side of the family. "Why didn't you just order a chicken salad?"

"Because," she began, then frowned as she apparently saw the error of her ways. "Hmm. I guess I should have."

"So, what are you going to do?" Tim asked me.

"Eat it." I shrugged. "I've got no beef with bread." I glanced down at the burger on my plate. "Well, that's not entirely true. There's some lean ground in my future."

"I think he's talking about the house," Dad said, dabbing his mouth with a napkin.

"Oh, I'm going to sell it," I said, waving the question away with one hand. I hadn't begun mentally spending the money yet, but there was plenty of time in the days to come for that.

Tim smiled, so I knew an evil comment was on the way.

"You're going to have to find out about taxes. See if you're stuck paying capital gains and all that."

Capital gains?

"Dad?" I asked.

"Not exactly my area of expertise, Laur. You know I did corporate work."

"No problem," I lied, brushing off Tim's negativity.

"I can probably refer you to someone," Dad said, grabbing a fry.

"It's okay. I'll have a poke around online," I told him, irked that Tim had brought the whole stinking issue up to begin with.

"No, you should see a *lawyer* or an *accountant*," Tim said. He paused to stare at me. "*Poke around online?*" He shook his head. "We're talking about the IRS, Lauren. This is hardly a job for Google."

"Well, you're the expert on virtually everything, aren't you?" I snapped. "Or is it everything virtual?" The guy spent more time in front of a computer than anyone I knew.

"Let's calm down," Mom said. "This is supposed to be a nice family dinner."

"All I'm saying," Tim said, through gritted teeth, "is that maybe Dad should recommend someone."

"Maybe someone single," Mom said, hopefully.

"What?" I asked, frowning.

"Mom, she's got to get her finances organized," Tim said. "Not hook up."

"Hook up?" Dad asked, clearly baffled.

"Meet someone romantically," I explained, then added, "and, once again, I'm *not* looking for anyone." Not quite yet, anyway. And when the time came, I certainly didn't want to be set up with someone from Dad's social circle.

"Well, that's the best time to meet someone," Mom continued. "You think I was *looking* for your father?"

I rolled my eyes. "Mom, I know for a fact you were. You met on a blind date, for crying out loud."

She cast a flirtatious look in Dad's direction, then took another run at it. "Well, we're probably a bad example. All I'm saying is that love usually strikes when you least expect it."

"So does diarrhea," I muttered.

"*Now* who's being negative?" Tim snapped, tossing his napkin onto his plate with a flourish. "And thanks, Lauren. That's really something I want to think about over dinner."

"You'll find someone," Mom said, reaching over to pat my hand. "I was thinking you should maybe try that speed dating."

"I'm not going to—"

"It seems like a good way to meet people," she said.

"Too much pressure," I told her. "Five minutes to make a good impression?"

"Well, why don't you try the computer?" she asked.

"Because Internet dating is for losers," I sniffed.

I'm not that desperate.

Yet.

"That's a ridiculous attitude," she scolded. "Tim met Beth on the Internet."

"No way!" I snorted.

"Thanks, Mom," he groaned, pushing his plate away again.

"What? It's true!" She shrugged at me, helplessly. "There's nothing wrong with it, Timmy."

"Mom, please. I'm twenty-eight. It's *Tim*."

"You'll always be Timmy to me," she said, winking at him.

"If it makes you feel any better," I said, giving him a cheeky grin, "you'll always be a Timmy to me, too."

"Anyway," Mom continued. "Beth sounds like a perfectly nice girl and you wouldn't have met her at all if it wasn't for the Internet."

"I realize that," Tim growled, his face flushed and shiny with either perspiration, a light layer of burger grease, or both. "But it's not exactly something I *tell* people."

"Why on earth not?" Dad asked, flagging down our waitress for yet more fries.

"Because it's for losers," I answered for him.

"Talk to me in a couple of months, when you've been 'out there' trying to meet someone, Lauren," he snapped. "You've got a rude awakening coming."

"I'll meet someone the old-fashioned way," I assured him, with my trademark false confidence. "With no technology *or* accounting involved."

"Good *luck*," Tim laughed. "Let me know how *that* works out for you."

We ate silently for a few moments, the din filling our ears, but it was only a matter of time before my brother spoke again.

"What am I supposed to do with a bunch of records, anyway?" he muttered. "I mean, what kind of logic would make her decide to give me a truckload of plastic—"

"Vinyl," I corrected.

"Whatever," he sighed. "I get something of no value, and Lauren gets a *house*? Was Ida out of her mind, or what?"

"Just sell the records on eBay or something," I suggested.

"Like I have time for that."

"Just trying to help." I shrugged.

"Come on, Lauren. Surely you see the unfairness here."

"Is that even a word?" I asked, frowning.

"What?" Tim scowled.

"Unfairness."

"Yes, it is," he assured me.

"It sounds weird." I looked to Mom. "Is it a word?"

"Yes!" Tim growled.

"Your father would know for sure," she said. "Did he tell you he's the reigning Scrabble champ of our whole complex?"

"It's a word," Dad assured me with a quick nod.

"*Unfairness*," I murmured. "No, it still sounds funny."

"So, look it up when you get home," Tim said. "Now, if we could just focus here for a second, you guys—"

"Say," Dad interrupted. "I've been meaning to ask, have you ever heard the phrase 'let's give it up for,' followed by someone's name, inciting a round of applause?"

"Uh, yes I have," I told him, puzzled by the question.

"Is it new?" Dad asked, frowning.

"No," I groaned. "Where did you hear it?"

"Your mother and I were watching the Country Music Awards last night and—"

"Rule of thumb, Dad. If it's on the Country Music Awards, it's not new."

"Back to the inheritance," Tim began, but I cut him off before he could get rolling.

"What do you *care* if she gave me the house?" I demanded. "You're the one who keeps saying it isn't worth anything."

"*Comparatively,*" he clarified, crossing his arms against his chest.

"Well, what are we comparing it to?"

"Other houses. When compared to *other houses,* it's not worth much."

"So there you go."

"I'm not finished, Lauren," Tim said, holding up his index finger, which happened to be the digit he used to lick and stick in my ear to torment me. "When compared to a collection of old 45s, it's worth a *ton.*"

"Okay, I'm not going to apologize for an inheritance just because you're pissed off."

"It's total bullshit," he hissed at me.

"Well, I think it's wonderful," Mom said, pretending not to hear him. "I'm amazed she thought of you."

"Yeah." Tim drummed his fingertips against the tabletop and frowned. "*Why you?*"

The question was asked enough times over dinner that by the end of the meal I was beginning to think Why You was my alma mater.

The bill was presented and I valiantly fought Dad for it while Tim skulked off to the bathroom. Dad eventually forced his MasterCard into our server's hand and Mom informed me that I had no responsibility to entertain the following night, as they would be spending the time catching up with old friends in Tigard. Somewhat relieved and guilty for feeling that way, I bid the family farewell in the parking lot, with the promise that I'd be ready to be picked up for the funeral at ten o'clock on Friday morning.

∾

Back at Rachel's apartment, I walked through the front door and past the cozy comfort of overstuffed living room furniture, making a beeline for the kitchen. Only mildly disappointed when I saw no blinking message light on the answering machine, the feeling was upgraded to distress when I found a note from my roommate, stating that she was spending the night at Steven's place.

Again.

Frustrated that I couldn't share my big news with her right away, I fed Gouda the cat, who was as unappreciative as usual, staring blankly at me while I waited for some sign of gratitude that never materialized.

Unsure of how to relax after my rather high-voltage evening, I decided to have a nice, hot bath, enriched by an assortment of scented salts and oils I'd purchased when I moved out of Daniel's condo, falsely believing luxury could overshadow loneliness.

As I wiggled my toes in the steaming water, creating teeny ripples on the surface, I thought about how much my life had changed in a matter of hours. Suddenly, doors I'd never known existed were flung wide open.

When I sold the house, I could go back to school, *if there was anything I wanted to study.* I could take a trip around the world, *but I'd have no one to go with.* I could go alone, *but I'd drive myself nuts.* I could buy a new car, *but mine was perfectly broken in.*

You've got all the time in the world to decide.

I lay back in the tub and closed my eyes, feeling more prepared to take on the world than I had since I'd broken up with Daniel and struck out as a soloist.

After an hour, when my skin was wrinkled and tight, and the

bathroom was filled with steam, I reluctantly climbed out of the tub and wiped the mirror clean. Hoping that my piece of good fortune would have somehow made me look younger and perkier, I peered at my image, but only saw the same faint wrinkles around my eyes and that damn crease between my brows.

Yup, still old.

I towel-dried my hair, then dipped my fingers into a melon cream, racing to distribute a small glob of it before the curls turned to frizz.

I rested my hands on the frayed elastic waistband of my flannels, disappointed by the sight of toneless flesh wherever I looked. I lifted one arm and attempted to flex my biceps, only to discover that I either no longer had one, or it was hiding out, working undercover somewhere else in my body.

I turned for a side view and frowned.

Like in my left butt cheek.

I seemed to recall a time in elementary school when I was picked on for being too skinny.

I forced a smile, exposing every orthodontically straightened tooth in my arsenal, awakening deep dimples in the process.

See, you look twelve.

Well, sixteen.

Twenty-five, at the most.

I abandoned the bathroom and approached what appeared to be a cabinet on the far side of the living room and gripped both handles. Using virtually all of my pitiful upper body strength, I slowly pulled the giant drawer open, exposing a brass-railed bed on wheels. I felt a sudden rush of cold air at my knees, and even though I knew it was just ductwork in the dark, cavernous space at the foot of the bed, it was still spooky.

I felt like I was sleeping in a morgue.

For the umpteenth time, I wondered what would happen if

someone snuck in during the night and rolled me into the wall. Would I ever get out?

There was nothing like an old building to keep you on your toes.

As I climbed into bed, excited, exhausted, and cold, I tried to plan my future.

Unfortunately, the couple above me had plans of their own, which included enjoying loud sex while listening to the *Top Gun* sound track.

I buried my head under a downy pillow, which couldn't block the sound of a series of grunts and the chorus of "Take My Breath Away."

"I'd love to," I shouted at the ceiling.

Four

THE NEXT MORNING I couldn't get it together to save my life. I'd run out of my favorite shampoo (which meant using Rachel's dry-scalp formula), my breakfast yogurt was well past its expiration date, and I tore three pairs of nylons before giving up the ghost in favor of pants.

By the time I hustled out the front door, on the cusp of late, I was gripping an almost-ripe banana and wearing a wrinkled outfit I hadn't had the chance to iron.

How is it I always forget how much I hate the rumpled reality of linen for just long enough to buy more?

When I was younger, I'd really cared about the state of my clothing. I was always playing with outfits and adding a splash of creativity to an existing jacket or skirt with the help of a beat-up Singer sewing machine and a basket filled with unusual remnants and notions I'd picked up at fabric store sales.

How was it that, just a few years later, I was driving to work in a wrinkled and ill-fitting light brown suit?

Sighing, I pulled into traffic, too busy concentrating on avoiding another late arrival to worry about the tragic loss of my personal style.

I glanced at the fuel gauge and saw that my gas tank was almost empty.

"Crap," I whined, checking my watch. I had no time to spare for a fill-up of either gas *or* my desperately needed coffee. "Driving slowly probably uses less fuel," I reasoned aloud. "But then again, wouldn't flooring it mean covering more distance before I run out?"

I decided to join Team Lead Foot, hoping it would not just get me to the office, but get me there on time.

What it got me was pulled over.

After about ten minutes of driving, I hit the brakes at the first sight of the police car behind me, but apparently the radar gun had spotted me first.

I moved to the shoulder, placed my half-eaten banana in my empty cup holder, rolled down my window, and reached for my wallet.

A female officer appeared beside the car. "Good morning."

"Hi," I said, attempting to convey an expression of respect, courtesy, and an innocent kind of guilt. My friend Gavin had given me a guidebook on how to weasel out of tickets for my birthday, and I found myself wishing I'd taken the time to crack it open.

The officer took off her sunglasses and gave me a steely look. "Do you know why I pulled you over?"

"Speeding," I said, nodding solemnly. "I'm late for work, so I—"

"Do you know how fast you were going?"

I tried to envision the sign I'd passed. *Was the limit sixty?* "About sixty-three," I guessed, figuring it was close enough for a warning rather than a ticket, "but—"

Her face was expressionless. "The limit's forty-five."

Shit.

"Really? I thought—"

"And I was actually pulling you over for an illegal lane change back there. Not speeding."

"Oh." I bit my lip, before I could do any more damage.

"Of course, we'll have to address the speed, too," she said, as I handed her my license and registration.

I endured public shame as the entire population of Beaverton drove past me. My Toyota was like a modern-day stockade and my fellow commuters offered me smug looks as they sipped their lattes and listened to inane morning radio shows. Every couple of seconds, I glared at the minute hand on my watch, which was ticking closer and closer to late o'clock.

When the officer returned, she wore a puzzled expression as she said, "You have a totally clean driving record."

"Yes," I told her. The three other cops who'd pulled me over in recent weeks had all said the same thing, and each had opted not to tarnish it.

Evidently, my luck had run out.

"Considering the excessive speed, I can't just let you off with a warning."

"I understand," I told her, my voice full of apology.

"I won't give you the maximum, but there'll be a fine for that and the lane change." She glanced at my license before handing it back to me. "There are a lot of drivers on the road, Ms. Peterson. You've got to watch the reckless behavior."

"I will," I assured her. Thoroughly relieved, I added, "It's a good thing you didn't see me a couple of miles back, when I was going closer to seventy and steering with my knee while peeling a banana." I chuckled, slipping my license back into my wallet.

"What did you say?" she asked, incredulously.

Shit.

Why are you such an idiot?

"Uh . . . pardon me?" I stammered.

She shook her head. "I'm going to pretend I didn't hear that."

"Thank you," I murmured. "I'm going to try keeping my mouth shut."

"Good luck with that," she said, tipping her hat.

∽

WHEN I ARRIVED at work, my desk looked even more loaded with stacks of paper, magazines, crumpled takeout menus, and far too many plastic figurines some goon in Claims had arbitrarily decided I "collected" than it had the day before.

I was greeted with a bright smile from Rachel, who had probably arrived ten minutes early and was already elbow deep in paperwork. A new day, and her black cloud of moodiness had blown away.

"I got a ticket on the way here," I told her.

"Geez, it's about time someone actually gave you one," she said, with a laugh. "I haven't been pulled over in the Bug yet."

"That's because you drive like a complete wuss," I reminded her as I dug past the claim carnage to find my date book so I could scribble in a dental appointment.

"I don't want anything to happen to it," she said, with a shrug. "You know it's the first new car I've ever owned."

"And you've only had it for six weeks. Just wait for that first ding, Rach."

"Let's not talk about bad things happening to something so gloriously yellow and so damn cute! I sent my folks some new pictures of it from Steven's last night."

"Speaking of last night," I paused dramatically, "you'll never believe what happened at dinner."

"You and Tim fought like children."

"*Small children*, yes, but something else as well."

I didn't give her more than two seconds to think about it before I blurted my news.

"A house?" she gasped, eyes wide. "She left you a *house*?"

"Yup," I said, grinning. "I'm going to sell it, of course. God, I have no idea what I'll do with all that money."

Rachel nodded slowly, moistening her lips with a perfect pink tongue. "Congratulations, Laur."

"I mean, the sky's the limit. I could travel, invest—"

"That's great," she said softly. "I'm really happy for you."

Her tone was off, and when I glanced at her I saw a weariness in her face. Without giving it a moment's consideration, the words flew out of my mouth. "I could pay off your Visa," I blurted.

"What?" she gasped, shaking her head. "No, that would be . . ." She stared at me with barely surpressed glee. "Really?"

"Why not?" I asked, laughing as her face lit up. I suddenly felt like the Oprah of Oregon.

"What's going on?" Candace asked. She'd abandoned the wind-chime bracelets in favor of what appeared to be stirrup pants and a thick turtleneck sweater that ended halfway down her thighs.

I remembered an ex-girlfriend of Tim's wearing a similar out-fit while we watched *Family Ties* in my parents' basement.

"What are you *wearing*?" I asked, incredulously.

Candace looked down at herself, causing the large silver hoops dangling from her ears to hit her in the face.

"Page sixty-four of *Vogue*'s Fall Fashion."

"From 1986?" I asked, stunned.

"Lauren," Rachel interrupted, "why don't you tell Candace your big news?"

"What big news?" Candace's cohort, Lucy, asked, appearing behind her.

Where Candace was tall, fair, and skinny, Lucy was petite, dark, and bookishly chic.

"I inherited a house," I announced, rather pleased to be the center of positive attention, for a change.

After the expected oohs and ahhs had been released into the air around us, Lucy suggested we all go out for dinner that evening, to celebrate.

"I can't," Rachel said. "I mean, that sounds fun and every-thing, but Steven and I have dinner plans."

"What about after dinner?" Lucy suggested. "We could meet up."

"We kind of have after-dinner plans too," she said, her pale skin turning bright pink.

"I see," I said, wondering if *I'd* ever have *after-dinner plans* again. "That sounds nice."

"So, the three of us will go," Lucy said, raising an expensively shaped eyebrow suggestively.

"Why don't you invite Gavin?" Rachel asked. "I'm sure he'd be up for it."

So, I placed a call to my oldest friend.

He'd nursed me through everything from vomiting fish sticks in the fourth grade to vomiting fish sticks *and* Jack Daniels at age twenty-two and there was no one I'd rather whoop it up with.

"It's Lauren," I said, when he answered on the second ring.

I imagined him sitting on the chrome and red vinyl barstool he'd bought from a bankrupted restaurant to park next to his black rotary-dial telephone. He was probably clutching a mug of tea with some soothing name like Elderberry Cloud that smelled divine but tasted like pond scum.

I gave him a brief overview of Aunt Ida's death and my subse-quent good luck.

"I think what *you* need to get over this incredible Aunt Ida grief is a night on the town."

"That's why I'm calling. Can you go out with me and a couple of girls from work tonight?"

The invitation was greeted with a moment or two of dead air.

"Laur, it's Wednesday," he said.

"You're a *freelancer,*" I reminded him. "You can work in your living room while wearing pajamas."

"I know," he sighed with satisfaction. "I'm talking about you."

"And I'm telling you I'm going out."

"Who *is* this?" he asked.

"Very funny, Gav. Are you in?"

"Oh, you know I'm always in."

I thought about the alcoholic component of celebrating and asked, "If I get a little loopy, can I crash at your place?"

"That's what the hide-a-bed's for."

"Okay, we'll pick you up at seven or so."

"Sounds good." He paused. "And Lauren?"

"Yes?"

"*I'm* fine, thank you."

I cringed. "Geez, I'm sorry, Gav, I just—"

"That's okay. You had big news and I didn't. I'll see you tonight. And make sure the girls are cute."

"See you, circa seven," I said, with a laugh.

AT THE END of the day, when everyone else was slipping into their coats and slinging purses over their shoulders, I stayed at my desk to make up for the morning's tardiness. Granted, tacking thirty minutes of reading stale magazines onto the end of my shift hardly cancelled out the hours I'd spent looking at the newspaper, surfing the Internet, chatting with my fellow employees, and generally *not* working, but Payroll measured time, not productivity.

After clocking out, I made my way to the parking lot in a sudden drizzling rain, the kind that didn't warrant digging an umbrella out of my knapsack, but left a light mist on everything.

On the way home, I stopped by a drive-through coffee stand and got myself a latte to warm my bones.

When the foaming cup was in my hand, the thought struck that I was just one insignificant person, surrounded by hundreds and thousands of others. Truth be known, all that made me stand out from anyone else who hustled and bustled around me were the special instructions for my daily coffee. I was reduced to identifying myself as a decaf, rather than regular, skim—not whole—milk, very light foam, and a hazelnut sprinkle.

Twenty-six years old, and defined by a fussy beverage.

I sighed as the deejay rattled off a bunch of concert dates and changed the station as the congestion ahead of me inched forward in stilted bursts, finally settling on country music.

Dear god.

Country music.

Maybe my new life will be all about trying new things.

After two annoyingly twangy songs, I threw that theory out the window, hit the Off button, and continued inching toward home with only the sound of an idling engine to keep me company.

When I reached the apartment, I grabbed a pair of pajamas, a change of clothes for work, my toothbrush, and some overnight staples. When Lucy and Candace showed up a few minutes later, I slipped out to the car, ready for a night of letting loose to begin.

If I'd only known what I was getting myself into.

Five

"SO, THIS GAVIN guy," Candace said, as I was buckling up, "he's single?"

"Pathologically," I told her.

"And cute?"

"So I'm told." As far as my Mom was concerned, he was downright dreamy.

"Why don't you go for him?" Lucy asked, peering at me in the rearview mirror.

I leaned between the two front seats. "Because I'm not ready to 'go for' anybody yet, and because he's more like my brother than my own brother."

"Sort of a Harry and Sally thing, huh?" Candace asked.

"More of a Ross and Monica thing, actually," I told her.

"We'll see," Candace sang.

"I sure hope so," I muttered, suddenly dreading the prospect of being pushed toward Gavin romantically.

For crying out loud, I was worried enough about the prospect of dating without everyone around me sticking their noses in for some matchmaking.

I directed Lucy to Gav's place and my two coworkers waited in the car while I marched to his front door.

I didn't bother knocking, knowing full well that he never locked it up. Instead, I walked right in and turned off the blaring stereo.

"My tunes!" he called from the bedroom.

"Your chariot awaits," I replied, gathering the dirty plates from the top of the television, bookcase, and coffee table to find them a new home in the sink. "You live like a pig, Gav."

"The ladies love it," he said, appearing in the doorway, looking as artfully disheveled as ever.

"How long did it take you to put that outfit together?" I asked, taking in the leather Converse, perfectly baggy white cords, and pale blue checkered western shirt, complete with snaps.

"Three minutes," he said, with a shrug.

"*Gav.*"

He smiled. "Twenty, tops."

"With hair?" I asked, gently prodding the tousled blond mass.

"Half an hour." He tucked his wallet into his back pocket and slipped into a denim jacket. "Rachel coming with us?"

"No."

"Really?" he asked, frowning slightly.

"She and Steven have plans."

"Man, when is she going to dump that guy?"

"Why would she?" I asked.

"Because I'm right here, waiting for her."

"Good grief," I said, rolling my eyes.

"She's a knockout, Laur."

"And nice, t'boot. Way too nice for the likes of you."

He grabbed his keys from the coffee table and led me to the door. Just before he turned the knob, he spun around to give me a quick hug. "I know you're not the big touchy-feeler, but humor me."

"Laugh it up, buddy."

He pulled away from me, hands resting on my upper arms, like a coach addressing his star player. "You're doing okay?"

"I'm fine."

"I don't mean the aunt." He looked more intently into my eyes. "I'm talking about you and Daniel."

"Understood, Gav. I'm fine."

"The idea is to have fun tonight, okay?"

"I know," I assured him.

"Well, knowing it and doing it are two entirely different things," he said.

"I need some fun," I agreed.

"Damn straight," he said, resting his arm on my shoulders as we approached the car.

Just the ammo Candace needs.

I introduced Gavin to the two girls as we climbed in the backseat. Candace grinned at the sight of him, while Gavin took in the details of her blonde bob and glittery halter top, then directed an A-OK sign at me.

This could be a long night.

I hadn't even considered the possibility of an intergaggle hookup, and really didn't want to.

"So, what do you feel like?" Gavin asked, as we drove toward Portland.

Starving, I was in the mood for anything, especially if it came with a big juicy steak.

Candace answered, "When I was in second grade, one of the girls in my class, Faye Cameron, came to school in a dress without underwear. She just forgot to put it on, you know? I've done the same thing as an adult. Not underwear, but I forgot to wear a bra to work a couple of months ago and all day I couldn't figure out why I felt so weird. It wasn't until lunch that I realized I hadn't spent the morning tugging at the strap. Anyway, it was the same thing with Faye Cameron. She was probably feeling strange all day, but didn't know why until we sat down cross-legged for an afternoon sing-along and Drew Scorden pointed out her naked bits to the whole class. Everyone laughed, the way kids do. I guess that's how I feel; kind of like Faye Cameron without underwear."

The car was silent for ten full seconds before Gavin spoke.

"I meant, what do you feel like for dinner."

A very long night.

"Oh," Candace sighed. "Anything's good."

"What about you, Lucy?" Gavin asked.

"Anything's fine with me."

"Great. That narrows it down."

"Just no meat on a stick," Lucy added.

"What?" Gavin asked.

Candace piped up, "You mean, like, a corn dog?"

"Yeah, a corn dog would definitely be on the list," Lucy murmured.

"You have a list?" Gavin asked, leaning forward, always intrigued by human oddities. He used to come up with crazy bets in our high school cafeteria, challenging classmates to eat an entire jar of mayonnaise for five bucks, or shotgun a severely shaken Pepsi.

"I can't eat a corn dog either," Candace said. "I mean, I could eat the wiener if it was made of tofu or something, but not the breading."

"That's riveting, Candace," I said. "Seriously, Lucy, you have a *list*?"

"Not written down or anything, but yeah."

"What else is on it?" Gavin asked.

"Kebobs?" Candace asked.

"No, I'd eat kebobs," Lucy said.

"Last time I checked," Gavin said, "a kebob was meat on a stick."

"Well . . ." Lucy hedged.

I watched the glowing lights of the city emerge in front of us, and thought about Mom's comments on branching out. The safe nest of Beaverton had been home for so long, I couldn't imagine starting over somewhere else. It was simply out of the question.

"I can't think of any other meat on a stick," Candace said.

"Me neither," Lucy agreed.

"So," Gavin sighed. "Basically you're saying you'll eat anything but corn dogs."

"Well, corn dogs and yellow food," Lucy corrected, and my head started to throb. "I've gone off yellow food."

"Jesus," Gavin groaned, though I knew he was loving every minute of bantering with the girls.

"I've stopped eating anything but *white* food," Candace said.

"You just ate a Snickers," Lucy said.

"No, I didn't."

"I *saw* you."

"It was only a Fun Size," Candace reasoned.

"It's *brown,*" Lucy snapped.

"It's barely a mouthful."

"You're an idiot," Lucy announced.

Candace turned toward the backseat. "That's a bit harsh, don't you think?"

"I think you're both idiots," Gavin laughed.

I think I want to go home.

Already.

"Geez, Lucy," Candace said, ignoring Gavin's insult and leaning back in her seat. "What gives you the right?"

"It's my car." Lucy shrugged and winked at me.

"I offered to drive," came a whine from the passenger side.

"You have a *scooter,* Candace," Lucy reminded her.

"But still . . ."

The car was blissfully silent for a moment, before Lucy said, "So, Rachel's getting married, huh?"

"What?" Gavin and I gasped in unison.

"Rachel who?" Candace asked.

"Rachel's getting married?" Gavin asked me, with an accusatory look.

I shrugged, utterly bewildered.

My Rachel?

She hasn't said a word about it to me.

"Yup," Lucy said, "and I hope she can find a dress that hides the fact that her torso is only about a tenth of her body."

"Ooh, she's leggy," Candace agreed. "I'd love to be leggy."

"She's leggy all right," Gavin sighed.

"She's high-waisted. Her belt could double as a necklace," Lucy said, and she and Candace both laughed.

"That's a little uncalled for," Gavin murmured.

"Are we talking about Rachel Padlow?" I asked. "Rachel who sits next to me?"

"Yeah," Lucy said, eyeing me in the rearview mirror. "You didn't know?"

"No."

"I thought you guys were pretty tight."

"So did I." My heart sank.

I thought we were best friends.

WE STOPPED IN at Mint, a small restaurant close in the north-east side of the city, a place Gav recommended because it was dimly lit and filled with jovial hipsters. While I navigated the narrow pathway between tables, my mind was spinning with the news of Rachel's engagement. I just couldn't believe that she hadn't told me.

"Get this girl a drink," Lucy demanded, once we were seated and our waitress was ready to take our order. "She needs one."

The next thing I knew, there was a martini glass filled with yellow liquid in front of me.

"What is it?" I asked Lucy, who was seated next to me with what she'd informed me was an avocado martini.

"It's lemon," she said. "And it's incredible."

I took a sip, and discovered she was right. So right that I had another in short order, accompanied by countless crab cakes and prawns with mango sauce. I switched to a gorgeous blackberry beverage, at the suggestion of Gavin, and didn't regret it.

By my fourth drink, I'd laughed so much my whole face ached.

"You know what you need to do?" Candace asked me across the table.

"Pee?" I asked, giggling.

How long has it been since I've had this much fun?

"No, I mean, the first thing you do as a single girl."

Single girl. How strange the title felt. "I have no idea."

"Buy a box of condoms," Candace gleefully shrieked, her blonde bob swinging as she raised one arm in the air.

I glanced at Gavin, who shrugged in response.

"She's right," Lucy said, matter-of-factly.

"I don't *need* any condoms," I hissed, mortified that we'd won the attention of a couple of yahoos at the bar.

"Not *yet*," Candace said, lifting a finger to point at me. "You don't buy them to *use* them right away. You buy them as a re-minder that *you will have sex again*."

"Someday," Lucy added, grinning.

"Thanks for the tip," I murmured, blushing furiously and tak-ing a big swig of blackberry.

"It's empowering!" Candace bellowed.

"Empowering!" Lucy echoed. "Go buy one in the restroom."

"No."

"Come on. The rule is a box, but one's a good start. It's a first step," Candace said.

"An important one," Lucy seconded.

"Hey, you might as well just do it," Gavin urged, nudging me with an elbow.

"I don't think so." I desperately tried to change the topic. "Does anyone need a drink? I'll buy the next round."

"*Come on,* Lauren," Candace said, grabbing my hand and dumping a load of change into my palm.

Gavin leaned over to whisper in my ear, "I don't think they're going to let it go."

And that was how I found myself in the women's restroom, trying to choose between strawberry flavored and glow-in-the-dark condoms.

I finally settled on the strawberry, and was met by a three person arena-style wave when I returned to the table.

"Ooh, ooh, I wanted to show you this," Candace said, digging in her purse for a full minute before she produced a folded slip of glossy paper. Once she'd smoothed it out, she held it up for all of us to see.

It was a magazine photo of a woman wearing a knee-length skirt and a wraparound sleeveless top.

"Noga's latest collection," she sighed. "I want it, but I'll never have it."

"How much?" Lucy asked.

"Three thousand."

"*Dollars?*" I gasped.

"No, pesos," Lucy said, dryly.

"Candace," I said, through the shock, "you could *make* that outfit."

She looked at me like I was crazy. "No, I couldn't."

"Sure you could." I studied the clipping, which was a little blurred around the edges. "It's a really simple skirt, and the top would barely take any time at all."

"Lauren, it's *couture,*" she said, looking at me like I was an imbecile.

"Candace, *I* could make it."

"You're crazy," she said, tucking the photo away and ordered another drink.

"You *could* make it, Laur," Gavin whispered in my ear.

"Never mind," I said, rolling my eyes and ready to abandon the subject.

"Remember," Gav continued, "I've seen you go hog wild on a sewing machine."

"True," I murmured.

Vision blurred and face flushed, I took a look at the rest of the patrons, noting a couple leaning into each other over a flickering candle, a mixed group in their mid to late thirties, apparently celebrating a birthday, and a group of what must have been football players, downing shots at an alarming rate. I glanced from one inebriated face to the next, wishing I could feel a spark of interest, but it just wasn't there.

Lucy and Candace urged me to talk to any one of the guys, but I firmly declined the opportunity. They strolled over on their own, leaving me with Gavin.

"What's wrong?" he asked, scooting his chair closer to talk.

"I'm too old for this."

"We're the same age, Laur."

"Well, I hate to break the news, but *you're* too old for it, too."

"The hell I am," he laughed, beating his chest. The effect was more chimp than ape.

"Seriously, Gav, I'm hurtling toward thirty."

"At the same rate as everyone else," he said, sipping his drink. "Everyone we graduated with is twenty-six, too."

"I'm no longer part of the hip, hep, and happening eighteen-to-twenty-five demographic advertisers are courting."

"Laur—" he laughed.

"And if advertisers won't even court me, why would men?"

"Geez, do you want me to set you up with one of my friends?"

"God, no! I don't need a man-whore, Gavin."

"Thanks a lot," he said, pursing his lips and studying me for a moment. "Where is all this coming from? What happened to the big fresh start canceling the wedding was going to give you?"

"My Aunt Ida *died,* Gav," I sighed. "I'm sad."

"Was she your Dad's sister? The one in Iowa?"

"No, that's Janet, and she's in North Dakota. Or South Dakota . . . maybe? Aunt Ida was my mom's mother's . . . no wait, my Dad's mother's sister." *Was that how we were related?* "I think."

Silence greeted me and I turned to face him.

"I can see why you're devastated," he said, dryly.

"Are you being sarcastic?"

"No."

"Yes, you are."

"Of course I am, Lauren. Yeesh, it's not the most tragic news I've heard this week."

"Okay, she and I weren't exactly close."

"You don't know that for sure. You might actually be first cousins. It's not like you've got your family tree memorized."

"It's still upsetting," I told him, getting irritated.

"Okay, okay," he sighed. "I'm really sorry, Lauren."

"You don't mean it," I said, my tone full of accusation and booze. "And now this Rachel thing. Why didn't she tell *me* she's engaged?"

"Maybe it just happened."

"I *live* with her, Gav." I shook my head, then pointed at Candace, who was perched on a football player's lap, giggling to the point of snorting. "*She* knew."

"Ask Rachel about it tomorrow, and in the meantime, let's have a good time, okay? Catch the train out of Downerville. You just inherited a freaking *house,* Laur."

"I know," I said, trying to smile.

After I'd had a couple more drinks, Candace and Lucy reappeared at our table.

"Next stop, the strip club!" Candace cheered.

I couldn't help laughing, because there was no way in hell they were going to get me into a peeler bar.

Clearly, I didn't understand the power of the martini.

I HAVE ONLY the vaguest recollection of the debate over whether or not Lucy was sober enough to drive and our lurching cab ride across the river. I don't remember exactly why the driver booted us out to walk the final few blocks, and while I *do* recall karate-kicking a couple of bushes on the way, I'm not sure what they'd done to deserve it.

"I think I'll head for home," Gavin said, swaying at the front door to the bar.

"Come on, don't be a wimp," Lucy said, grabbing his elbow and propelling him forward.

"Guy strippers aren't my thing," he said, but it was too late.

We stepped into smoky darkness, a gaggle of gigglers, and found an empty table at the center of the room. Lucy promptly waved a waiter over and ordered a round of Lemon Drops, while I tried not to look at the stage, where a slender guy with a buzz cut who couldn't have been too far out of his teens gyrated in a shiny silver G-string.

Oh dear.

I noticed an older man, paying rapt attention.

"That guy looks like my dad," I said.

"It is?" Candace gasped, staring at the stripper.

"Not *him*. For crying out loud, that guy looks like a college student."

"Majoring in sex ed," Candace said, breathlessly, as he molested the pole at center stage.

Members of my party wolf-whistled, and I was embarrassed for him, though he took it in stride (or *thrust,* to be more accurate). When his song ended, I watched as numerous women and a couple of older men walked up to the stage to slip dollar bills under the shiny confines of his limited underwear.

I'd never been to a female strip club, but I suspected they were more glamorous than the bar's bare wood stage, never mind the poles, which looked like stolen playground monkey bars, in the middle of it. Any movie I'd seen containing strippers involved tassles, boas, high heels, and carefully choreographed dance numbers, but the male version of events was drastically different.

I noticed a guy leaning against the bar in a baseball cap. He had a swimmer's build, covered by a Chicago Cubs T-shirt and a pair of track pants. He was handsome enough if not to be the *star* of a movie, than to be the star's buddy or sidekick. He didn't look gay (not that I was especially skilled at determining such things), and I wondered what on earth he was doing there.

Gulping my Lemon Drop, I leaned over to ask Lucy if he was as cute as I thought he was, but the high volume of a new song cut me off.

To my shock and dismay, the guy at the bar walked toward the stage, hopped onto it, and started to dance. I watched, stunned as he slipped out of a pair of flip-flops and yanked off his T-shirt with neither grace nor panache.

I mentally willed him to go no further. I feared sleazy gestures and butt jiggling were on the horizon, and I didn't want to see a nice-looking guy demean himself for Candace's cash.

Or, if I were going to be honest with myself, I didn't want to think that the first guy I'd found attractive in years was about to get naked for a bunch of suspiciously crusty one-dollar bills.

Against my better judgment, and with the help of another drink, I watched.

I snuck a peek at Gavin, who was alternating between looking vaguely jealous and checking his watch.

I'd always felt that there was something to be said for a slow reveal when it came to intimate body parts. I'd always been a great fan of men's forearms, or the napes of their necks. When the entire audience learned, with a snap of the wrists, that the track pants were tear-away Velcro, and what lay beneath was a tiny scrap of leopard print fabric, I found myself drunkenly pining for a more delicate time and place, like Victorian England.

Once his song ended, another guy jumped onstage, this one dressed as a cop, a costume that went over like gangbusters with the crowd.

There were only six or seven dancers, and they cycled through their rotation several times while my table got louder and drunker.

It was hard to say whether it was the booze, the atmosphere, or the amount of stress I was under, but the third time my guy danced, Candace and I were at the foot of the stage, ready to tuck bills into his underwear. When the time came, I'm pretty sure I winked at him when I followed the lead of the women I'd watched with the others and gave him a friendly slap on the ass.

We stayed at Three Sisters until closing time, when Gavin and I took a cab back to his place. I was drunk and giddy enough that I didn't give a thought to how I was going to get to work in a handful of hours, or what I might face when I got there.

A fool, plain and simple.

Six

"WANT THE BED, or the hide-a-bed?" Gavin asked, once we'd safely made it home.

"Doesn't matter," I mumbled.

"I'm warning you right now that no woman *ever* wants to leave my bed."

"Get over yourself," I snorted.

"I'm talking about *linen*," he said, defensively. "I've got the softest sheets on the planet."

"How could I turn down that kind of a claim?" I asked, moving toward the bedroom and leaving him to what I knew from previous experience was a creaking, backbreaking pullout in the living room.

"We could always share," he called after me, clearly wishing he hadn't offered his boudoir.

"No, we couldn't," I sang back as I pulled back his comforter and ran a hand over his blissfully soft sheets.

This will be like sleeping on kittens.

Well, minus the visit from the Humane Society.

MORNING CAME SCREAMING into my life with the ungodly bleating torment of Gavin's alarm clock, which I'd miraculously managed to set in my drunken stupor. I slipped a hand out from under the twisted, sweaty blankets and slapped the machine until I hit the right button, effectively bringing an end to the alarm, but not the pounding in my head.

Rolling onto my back, I stared at the ceiling and let out a low groan, which came out raspy. The inside of my mouth tasted liked rotten produce and cigarettes. I tried to sit up, but every muscle and joint I possessed ached like I'd spent the night either wrestling an entire varsity boys' team or doing Pilates.

How many Lemon Drops did it actually take to drop you?

You aren't twenty-one anymore, you know.

I closed my eyes for a moment, soothed by the darkness my lids provided.

Is it Saturday or Sunday?

My eyes popped open.

"Holy shit, it's *Thursday!*" I cried, leaping from the bed. I tripped over the comforter and lurched into the wall with one shoulder, sending shooting pain to my collarbone.

I wasted valuable minutes trying to decide whether I had time for a shower, and once I was under the hot spray, I tried to hustle through my daily regimen as quickly as possible, but only managed to do everything half-assed, including rinsing the shampoo from my hair. I didn't notice the soapy bubbles still clinging to one side of my head until I looked in the mirror, and ended up shoving my head under the bathroom faucet to finish the job.

I threw on the chinos and black hooded sweater I'd packed the night before and tied my hair in a loose ponytail, figuring it could dry on the way to work. Checking my watch as I raced downstairs, I cringed and picked up the pace, grabbing a banana and a bottle of water from the kitchen, slipping my keys from the front pocket of my purse and throwing open the front door to find . . . no car.

My first thought was thieves, then joy riders . . . then *Lemon Drops.*

I froze for a moment, closing my eyes until the car's location came to me. Sitting in front of Rachel's apartment building.

Cursing the fact that the responsible behavior of not driving while drunk the night before was going to result in the irresponsible behavior of showing up late to work that morning, I zipped back inside to wake Gavin.

"I need a ride, Gav!" I cried, banging on his door.

"Where?" he moaned.

"To work!"

"Call in."

"I can't."

"Why not?"

"Because I *can't*."

"Bus?"

"No time! I'm going to be late."

"All right, already. Gimme five minutes."

Five turned into fifteen, then twenty, and by the time Gavin was dressed and locating his keys under the coffee table, I was nearing meltdown status.

"Shake a tail feather there, guy," I muttered, opening the front door for him.

He wasted precious seconds searching his overburdened key ring for the magical item that could lock the front door behind us, and once he'd done so, he turned and froze on the stoop.

"Where's my car?"

I stared at the empty driveway. "In the garage?"

"What garage?"

"Your garage."

He frowned. "I don't have a garage."

"Then where's your . . . Lucy drove, so where's your . . . ?"

"Aha!" he said, smacking his forehead. "I parked it in the lane out back, since the folks next door were having a dinner party last night."

"Thank god," I sighed. "You're an idiot, Gav."

Within a couple of minutes we were on the road, which was great, aside from the fact that every time Gavin hit the brakes, my stomach lurched toward my tonsils, as though it was taking swings at a candy-filled piñata. My head was pounding, and my mouth had hit a new low, tasting like something had died in it.

Gavin darted in and out of traffic, muttering and cursing at the cars surrounding us. We came to the agreement that every vehicle emblazoned with the word *turbo* that was driving under the posted limited should be repossessed. And there were a lot of them that Thursday morning.

"Can I check out the house with you when you go?" he asked, between erratic lane changes.

"Sure. How about Saturday?"

"Works for me," he said, grinning.

When I did finally make it to work, I was only twenty minutes late, and the first people I saw were James and Elizabeth from Claims chatting in the foyer and sipping takeout coffees.

"Knutsen's in Sacramento for a couple of days," James told me, with a smile. "You're safe."

"Thank you!" I said, grinning and giving a thumbs-up to the gods above me.

Well, to the false ceiling and sputtering fluorescent lightbulbs, anyway.

"Your posse's in the back room," James added, with a grin of his own.

My posse?

I dropped my bag at my desk, next to Rachel's empty chair. Curious about the comment from James, I headed for the break room, and the closer I got, the louder the buzz of conversation and short bursts of giggling.

When I arrived at the doorway, I saw a group gathered around Candace and Lucy at the watercooler.

"There she is!" Candace cried.

They all turned in my direction and I couldn't help looking over my shoulder to see if there was someone standing behind me.

There wasn't.

"We didn't expect to see *you* today," Candace teased. "I figured you'd be nursing the hangover of the century this morning."

"I am," I croaked, which sparked another wave of giggling. Shrill, painful, and unwelcome giggling.

"Who knew you were such a party animal?" Lucy asked.

Party animal?

I couldn't decide whether I was more baffled by the fact that the term was being applied to me, or the fact that it was used at all.

"We were just telling everyone about it," Lucy said.

"About what?" I asked, moving toward the cooler to get some water.

"'About what,' she says!" Candace laughed.

"*What?*" I asked, getting irritated.

"The strip club," Mary said, eyes sparkling as though she'd been there.

"What about it?" I poured a paper cup of water and guzzled it in a matter of seconds.

"The Velcro pants guy," Lucy said.

I felt a blush take over my face and turned to pour myself another drink. Wincing, I closed my eyes and could clearly see a hand that looked incredibly like mine reaching out to tap . . . well, *pat . . .* okay, *spank,* his naked buttocks.

Mortifying.

"We thought you were this quiet little mouse at the front desk, and instead, you're—" Lucy began.

"Hey," I interrupted, casually sipping my water. "He was cute, right? And I'm not the only one who, uh—"

"Slapped his ass?" Rachel asked, stepping out from behind the group and making no effort whatsoever to stifle a laugh.

Thanks for the support.

"Well, yeah," I said, taking another sip.

"But we hear you were the only one to climb onstage," Susan said.

Onstage?

"You almost got us all booted out," Candace chortled.

"What?" I asked, but even as the tiny question was voiced, I remembered looking for a set of stairs, becoming frustrated, and finally hoisting myself onto the wooden planks of the stage.

What on earth had I done that for?

As the women around me laughed and joked, I tuned them out as I tried to piece the scene together. Someone had handed me a bottle of beer, and I felt a bit dizzy under the hot lights. The tear-away pants had been . . . torn away. The music was loud and guitar-heavy. Something from the Seventies? The cute guy was slowly writhing against the central pole of the monkey bars while the women screamed.

What did I tell him?

He couldn't hear me, so I repeated it, but he still couldn't hear, so I shouted it. I remembered him shrugging apologetically to indicate he couldn't hear, just as a bouncer approached me. I moved away, clumsy on my feet, and shouted to him one last time, at the very second the song ended and silence filled the bar. What was I trying to—?

" 'I wanna be the pole!' " Candace shrieked, and the entire break room erupted in laughter.

Of course.

I cringed, hoping my face wouldn't burn bright, but it was too late.

Lemon Drops.

Strippers.

I wanna be the pole.

"Oh my god," I murmured.

"We need to go out more often, girl," Lucy said, patting me on the back as she headed back to her desk.

The rest of the women followed her, murmuring their approval. I heard snippets along the lines of "You go, girl," and "She's an animal," and did my best to smile politely and pretend I wasn't bothered by any of it.

THROUGHOUT THE MORNING a few comments were made about the stripper debacle, but I would have been terribly naïve to think there was a chance the subject would be abandoned. I was winked at, called "Wild Girl," and even invited to poker night with the guys from the legal department by ten o'clock.

"What were you thinking?" Rachel asked, with a laugh.

I'd been gearing up all morning to ask about her engagement, but between fielding comments from the peanut gallery and nursing the hangover from hell, there never seemed to be a good time. I didn't want to get into a big emotional discussion, but the truth was, my feelings were hurt and I needed to know why she hadn't told me.

"I guess I wasn't thinking at all," I said, shaking my head. Just as I was about to finally broach the subject, my stupid phone rang.

"I wanna be the pole," Kathy Hanlen sang as she passed my desk.

"Hi, honey, it's Mom."

My head, my head, my pounding head.

"How are you?" I asked.

"Have you got a cold?"

"No, I went out last night, and now I'm kind of hungover."

"Oh, dear. Well, I was wondering whether the four of us should get together tonight."

"That would be fine," I told her. "Just come over to Rachel's and we can visit there."

When I hung up the phone, Jeanette from Accounting was waiting to not only introduce me to two new hires, but to regale them with the tale of the pole.

Thankfully, we had a bomb threat just before lunch that afternoon, during which our main switchboard operator managed to ask all of the fourteen questions from our posted Bomb Threat Checklist, including "Why are you doing this?" She only received one answer out of fourteen queries, and that was reportedly the clichéd but always effective "Fuck you."

During the evacuation, the police arrived with dogs and thoroughly searched the building while we peons sat on the grass and tried to absorb whatever sunshine we could.

Just after lunch, one of the guys in Accounting was fired for spending most of his time on the clock looking at Internet porn. Thanks to Human Resources' own Cynthia "The Vault" Tolnik and the wonders of e-mail, the news took a mere seven minutes to circulate through the entire company.

By the time the blushing, scrawny guy was escorted out the front door by not one but two security guards, there was practically a farewell party in the lobby.

By one-thirty, "I wanna be the pole" was a distant, faded memory.

MOM, DAD, AND Tim were waiting outside Rachel's building when I got home, which meant I had no time to tidy up or zip down the block for some groceries. I couldn't see offering them tap water and cat biscuits, but it was their own damn fault for arriving earlier than the six o'clock we'd agreed upon.

"You're here," I said, grimly.

"With booze and snacks," Dad said, lifting a paper bag I hadn't noticed.

Thank god.

I led them upstairs and gave them a quick tour of Rachel's unit before Mom and Dad settled on the couch and Tim took the rocking chair.

"Would you like something to drink?" I called from the kitchen as I unloaded their bag of wine, cheese, and crackers.

"*That* would be wonderful," Mom said. "Red for all of us."

I managed to break the cork while trying to get the bottle open, then couldn't find any wineglasses. Mom and Dad ended up with the matching set of Tom Peterson Furniture mugs Rachel had received when she bought her glass-topped coffee table and I found a small juice glass for Tim.

I briefly contemplated having a pop, but the phrase *hair of the dog* leapt to mind and I chose to imbibe instead.

When I returned with the beverages, everyone looked both comfortable and relaxed.

"This is fun," Mom said, admiring her mug. "Different."

"We drove by Ida's house today," Dad said, settling back against the couch cushions. Within seconds, Gouda had jumped on his lap, coating his dark slacks with a light layer of white fur. Dad didn't seem to mind, absently petting the cat as he spoke. "It looks good from the outside. I think she's had a gardener in."

"No, it was all her doing, Bill," Mom said, resting her hand next to the cat on his knee.

"It looks like it needs a new roof," Tim said.

"Hard to say from street level," Dad told me.

"It's just a lovely home," Mom assured me. "And *this* sure seems like a secure building," she said. "And a nice neighborhood." She cocked her head to one side for a couple of seconds, then nodded her approval. "Quiet." She smiled and her green eyes sparkled. "I like it."

"It's not too bad," I said, taking a seat on one of Rachel's hard-backed dining room chairs. I shifted from one butt cheek to the other in an effort to get comfortable.

"What's that look for?" Mom asked.

"What look?"

"That 'the world is coming to an end' look," she said, eyebrow raised. "Look, you're a woman *in transition.*"

"Oh god, here we go," Tim groaned.

"You're going through some major changes right now and starting a brand new life. Your dad and I have talked about it at length and—"

"Talked about what?"

"*You,* honey. The split, the move, all of it. Michelle says these are very stressful events, and to be going through them all at once is very hard on you."

I placed my beer on the carpet at my feet. "Who's Michelle?"

"One of the gals at our condo. She's a retired counselor."

"Great," I sighed.

"A counselor might not be a bad idea, you know," Dad offered.

"I'm sure your pal Michelle appreciates *that* vote of confidence."

"He meant that it wouldn't hurt *you* to see one," Mom explained, unnecessarily.

"Actually, it probably would."

"You're lonely and—"

"I *know,* Mom. I'm living it. In fact, every night, I lay two pillows behind me, so it feels like someone's there," I blurted, then gasped, as though I could suck the words back in. I hadn't planned to reveal that particular detail of my isolation, and frantically blinked in an effort to hold back the sudden approach of tears.

Dad and Tim both looked like they wanted to bolt.

"You know," Mom said, responding to the quiver in my voice, "I saw a great big, long pillow at the mall the other day and I *wondered* what it was for. Now it makes perfect sense. Would you like me to mail you one when I get home, or look for one here?"

I closed my eyes.

Oh my god.

"No, thank you."

"They came in all sorts of garish colors, geared toward college students, I think."

"I appreciate the thought, but—"

"It had a catchy name, like Body Bag, though that can't be it. Too morbid. Was it a—"

"Mom, I don't need one." Though it would certainly suit the morgue gurney I climbed onto every night. I slowly rubbed the back of my neck and took a shaky breath. "Look, I shouldn't have even mentioned the sleeping thing. It's just a temporary measure, I'm sure. I don't need a . . . special pillow."

"Well," Mom said, drawing the word out into two syllables, "I think it's perfectly *normal* to want to feel like someone is there, honey. When Linda's husband died, she said—"

"Mom, Daniel didn't die."

I could only imagine my deceased grandmother, arms folded across her bony chest as she scowled at me from Heaven, resenting not only the sympathy I received, but the fact that I'd committed the unspeakable act of tossing away a perfectly good fiancé. "Can we talk about something else?" I asked, lifting the mug to my lips.

"Let's see," she murmured. "Well, your father's prostate exam went well."

"Are you *kidding*?" I sputtered, beer droplets spraying all over my chest.

"No," Dad informed me, "the doctor said he—"

"No, *no*! I mean . . . oh my *god,* can we talk about *anything* else?"

Mom took another sip of her drink. "We could talk about Ida."

"Perfect, Mom," I said, rolling my eyes. "Death is a nice, bright subject."

"Do you have any special words you'd like to say tomorrow?" Dad asked.

"Special words?" I asked, looking to Tim, who appeared as uncertain and uncomfortable as I was.

"Anything you want remembered about her?" Mom asked.

There wasn't much to draw from. Despite her close proximity, I hadn't seen Aunt Ida for years. It was shameful, really, but driving across town to see her had never been high on my to-do list. I tried to imagine what I'd been too busy doing, but the only image my mind was willing to transmit was Daniel and I zoned out on the couch.

"I don't think I have any special words," I told Mom.

"Well, to be quite honest, I don't know quite what to expect tomorrow."

"I'm sure it will be a standard ceremony," Tim said, "just like every other one you've been to."

Of course, he was way off.

Seven

WHEN I AWOKE to the sound of the alarm the next morning, my first response was to groan at the thought of work, until I realized I had the day off.

Well, maybe not *off*, exactly. There was still the matter of laying the dead to rest.

Deciding I had time to indulge in yet another steamy bath, I filled the tub with hot water and at least half of the bottle of peach-scented bubble bath. As I soaked, I tried to empty my mind of everything but the smell of peaches and the comforting sensation of being submerged in warm water.

When the temperature cooled, I just added more hot water, again and again.

I thought about my new life, and the money that was coming my way, courtesy of Ida.

What will I do with it?

The world was my oyster, but I wasn't sure where to start looking for pearls.

I dressed in the pleated black skirt and jacket Mom had brought for me from Florida, having assumed, correctly, that I possessed no mourning attire. I glanced at myself in the full-length mirror on the back of the bathroom door and figured the outfit would come in handy for future job interviews, if I ever left Knutsen Insurance.

After applying a little eyeliner and shadow, I slipped into some low heels and waited for the Peterson family to claim me.

When Tim pulled up outside he didn't offer much more than a brusque "good morning" when I climbed into the backseat, next to Mom.

"Let's just do our best to make today as pleasant as possible," Mom suggested.

"After all, it *is* a funeral," I muttered.

I saw Dad nudge Tim with an elbow.

"You look nice," my brother told me, clearly under duress.

"You sound surprised," I told him.

He didn't speak for a moment. "I guess I still think of you in those kooky outfits you used to make for yourself in high school. You know, the sort of patched-together look, where you didn't even use a pattern."

"I came up with some cool stuff," I said, remembering a calico skirt I'd worn to shreds.

"Right, Laur." He laughed. "Like the velvet cape."

"I never wore a *cape*." I glared at him in the rearview mirror.

"Sure you did."

"It was a velvet *cloak*."

"Semantics." He shrugged.

"Well, what about that vest I made out of bits of embroidered fabric? I received constant compliments on that."

"That was a terrific vest, Lauren," Dad said. "Very *creative*."

"Constant compliments?" Tim asked, tone packed with doubt.

"Well maybe not *constant*," I allowed. "But frequent."

"From your classmates?" he asked, knowing full well what the answer was.

Geez, could he just let it go?

"More from . . . well, teachers, I guess."

"I like how you used the plural, there. *Teachers?*"

I shot him another dirty look in the mirror, but he wasn't even looking at me. "Okay, okay. Ms. Traskett, the nutty drama teacher liked it."

"Point made. Anyway, all I'm trying to say is that it's nice to see you dressed like a normal person."

"You'll need to take a left up here," Mom said. "Then a right at the light."

Tim had to change lanes within half a block to make the left, and when he did, it was a very sharp turn.

"Welcome to Daytona!" I called from the backseat. "Make sure you don't take out your pit crew on the next lap."

"Very funny," he snapped.

"Your Dad gave me a backseat driver's license in my Christmas stocking last year," Mom said, with a smile. "It has my photo and everything. He made it himself."

"I bought a laminating machine on eBay," Dad explained.

Who are these people?

When we reached the cemetery, we parked and made our way to a small group gathered midway up a small hill.

"What the hell?" Tim murmured, as the full spectacle came into view.

Most of the mourners were senior citizens, and all looked appropriately solemn, dressed in varying shades of grey, black, and navy, but it was the twenty or thirty helium balloons bobbing over their heads that looked out of place.

"What's going on?" I whispered to Mom.

"I'm not sure, but it seems *very* Ida."

We walked closer, and soon enough I could make out "Good Luck" printed on a silvery orb and "I Love You" on another, tinted red.

"Well, this certainly puts the 'fun' in funeral," I murmured.

The three of us joined the back of the crowd, and were

acknowledged by a quick nod from two of our fellow mourners before a tiny, wrinkled man in a suit at least two sizes too big introduced himself as Jim Reynolds, a neighbor of Ida's.

"You're relatives?" he asked, smiling politely as Mom explained that Ida was her aunt and Tim and I were her great-niece and nephew.

Not that great, I thought, guiltily.

Mom and Jim chatted for a few minutes and when the opportunity arose, she asked him about the balloons.

"Ida always said she wanted them instead of flowers when the time came," he said, with a shrug. "So, we hit the local florist and here they are."

Tim cleared his throat. "Does that one say 'Get Well'?"

Jim peered over his shoulder. "Not quite fitting, under the circumstances, but the gal only had so many in stock."

" *'Congratulations'?*" I asked, pointing to a teal balloon with pink cursive script over Mom's shoulder.

"We did our best," Jim said, coldly, and turned to make his way to the front of the crowd.

"Do we know any of these people?" I whispered in Mom's ear, checking out the rest of the crowd.

"I don't see any relatives," she whispered. "I think that little oldie in the two-piece outfit is a longtime friend of Ida's, but I don't recognize anyone else." She sighed. "It's a shame I didn't keep in better touch. Annual Christmas cards and a birthday phone call were pretty well the only communication we had for the past few years."

"But you were much closer to her before, right?" I asked.

"Not really."

"Mom, you left us at her place when you went on vacation."

"Well, she was . . ." Mom searched for the right word.

"Available," Tim finished for her.

"Yes," Dad said, with a soft chuckle.

"Great criteria for child care," I muttered.

"And free," Mom added.

"It only gets better," I whispered, rolling my eyes at Tim, who gave me a wry smile. For a split second, he looked like the boy I'd spent my childhood with, until the minister cleared his throat and Tim's expression turned to the carefully neutral mask he'd been wearing since high school.

What happened to him?

We used to watch cartoons together, each with a plate of cinnamon toast we'd made for our dining pleasure. We ran through the sprinkler, sold our old comic books from a little table at the end of the driveway. He used to sleep in my room on Christmas Eve, so whoever woke first could wake the other for the festivities.

My thoughts were interrupted by the deep baritone of the minister, who could have passed for twelve, with a protruding Adam's apple that looked like it was about to break through his pasty skin and make an escape at any moment.

"Welcome," he said, glancing nervously from one face to the next, as though he was hoping for cue cards. He blinked hard a couple of times, then seemed to recall that he was not without material. His shoulders relaxed as he fingered one of two cloth bookmarks and opened familiar gilt-edged pages.

He cleared his throat and began, "Dearly beloved, we are gathered together here in the sight of God, and in the face of this company, to join together this man and . . . *dang!*" His face ripened with color as he scrambled for the other bookmark to locate the correct page.

"Maybe he was that winning combination of *available and free,* too," I whispered.

"Well, Ida never *did* marry," Mom murmured.

"So maybe this is a two-for-one ceremony?" I asked, only to be elbowed by Tim.

"Sorry about that," the minister said, voice cracking. "Let me, uh . . . let's just . . ." He closed his eyes for a moment, then opened them to begin, taking a deep, shaky breath before doing so. "While we are sad to lose one beloved in the Lord, there is reason to rejoice when a child of God goes home." He took another breath, this one steadier and filled with an apparent relief, then carried on.

I tuned out the sermon, which only reminded me of all the family members and friends I'd heard sent off in similar ways. It made me think about all of the funerals I'd have to attend in the future and all of the people I had yet to lose.

What would I do without Mom and Dad?

What would happen when Tim, the only witness to my childhood, was gone?

Shaking the thoughts out of my head, I considered the bright side of my own demise. Along with "Cum on Feel the Noize," my event would feature delectable snacks. Mini egg rolls, crab cakes, and chicken satay with peanut sauce. Light and fluffy lemon mousse. Fudge brownies, loaded with walnuts. My mouth watered at the thought. And it wouldn't be in a church or reception hall, but somewhere familiar and comfortable for everyone, a place that reminded mourners of the real me, rather than the sick or dead version. It should be in my own home, wherever that might be at the time, amid all of my things.

I shook my head, slowly, and bit my bottom lip.

This is morbid.

It sounds like you're planning the creepiest party ever, featuring a warm house and a cold corpse.

The next thing I knew, the minister had finished speaking. We all watched in silence as the casket was lowered into the ground in a jerky fashion that reeked of "technical difficulties," holding our collective breath until Ida was safely parked in her final resting place.

As soon as I heard the first clump of dirt hit the mahogany, I was ready to leave, but I waited for others to depart before making a move. After a couple of minutes, I glanced at Tim, who looked as anxious as I was, and tilted my head toward the car. He nodded and we both turned, just as Mom grabbed my arm.

"I see Ida's old neighbor over there. I'm just going to pop by to say hello."

"We'll wait here," Dad told her.

"Have you got any gum?" Mom asked me, reaching for my purse. "I need to freshen my breath a bit."

"I'm not sure," I said.

She unzipped the bag and started rifling through it while I watched the balloons bob in the wind.

"A mint would do," she murmured. "Aha! A hard candy!"

There was a strange pause, and I turned toward Mom just as Dad asked, "What's wrong, Cecile?"

Her pinched smile confused me for a split second, until I saw the strawberry condom she was clutching.

"*Not* a hard candy," she murmured.

Dad's lips thinned to the point of invisibility.

"Geez, I'm sorry, that's not—" I began, only to be interrupted by Tim.

"What have you got there?" he asked, leaning in for a closer look, then wincing. "Oh." He cleared his throat, eyes widening. "*Oh*."

Mom looked at me as though she was frightened, then turned to see Tim staring at her in mortification. She looked at the purse in her hand, then the condom, and finally back at her son before blushing furiously. "It's not *mine*!"

Tim's broad shoulders relaxed. "Thank god."

"It's your sister's," she continued, shoving the purse at me.

My big brother looked like he was going to pass out.

"It's not mine," I stammered. "I mean, it is, but it's a joke, you know? The girls put me up to it Wednesday night, just before we went to the strip . . ." I caught myself just in time, with a slightly breathless, "*mall*."

"It's always a good idea to be prepared," Mom said, through the gritted teeth of the fakest and most unnaturally bright smile I'd ever seen.

The poor woman.

THE DRIVE TO the reception at the seniors' center was remarkably quiet, but every time I opened my mouth to start a conversation, I remembered the discomfort I'd seen on Dad's face at the sight of the condom and zipped it.

Maybe that's what my new life will be all about: knowing when to keep my mouth shut.

The four of us ended up standing together in the middle of a decorated hall, sipping punch and eating cookies while the local geriatrics stared at us like we were from outer space. The strange part was, I was one of the only people on the planet genetically linked to Ida, and I was sure I knew less about her than anyone in the room.

Mom and Dad ventured out in an effort to mix and mingle, leaving Tim and me stranded together. We silently agreed on a temporary truce and chatted like real live adults. It didn't take long to realize that the only thing we had in common was the past. Almost every sentence began with "remember when . . ." but, thankfully, most of the stories ended with a laugh.

Of course, Tim was a plotter and planner, so it was only a matter of time before the question of my future came up.

"What are you going to do?"

"When?" I asked.

"Now. With your new life."

"Everyone keeps calling it that, but you know what? It's the same life I've always had, minus Daniel."

Mom appeared with fresh drinks for both of us.

"Why don't you teach English in Japan?" Tim asked.

"What?" Mom spilled her punch and set to work dabbing at the carpet with a hand towel.

"Because I don't speak Japanese," I reminded him, irritated that he couldn't just let things lie.

"But you speak *English*," he said.

"That sounds like *almost half* of a terrific plan, Tim, but not quite feasible."

"Why not? You're in the prime of your life. You're twenty-six years old, with a job you hate—"

"Dislike," I interrupted. "And that's not all the time."

"Whatever. You're in good health, with some money in the bank. You've got no one to be responsible for but yourself."

"I was thinking about getting a cat."

Only for about three seconds, but it seemed like a good comeback.

"Cats are nice," Mom said, ever supportive. I was beginning to think that if I were a serial killer, she'd find a way to commend my ability to chop up and hide bodies.

"You've got to be kidding," Tim said, with a roll of the eyes. "The last thing you need is to be tied down by kibble and a litter box. You need to take a bite out of life, Lauren."

"I don't know," I hedged.

"See the world."

"I don't have a passport."

"*Get one.*"

"But—"

"You could learn another language, experience a different culture—"

"I don't need a different culture. I need my own life."

"You could go to Vietnam, Australia, Italy—"

"Why are you so determined that I leave the country, Tim?"

"I'm not. Geez, there's no pleasing you, is there? You always say we don't communicate, but when I start tossing ideas and options at you—"

"I feel like I'm being attacked," I finished for him.

"I'm not *attacking*. I'm just trying to get you motivated."

"Kids." Mom's tone made me feel about nine years old.

"I don't need a life coach, Tim."

"Lauren," Mom warned.

"Well, you need to get off the bench."

"Nice one," I sneered.

"I just think that when opportunity knocks, you should at least consider opening the door."

"Do you have a cliché quota to fill for the day?" I paused. "And if so, please tell me you're getting close."

"I think that does it for now," Mom said, pulling me toward the door. "Bill, we're ready to head along," she called to Dad, who practically dropped his drink to join us.

We piled into the car so Tim could drive me home then take the vehicle and my parents back to the airport.

"That was . . . interesting," I offered.

"Unusual," Dad agreed.

"I've got something for you, Lauren," Mom said, digging into her purse." She handed me a silver keychain with an army of keys hanging from it. "Opportunity is officially in the palm of your hand."

Eight

On Saturday morning, I rolled out of bed and slipped into some sweats for my first visit to Ida's house in at least ten years.

Ten years! If I were her, I would have left myself a nasty note before I started doling out real estate.

I hopped into the Toyota, remembering as I started the engine that I hadn't mailed my monthly payment in yet. I spent the drive to Gavin's trying to think of a single aspect of my life for which the word *late* didn't apply.

My period, but only because I'm not having sex.

I stopped by Gavin's and, for the first time that I could ever recall, he was ready and waiting for me on his front step.

"I still can't believe she left you a *house*! That's like winning the lottery or something."

"I know," I said, with a grin. "Granted, we haven't seen it yet, but it has to be worth something, right?"

"Hell, yes!"

We cruised along the highway with amazing ease, considering that weekday mornings saw my feet aching from depressing and releasing the clutch as traffic inched forward in slow bursts of four and five feet.

I passed the zoo exit, shot through the tunnel, and there we were, in the midst of Bridge City's finest curves. I circled town, admiring the play of the sun off the Willamette River as I crossed it and merged onto Highway 84.

"The East Side," Gavin said, in a ghoulish voice.

"Yes, there is life across the river, despite what Tim thinks."

"Is he still pissed about all of this?"

"Who knows," I said, lifting my shoulders in a shrug. "And it's not my fault, anyway."

After just a couple of minutes, I slipped onto the Hollywood exit ramp, just as MapQuest had directed me to, and made my way to Sandy Boulevard, noting with pleasure the presence of a Starbuck's, a Trader Joe's grocery store, and a gorgeous old movie theater. At the same time, I tried to ignore the transient character holding a sign for spare change, wearing a pith helmet and what appeared to be a sequined blouse.

When I drove past him, he flipped me off.

Welcome to the neighborhood.

I continued along Sandy, observing countless yuppified couples walking well-behaved yellow labs and pushing high-tech baby strollers, complete with joyful and boisterous cargo. I wasn't sure why I'd expected the area to be drastically different from where I'd been living, but the similarities were both reassuring and disconcerting. I was alone and uncertain about what was to come and, clearly, the loneliness would move with me.

"That's the third porn shop we've passed," Gavin said, pointing to an XXX sign.

"Is there a reason you're counting?"

"Well, I can also tell you we've passed four coffee shops and two pho restaurants, so it's not about me being a perv or anything."

"Sure it is," I laughed.

After a few more blocks lined with Vietnamese restaurants and various small businesses, including a purple antique shop that looked more than slightly compelling, I pulled onto Ida's street, which was lined with a seemingly endless variety of bungalows built in the 1920s. Each home was painted three or more colors, accentuating the kind of vintage details that simply weren't present in Beaverton. They all sat back on rich green lawns, populated with rhododendrons, azaleas, and lavender bushes, most of which had already bloomed but appeared full of promise for next year. Some of the yards featured stone walkways, or fancy brickwork, while others were lined with boxy hedges, cut to waist height.

"Nice," Gavin confirmed. "Really cute little places, Laur. And I love how the tree branches reach over the street and meet in the middle."

As I cruised down the block, I vaguely recalled playing hopscotch with some neighborhood kids during that fateful Ida visit, and remembered the lopsided chalk grid we were unable to wash away with a garden hose.

Each house was more darling than the next, and I found myself holding my breath with anticipation. I couldn't visualize Ida's place, so I counted off the address numbers until I found hers.

I slowed down to pull into the driveway.

A Craftsman, just like Mom said.

Beautiful.

"No *way*!" Gavin squawked, unlocking his door and leaping onto the pavement.

I climbed out of the car and examined my inheritance.

The steps leading to the front door each held a terra cotta planter I pictured filled with blooming perennials, and while the white trim around the windows and tracing the shape of the house contrasted nicely with the weathered cedar shingles, a fresh coat of paint wouldn't have hurt.

The windows were shielded by white lace curtains, and the covered front porch housed a solid bench with plump and welcoming striped cushions in blues and reds. As I climbed the steps I saw that the brass door knocker, in the shape of a smiling whale, could benefit from some polish, and the roof appeared to have a couple of loose shingles, but overall the house appeared to be in great shape.

Ida's house.

My house.

"If the inside's as nice as the outside, you're *golden,* Laur. You'll make a mint."

Getting inside the house proved far more difficult than locating it had been. The locks on the front door were not only rusty, but numerous, and the key chain was loaded with prospective mates.

As I wrestled with the keys, I noticed movement next door, in the form of a brief parting of curtains, but whoever was there was quick to hide from view.

Interesting.

Each lock took at least three attempts and five curses, but the door did finally swing open, and I stepped over the threshold, Gavin right behind me.

The first thing I noticed, aside from the bright sunlight shining through the living room windows and bouncing off the hardwood floor, was the smell of citrus hanging in the air. I don't know why I expected all of the furniture to be covered with ghostly sheets and layers of dust, since Ida hadn't been gone long, but the cheeriness of the room came as a surprise.

A welcome one.

"Sweet," Gav whispered.

Against pale blue walls, an off-white sofa housed a collection of brightly colored pillows I guessed my aunt had embroidered herself. A small stack of cork coasters sat on the table, awaiting tumblers or coffee cups, and a thick but well worn red rug tied the room together.

A display of black-and-white framed photographs, lined up next to the reaching limbs of a rather delicate-looking ficcus,

traced my family history backwards to the early 1800s, each generation scowling a bit more than the last, ending with a stodgy
couple in high collars who appeared to be passing a matched set
of kidney stones at the precise moment the photo was taken.

A weathered but impressive grandfather clock in the far corner
ticked with each passing second.

"This place is gorgeous, but that thing would drive me nuts,"
Gavin said, taking a closer look.

"Yup. That kind of noise would invade anyone's dreams," I
agreed.

I stepped away from him and promptly screamed.

There was a fucking *squirrel* on top of the bookcase.

My shriek was no less real when I realized the animal was dead.

"What? What is it?" Gavin asked, hustling away from me and
toward the door, apparently more inclined to make a run for it
than save me.

I caught my breath and pointed to the beast. "*That.*"

"What the hell?" he murmured, taking a few cautious steps
closer. "What's it supposed to be *doing*?"

As I waited for my heartbeat to return to a normal pace, I
gazed at the creature. It was positioned in a most unnatural way,
on its hind legs, head titled to one side as if asking a question, delicate front paws raised in supplication.

"I have no idea," I told him.

"Did she buy it like that, or commission it?"

"I have no idea."

"Did she kill it?"

"No!" I gasped.

Or did she?

I moved away from the squirrel, and stepped into a short hallway, where I was stunned by the presence of a stuffed raccoon.

"Holy crap. There's more, Gav!"

This second taxidermy treat was also standing on hind legs, mouth slightly open in something halfway between a smile and a grimace, as it appeared to be preparing to eat a small and equally dead fish.

In a matter of minutes, the ghostly menagerie had grown into a small and furry army, new critters stashed in all kinds of unexpected places.

"You need to schedule a garage sale, Laur."

"Tell me about it."

I wandered onto the checkered tile of the kitchen floor, first glancing above the sink for the dreaded flypaper. I wasn't disappointed. The brown tape dangled listlessly, but only three dead bugs adhered to the sticky surface. In light of the unfortunate beasts I'd already encountered, I was relieved not to find a fly-populated diorama on the kitchen counter.

I peered at Ida's grocery coupons, anchored to the fridge door with a magnet advertising lawn care. Judging by the number of Starkist clippings, it was clear that the woman had loved her tuna.

Looking out the back window, I saw a couple of fruit trees and a brick patio that would be perfect for a barbeque. All the backyard needed was a strand or two of tiny, twinkling white lights to illuminate it at night.

"What's upstairs?" Gavin asked.

"Bedrooms, I think. Let's check it out."

I stepped back into the living room and climbed the stairs, noting a loud creak just before the landing.

A flash of memory shot through me. "When Tim and I stayed here as kids, we always skipped that step during hide and seek."

"You know, I don't even remember you coming here."

"It wasn't often," I told him. "That's why this whole thing is so weird. I mean, why leave it to me?"

The soles of my sneakers sunk into the plush rugs lining the hallway and I was surprised to see that Ida had removed the yellowed plastic runners, which I suddenly remembered used to cover them like a layer of shellac. I passed the inlaid armoire where I vaguely recalled she stored her countless decks of playing cards and mismatched dice.

Reaching the second-to-last doorway, I peeked at the single bed and rolltop desk occupying the little alcove where I'd slept. The lack of ornamentation redefined the term *spare room,* and when I stepped onto the dusty hardwood, it produced the same hollow sound I recognized.

It was all coming back to me.

The lace curtains were in good shape, though they could use a soak in bleach, and I doubted the folded quilt at the end of the mattress had warmed a body in at least a decade. Hands on my hips, I tried to decide whether it was comfortable or spooky.

"Oh, it's spooky," Gavin assured me, "but it *could be* really cozy, with the right touches."

I walked to Ida's bedroom door and barely stepped inside, staring at the combination of a sagging canopy over the bed and the porcelain pan below it.

"Ida's bed," I whispered.

"*Her deathbed,*" Gavin moaned, in the same ghoulish voice he'd used earlier.

"She died at Safeway," I told him.

"Seriously?"

"Yeah."

"Hmm." He rubbed his chin like a crime scene investigator. "Not *quite* as safe as they'd have us believe."

"You're a tool, Gav." I laughed and started to leave the room just as my phone rang.

"Lauren, it's Tim," my brother said, when I answered.

"Hi," I said, cautiously.

For crying out loud, didn't I see him just yesterday?

"How's it going?"

"Fine, I guess." I mouthed his name to Gavin, who nodded.

"How's work?"

"Okay, I guess."

He sighed. "Hey, have you given any thought at all to my suggestions about jump-starting your life?"

"I haven't applied for a passport, if that's what you mean."

"You know, it doesn't make a whole lot of sense to waste an opportunity to change your whole life."

"I *am* changing it," I told him.

"But you don't want to *do* anything."

"That's not true," I argued.

What the hell does he want from me?

"You want to know what I think?"

Uh-oh.

"Sure," I said, reluctantly.

"I think . . ." He paused for a moment and I let the silence hang between us. "That we should pool our resources."

"What resources?" I asked, watching Gavin peer inside Ida's closet doors.

"Our inheritances, Laur. Now, hear me out," he said, his pace quickening. "Surely you agree that we did *not* receive an equal share from Ida."

I didn't say anything.

"Lauren?"

"I'm listening," I told him, my whole body tensing up.

"I think we should pool our inheritances together. You sell yours, I sell mine, and we split the profit equally. That's the fair thing, don't you think? You could travel the world, or go back to school."

"I don't want to go back to school."

"You could start a business—"

"Doing what?" I asked.

What kind of a cockeyed plan was this?

"Use your imagination, here. This is a *huge* opportunity."

"Tim—"

"Seriously, Laur. Don't you think that's the fair thing to do?"

"You're kind of catching me off guard here, you know."

Gavin raised his eyebrows and whispered, "Should I leave?"

I shook my head.

"Lauren, just think about it," my brother continued, a note of urgency in his voice. "This is the right thing to do, don't you think?"

He carried on, but I stopped listening to him as an idea formed in my head. A wonderful idea that would take the fraternal and housing pressures off of me in a heartbeat. A wonderfully simple idea that I hadn't given more than four seconds' thought before blurting out a commitment to it.

"I'm moving into Ida's house."

"What?" he choked.

"What?" Gavin whispered, his eyes bulging.

My brain might have been in overdrive, but my mouth was way ahead of it.

"The thing is, it's just sitting here. I mean, I'm standing in the house right now, and it's totally livable." It was fairly true. Sure it needed a bit of elbow grease, but it was a solid, lovely house. "And it's mine," I reminded him, as gently as I could.

In light of everything that was going on in my life, throwing myself into a new and positive project seemed like the perfect plan. There would be no time for loneliness and second-guessing if I was up to the elbows in home improvement. After all, I was no multitasker. I couldn't wallow *and* wallpaper.

"Lauren, you can't—" my brother began.

Can't was the word that sealed the deal.

"My fresh start," I murmured.

"You're nuts," Tim told me.

"It's the best idea I've had in months," I told him, pushing the possibilities of decommissioning an oil tank or removing asbestos insulation from my mind. "Maybe even years."

That was pushing it, but I was on a roll.

A borderline manic roll.

"Talk to Mom and Dad first," he sighed. "Don't just jump in like you always do."

It was too late.

I was already neck deep, and I'd barely looked at the place.

Nine

MOM AND DAD tried to be enthusiastic about me taking over Ida's place, but they were a tad concerned about how much work the house might need. I'd already considered the issue and if there were any substantial expenses, I figured I could hire a contractor with a cash advance on my credit card.

Easy, peasy.

"All it needs is some paint and maybe a couple of shingles," I assured Mom. "Gavin looked at it with me."

As if that means anything.

He was a graphic designer, not a contractor, though he was male, which counted for a lot in Mom's home repair book.

"So, what's he up to?" Mom asked.

"Gavin? Maybe a buck fifty, soaking wet."

"You know what I mean."

"Oh, I don't know," I shrugged, even though she couldn't see me. "He's still working from home and seems to be doing pretty well with it."

"And?"

"And, like I said, he checked out Ida's house with me."

"So, you two have been . . . *hanging out* lately?"

"We've always hung out, Mom."

"I like Gavin," she said, with a strange wistfulness.

"So do I." *Obviously.* The guy was one of my closest friends.

"You know, when you broke off the engagement, it took your

Dad and I by surprise, and we couldn't help wondering if it was Gavin."

"If *what* was Gavin?" I asked, loading sweaters into a box for the big move.

"You know . . . if it was Gavin."

"What are you talking about?"

"We wondered if maybe you and Gavin—"

"*Oh my god.* No!" Had she gone completely bonkers?

"Well, you've always been close, and—"

"Not like *that*!"

"Why on earth not? He's a very handsome man, and—"

"Mom, I just don't think of him like that."

"That doesn't mean you *couldn't*."

"How about we just drop it?" I asked.

She paused. "Fine, but I think you should at least consider it."

"I consider it out of the question, Mom."

Dad picked up the extension. "Are you on here, Cecile?"

"I'm talking to Lauren," she told him, then said to me, "Your dad is more than willing to come out and help with the house, you know."

"That's right," Dad agreed, though I could barely hear him over the static.

"What phone are you on?" I asked.

"A new one," he said. "I picked it up at Wal-Mart for seven dollars."

"Seven dollars," Mom repeated. "Can you believe it?"

"Yes, I can. It sounds like you're calling from your car trunk."

"Close!" Dad exclaimed. "I'm in the garage."

"It's a *portable*," Mom explained, as though I wouldn't be able to put the pieces together.

"Can it be stationary, too?"

"What?" Dad asked.

"Any chance you might stop moving?" A headache tingled at the center of my forehead.

"What did you say?" Dad asked, his voice scrambled by crappy technology.

"*Stop moving!*" I nearly shrieked.

"Honey, what's wrong?" Mom asked.

"Nothing." I looked at the flattened cardboard boxes leaning against the wall of Rachel's apartment, waiting to be filled.

The thrill I'd felt when I moved in with Daniel was markedly absent. There was something alien and sad about going it alone, and I wasn't looking forward to it.

"Lauren?" Dad's voice broke the silence.

"Nothing's wrong. I'm just exasperated by this conversation, okay?"

Neither of them said anything.

I cleared my throat. "Are you still there?"

"Yes," Mom sighed. "Do you want us to come and help or not?"

I'd taken up enough of their time with lengthy phone calls during the split, and the last thing they needed was to miss their upcoming Yahtzee tournament in favor of unpaid manual labor.

"No, I've got friends helping me," I assured her, though I hadn't actually asked anyone yet. I did plan on offering pizza and beer to whoever was game, however.

"Daniel?" Dad asked.

"No," I said, through gritted teeth.

"What did he say about the house?" Mom asked.

"Ida's?" I asked. "Nothing. We haven't talked for a while."

"Maybe when he helps you move—" Dad began.

"*Dad,* he's not helping me move."

"I don't see why he wouldn't help," Mom murmured.

"Because we're not together, Mom."

"That doesn't have to mean—"

"Yes," I interrupted. "Actually it does."

"Marg's ex-husband still drops by with cinnamon buns a couple of days a week," Mom told me.

"Who's Marg?" I asked, head pounding.

"The woman two doors down."

"That's not her ex-husband," Dad said.

"What?" Mom asked. "Of course it is."

"The guy with the goatee?" Dad asked.

"Yes, the goatee, the cute little beret, and the cinnamon buns."

This is costing me eight cents per minute?

"That's not the ex-husband," Dad politely informed her. "That's the fellow she left him for. The baker."

"Then who is the man with the red sports car?"

"The one she's leaving the baker for."

There was a static-filled pause before Mom spoke again. "How do you know all of this, Bill?"

"Ernie told me."

"Hey, guys?" I interrupted. "Maybe I should get going and let you talk."

"Talk?" Mom asked. "There's no time. We've got about . . . five minutes to make it to our Thai cooking class."

"It's vegan," Dad added.

"That sounds great," I sighed.

"But I'm sure we could add meat when we make it ourselves," Dad clarified. "Chicken and so forth."

"We'll call you in a couple of days, sweetheart," Mom said. "Good luck with the move and everything."

"Thanks," I whispered, my voice filled with its own brand of static.

I wished I was retired and living large in sunny Florida, sipping orange juice and waiting for my turn at shuffleboard.

I lay down on the couch, suddenly overwhelmed by the prospect of all of the things I needed to do in order to move. If nothing else, at least Rachel would be relieved to have me out of her hair.

We weren't even ships passing in the night anymore, but two vessels docked in different ports. She spent almost all of her time at Steven's while I was at the apartment, and when I did see her at work, I could never quite manage to ask about the engagement.

I had to move on with my new life, however, so I decided to approach her on Wednesday afternoon, after my meeting with Ida's lawyer, when I signed papers and truly took over the house.

I RETURNED TO my desk after the appointment and found Rachel studiously filing her paperwork. I wasn't sure how to broach the subject of the move, which was due to take place in a matter of days, so I just did what came naturally and blurted, "Hey, I just wanted to let you know that I'm moving out this weekend."

She clutched a file against her chest and gaped at me. "What?" She shook her head quickly, as though she were jump-starting her brain. "Where?"

"Ida's house," I said, smiling brightly.

"But you're selling it," she frowned.

"I changed my mind. It needs a bit of work, but that's no big deal." I widened my smile, but she was still frowning.

"But you live with me." She paused, then unnecessarily added, "at my place."

"Which has been *great*, and I've totally appreciated it, but now you can have your own space back, and—"

"Lauren, you were helping with my mortgage."

"Hey, it was no problem. You helped me so I helped you. That's friendship, Rach."

"No," she said, with an unexpected flash of anger. "I mean, you were helping with my mortgage, so I was able to buy the Bug."

"Sure," I agreed.

She stared at me. "So, I can't afford the car payment and the full mortgage alone, Lauren."

"Oh," I said, biting my lip.

This, I didn't anticipate.

"*Oh* is right. I thought you were going to stay for a while."

"It *has* been a few months, already," I reasoned.

"And you're moving *this* weekend? I get . . ." She glanced at her lighthouse calendar. ". . . *three days' notice?*"

"Hey it's not like I signed a *lease,* Rach," I snapped. "This was a temporary solution, a convenient arrangement for the time being."

"Convenient for *you,*" she barked.

"What, were we supposed to live together forever? We're not the fucking *Golden Girls,* Rach."

This certainly isn't going as planned.

Yeah, as if you actually plan anything.

"You don't even see that you've totally screwed me over, do you?" she asked, shaking her head with wonder.

"Rachel, I haven't done *anything* to you!"

She rubbed her forehead. "If you're not selling the house, that means . . . it means that—"

"What?"

"It means you won't have all that money."

"Of course not." I shrugged. "I'll have the house instead."

"But you . . ." She paused, her lower lip quivering slightly.

"What?"

"You said . . ." Her voice tapered off.

My god, knowing my mouth, it could be anything.

"What, Rachel?"

"You said you were paying off my Visa card."

That one hit me right in the stomach.

Shit.

I did.

All I'd wanted to do was to make her feel better, and I would have paid off the card (probably), if I had the money, but obviously my circumstances had changed.

Surely she doesn't expect me to do it now.

Or does she?

"Listen, Rach. That was an off-the-cuff remark, and—"

"Never mind," she said, softly, shaking her head and looking wounded.

"Rachel, I—"

"I *said* never mind," she snapped. "It's my own problem."

"But—"

"I should know by now that everything you say should be taken with a grain of salt."

I frowned. "Well, that seems a little uncalled for."

"I disagree."

"Look," I said, searching for the words that would smooth things over. "I didn't mean to . . . I guess what I . . . well, I'm *sorry*, Rach."

It wasn't a word I used very often, and she knew it. I preferred to stand behind my outbursts at any cost rather than back down.

She leaned forward in her chair and rested her gaze on me. It was uncomfortable, but I stood still and let her stare without saying another word, even though every cell in my body wanted to confront her about the wedding. For once, I managed to contain a candid outburst.

"Thank you, Lauren," she finally said. Looking down at her hands, still tightly clasping the file, she spoke both softly and carefully. "I guess I overreacted a little, but you really caught me off guard."

Sensing it still wasn't entirely safe for me to speak, I bit my lower lip.

She took a deep breath. "I shouldn't have raced out and bought the car," she said, quietly.

"But since you did," I said, unable to maintain my silence, "can you help me move on Saturday?"

She stared at me, her expression defeated. "I guess so," she shrugged.

IN THE FOLLOWING days, I stopped by the post office to forward my mail, then spent a ridiculous amount of time wrestling with automated phone services, trying to set up accounts for all of my utilities.

While preparing for Operation Relocation, a recurring question kept pestering me, like a loose bra strap in constant need of adjusting. It interrupted as I ate my third Pop-Tart, straight from the box, barely registering the stale crust. I tried to ignore the buzzing insistence, but failed. Whenever I had a spare moment, and even when I didn't, the same little voice in my head continued to ask, *What the hell are you doing?*

I didn't have an answer.

Why had I told Tim I was moving to Aunt Ida's house in the first place? What lapse in logic caused me to make the leap? My plan barely lived up to the word, conceived in a moment of stupidity and never fully thought through in the days that followed.

By Saturday, I'd managed to corral Gavin, Rachel, and Steven, the secret fiancé, into helping, which was a huge relief. If many hands made light work, a few would make it less heavy, if nothing else.

Standing in the middle of the Beaverton storage unit on moving day, with an open box of my personal history in front of me, I glanced from the Valentine's card Daniel had given me when we were first dating to the carefully dried and tissue-wrapped rose bouquet I'd saved.

Starting over?

No, I was far better versed in hanging on to the past.

"Ready to start loading?" Rachel asked, quietly.

"Sure," I said, forcing a smile.

With Steven's expertise, gleaned from a summer working for his uncle's moving company in San Francisco, we had the U-Haul loaded in a couple of hours. We set off as an awkward convoy: Gavin at the wheel of my packed Toyota, Steven and Rachel in her Bug, and me steering the mother of all clumsy trucks.

Irritated that I hadn't possessed the foresight to insure Steven as the driver, I bit my lip as I pulled out of the driveway and hoped like hell that all other vehicles would stay out of my path.

The drive to Ida's felt about 468 times longer than what it had been when I paid my first visit to the house, and Gavin's constant cell calls, checking to make sure that everything was okay, did nothing to alleviate the tension.

Once I got onto the highway, the curling nonsense and absurdly skinny lanes of the road might as well have been engineered by a pack of Ritalin-deprived first-graders.

The plan, which had originally made me euphoric, had left me deflated.

Deflated, annoyed, and anxious, actually.

Of course, my mood wasn't helped by the fact that Steven hadn't secured my truckload of belongings with rope, as advised by the assistant manager of the local U-Haul outfit, a balding know-it-all with Exacto knives and felt markers peeking out of every vest pocket. He'd gripped a staple gun with one hand and had a roll of packing tape secured to each hip, like he was Kevin Costner in *Dances With Cardboard*.

"Just tap the brakes," he'd advised me. "And keep her slow. That's a heavy load you're carrying."

Didn't I know it.

Every time I cautiously approached a corner, the beast of a vehicle swung wide and I practically heard the terrified screams of the

Royal Doulton I'd been left by my grandmother. I tried to shrug off the possible destruction of place settings, passing so many trees I figured it didn't really matter if the dishes made it; Oregon was an endless forest, begging to be converted into paper plates.

I slid the radio dial from one station to the next, but whenever I managed to hit something worthwhile, static rolled in. When the traffic ground to a halt, I tried to entertain myself with license plate games and guessing at the identities of various lumps of roadkill, but I wasn't six anymore.

As I slurped the watery contents of a dying Big Gulp and checked my watch, it struck me again that despite the precarious, shifting load in the back of the truck, I had virtually nothing. Perhaps it was this sour mood that turned my stomach, rather than the endless stream of Cheetos, choco-treats, and carbonated beverages I'd poured down my throat for days. Then again, maybe the gnawing pain in my chest had more to do with heartburn than heartache.

When I finally reached my exit, I pulled onto Sandy Boulevard and saw the image of my U-Haul reflected in the windows of a florist, fabric shop, then grocery store as I chugged toward my new home, the garish illustration of cacti and sunset filling the glass with flashes of color.

When our three vehicles pulled onto Ida's street, curious stares and the occasional wave were all that greeted us, until a boy of about eleven or twelve on a ten-speed appeared next to my window, feet furiously pedaling as he raced me. He was soon joined by a couple of younger kids on skateboards and some girls on mountain bikes within moments, all of whom tried to keep pace with me while blatantly staring. Some of them smiled, while one boy called out, asking where I was going.

"Just a couple of blocks down," I shouted, over the sound of the engine. I felt like the only float in the world's lamest parade, but the kids stuck with me. One of the girls said something, but I couldn't make out the words.

"What?" I asked.

"You got kids?" she shouted.

"No," I said, shaking my head.

"Crap."

"I told you!" her friend sang.

At that precise moment, my enthusiastic entourage collectively came to an abrupt halt, turned, and headed back to wherever they'd come from.

I hadn't been in my new neighborhood for five minutes, and I was already a disappointment.

"SO, THIS IS it," Rachel said, shoving her hands into the back pockets of a pair of distressed jeans as she stood in the driveway, staring at the house.

"Yup," I said, having trouble reading either her expression or her tone.

"It's cute," she said, with a smile. "Really cute."

As cute as a secret engagement?

That one was eating me alive.

"You know about the foundation problem, right?" Steven asked, pulling off his sweatshirt and tying it around his waist.

"Foundation?" I asked.

"See the front steps, how they're kind of lopsided and pulling away from the house?" he asked, pointing beyond the lovely planters that had distracted me during the last visit, to a substantial gap.

"I see," I told him, heart sinking.

"Foundation problem," he repeated.

"Yup," Gavin agreed, although I knew he had no idea what he was talking about.

"Oh." My voice was so soft, I barely heard myself.

Steven peered upwards. "You need some flashing replaced," he said, pointing to the right side of the roof.

Before I knew what he was doing, he'd zipped around to the back of the house, and in a matter of seconds, he appeared above us on the edge of the roof.

"Jesus," he said, shaking his head as he knelt to fiddle with the shingles. "You've got some serious moss happening here."

"I do?"

"Yeah." He stood and walked to the edge of the roof. "And your gutters are toast."

"Can you come down from there?" Rachel asked, nervously.

"Please?" I begged, not wanting to hear any more bad news.

Steven returned to earth and I led the three of them inside the house.

"Holy shit, what is *that*?" Rachel gasped, staring at the top of the china cabinet.

"A gopher, I think," I told her. "Ida seems to have been a bit of a . . . collector."

"Creepy," Rachel said.

"You don't know the half of it," I assured her, with a grim chuckle.

I toured them through the house, and with each room came new concerns from Steven about repairs that needed to be made. When he started using words like *safety* and *liability,* my inner monologue was limited to words like *oh* and *shit.*

How had I missed all of the problem areas?

Easy: I hadn't even looked.

Rachel wasn't much help, frowning over cosmetic issues like Ida's choice of a dismal Bismol pink toilet in the upstairs bathroom, peeling yellow linoleum in the laundry room, and the lace curtains I didn't mind but she deemed dreary.

I tried to be a "glass half full" kind of gal, but it was hard going up against Ms. Glass Half Empty and Mr. Glass Shattered on the Floor.

When the tour was complete and we'd returned to the front room, Rachel cleared her throat before speaking.

"Lauren, you know I want to support whatever you do, and I know you're coming out of a rough patch, but are you sure about this?"

Hell, no. But it was too late.

I shrugged and smiled as earnestly as I could, hoping to fool her. "Hey, if I don't do spontaneous things when I'm young, when am I supposed to do them?"

She glanced at me and winced. "You're almost thirty."

"Exactly," I said, pretending it had been an affirmation. "I'm under thirty and ready to take on the world." I nodded briskly toward the door. "Let's start unloading."

Before I change my mind.

Ten

As WE SET to work unloading the truck, I did my best to smile and nod to anyone passing on the sidewalk, figuring it couldn't hurt to be as friendly as possible on day one. In return, I was tossed a few greetings and repeatedly asked whether I was moving in. Why they'd pose the question to someone unloading a moving van, I wasn't sure, but I had the feeling that sarcasm wouldn't be appreciated. Instead of making any number of obnoxious remarks that came to mind, I adopted what I hoped was a peppy grin (though it was more likely idiotic) and said, "I sure am!"

Considering the nagging doubt that increased every time Steven pointed out a new problem (including, but not limited to, dry rot, windows in need of new sealing, the "wrong" type of insulation, and a running toilet upstairs), it was an Oscar-worthy performance, and as Rachel and I carried a small bookcase between us, I mentally practiced my acceptance speech.

A couple of hours slipped by, marked only by the growing dark stains under Steven's and Gavin's arms and my increasing thirst. The more we carried, the more clear it became that I'd accrued far too much "stuff" during the course of my relationship with Daniel. Between the grunts and groans of lifting boxes of dishes, linen, and photo albums, not to mention books and furniture, Gavin suggested that since pairing up had failed, perhaps paring down was a good idea.

"Seriously," he asked, "do you really need two whole boxes of cookbooks?"

"Well, you can't have too many recipes," I told him.

"Yes, Lauren, you can," Rachel responded for him. "Just like you can have too many placemats, vases, and what was that last box? Didn't we just move in a whole *box* of cookie cutters?"

"I have shapes for every holiday," I reasoned.

"You never make cookies."

"But I *might*. Maybe my new life involves lots of time in the kitchen."

"Make sure you leave enough time in your new life for therapy," she muttered.

"Look, a lot of this stuff belonged to my grandmother," I told her. At least I thought it did. Granted, I had no idea where the metal stars, squares, and circles had come from, but that didn't mean they were without sentimental value.

Or maybe it did.

"I'm willing to bet Great Auntie Ida has a drawer packed with even more of them." Rachel paused to genuflect, and added solemnly, "May she bake in peace."

"That's not funny," I told her, stifling a laugh.

"If you say so," she shrugged.

"My new life *might* involve a new best friend," I said, chuckling as we placed the bookcase next to the far window.

"You're new life *might* involve writer's cramp from signing checks," Steven said as he returned from the basement, dark hair curled with sweat. "That circuit breaker just screams amateur wiring."

"Great," I sighed, liking him slightly less with every new and unfortunate revelation.

"Hey, it's not the end of the world," Gavin said, patting my back, "but it's close."

"Yeah," Steven agreed. "You can definitely see it from here."

"Where was your expertise last week, Gav?" I asked, sweetly.

He wisely pretended not to hear me.

Steven wiped the sweat from his brow with the back of his wrist as Rachel approached him from behind and slipped her arms around his waist. He rested his hand on top of hers and gave it a squeeze, then gently loosened her grip and pulled her forward to face him. With a gentle smile, he drew her close and she rested her head against his chest.

I had to look away, and when I did, my gaze met Gavin's. He looked just as uncomfortable as I felt.

I awkwardly cleared my throat and checked my watch.

"Want to break for lunch?" I asked, out of desperation.

The next thing I knew, Steven and Rachel were off and running in her Bug to pick up beer and pizza with every last penny I had on me and Gavin was having a cold beer and a smoke on the back steps.

I sat down to rest on Ida's overstuffed couch, surveying the piles of boxes around me. As I read the contents scrawled on the side of each, I saw that a fair amount of what I'd held onto could be filed under the heading Life Before Daniel.

I had boxes packed with sticker books and Hello Kitty products, stuffed animals, and a shoebox collection of Smurfs. I could still remember my eight-year-old self, a couple of crumpled bills clutched in my fist as I tried to choose between a two figures while Tim relentlessly badgered me to buy both of us some candy instead.

In light of his recent attempts to commandeer my inheritance, it was clear that not much had changed.

From the high school years I'd kept books, swimming ribbons, and strips of black-and-white pictures from the days when five girlfriends would cram into a booth built for one or two at the mall, a riot of giggles and lip gloss.

I'd watched Steven carry a box labeled "Lauren—journals," and cringed at the sight of pound upon pound of pubescent angst and dreams tucked under his arm. I couldn't think of a single reason I'd kept them, beyond saving the spiral bound notebooks from the filth of a waiting garbage can. Would I ever read them again?

Maybe, with a bottle of dark rum.

How many dreams had I failed to achieve so far?

How many had I forgotten I'd ever dreamt?

I glanced at the chair Gavin and I had squeezed into the corner. It was an unfortunate shade of beige, and the kind of furniture that looked perpetually desperate for a pillow, an afghan, or even a stain or two.

Of course, I hadn't really considered the contents that came with Ida's house when we'd loaded the truck. Judging by the fully furnished rooms, I doubted I had space for it all.

Then again, I figured the square footage could open up quite a bit when I got rid of the furniture I didn't want and, of course all the dead stuff.

I glanced at the squirrel. "No offense."

I could have sworn the little beast glared at me.

My gaze shifted to the frame I'd wrapped in a wool blanket for protection. It was a Van Gogh print Daniel had given me for Christmas a couple of years earlier. I wasn't sure where the green vase filled with white roses would fit into Ida's décor, but I knew the print would make the house feel like home to me. I stood to slip the blanket off and while I waited for Rachel and Steven to return with lunch, I carried the print from room to room, looking for the perfect spot.

"We're ba-ack," Rachel called from the living room about twenty minutes later.

I had just decided that the print belonged at the top of the stairs, so I gently laid it to rest against the wall and joined my friends for pizza.

"So," Steven said, through a mouthful of Hawaiian. "Do you think you'll fix the place up and sell it?"

"I don't think so," I told him, breaking a long strand of mozzarella to free a slice for myself.

"You could probably make some pretty good bank if you did," he said.

I glanced at Rachel and wondered if she'd told him about my rescinded credit card offer.

"We stopped to check out a couple of houses for sale while we were gone," Rachel explained, handing me a small stack of flyers along with a bottle of beer. "Prices are getting up there."

I couldn't tell whether the lack of direct eye contact was deliberate or not.

I flipped through the pages, but didn't really look at them.

"I don't exactly have the budget for a big renovation," I told them.

"But you could take out a loan," Steven suggested. "Then think of the profit you'd make off the back end."

All I wanted was a place to call my own.

Dry rot or not, this was it.

"I'm going to live here," I said, with a slight quiver in my voice. I took a deep breath and, with as much force as I could muster, said, "I'm going to be happy right here."

"Seriously?" Rachel asked, reaching for a stray slice of pepperoni.

"Maybe forever," I told her, bravado taking over, as usual.

"You should think about one of those lofts in the Pearl District," Steven said. "Nice and modern, close to restaurants . . ."

"No yard to deal with," Rachel added.

"I *like* gardening," I replied, though that wasn't entirely true. I liked *looking at* gardens.

"When?" she snorted.

"More pizza?" Steven asked, hurriedly pushing the box in her direction.

"When the sun's out." I took another bite of Hawaiian.

"Lauren, your old place had a landscaper," Gavin reminded me.

"True, but he only came a couple of times a month."

"He did *all* the weeding, pruning, and mowing," Rachel added.

"I planted some stuff," I told her.

"When? *Once a year?*"

"Gavin, more pizza?" Steven asked, looking more than slightly uncomfortable.

"I'd *love* more pizza," he said with unnecessary zeal as he reached for a slice.

"Hey," Rachel said, resting a hand on my forearm. "I just think that you've gone through a lot in the past few months, and you should be trying to simplify your life."

"I am," I told her, trying not to sound snarky.

"You told me just yesterday that you'd signed up for tap lessons."

"So? What's simpler than heel-toe-heel-toe-clap-clap-clap?"

Another spontaneous decision.

"Lauren, you should be taking this time to get yourself together."

Easy for her to say, fabulous *fiancé* and all.

"I *am* together, which is not an easy task for *one* person."

She sighed, pushing the pizza away. "Why does everything have to be a joke with you?"

"What's wrong with a little levity?"

Rachel tucked her perfect golden hair behind her perfectly formed ear. "I've got a friend who's a—"

"Look, I don't need a counselor, a therapist, *or* a shrink," I snapped.

Rachel stared at me, her plump lips shining with pizza grease. "She's a yoga instructor."

I stared at her. "So, I'm not allowed to take tap, but I can do yoga?"

"It'll relax you."

"No, Rachel. It *won't*."

"Maybe we should get back to unloading," Steven said, rising to clear the pizza boxes from the coffee table.

"I *can't* relax," I told her.

"Which is why you need help."

"*I need help?*" I choked. "Did I tell *you* that you needed help when you were dating that married guy in Tigard?"

Oh, shit.

I wished I could take the words back as soon as they flew out of my mouth.

Rachel's face turned white and her lips were pressed tightly together, like they were trying to contain a hellacious and powerful message.

I couldn't look at Steven, but noticed from the corner of my eye that he was standing utterly still, pizza box in hand.

"Married guy?" he repeated.

"Rachel—" I began.

"Don't!" she barked, rising from the couch in a swift and angry motion. "Don't say another word right now, or god help me, I don't know what I'll do."

"But—"

"*Don't*," she said, eerily calm as her eyes glazed over.

She moved toward the door as Steven laid the box on top of the dining table then turned to follow her. His cheeks were flushed with color and I could see his jaw pulsating.

I followed them to the door, my mind racing through every word in my vocabulary, frantically searching for the right combination, the right sentiment to repair the damage.

I came up empty.

They left without saying a thing, closing the door behind them with a quiet click.

"Shit," I groaned, leaning against it, fists clenched with frustration over my stupidity.

"What the hell just happened?" Gavin asked.

"I blew it," I sighed. "Her relationship with Kevin was years ago, and I know she's totally ashamed of it."

I was pretty sure she hadn't told anyone, aside from me, about it, and what had I done?

Opened my big mouth, yet again.

"Why would you even bring it up?" he asked.

"I don't *know*, Gav. Because I'm a horrible person?"

"Hey, I didn't say—" he began.

"But you were thinking it," I finished for him.

"Call her," Gavin urged.

"You think she'll answer?" I snorted.

I sighed as I cleaned up the mess from lunch, then did dial her cell phone. Of course, she didn't pick up.

What do you expect?

I left a lengthy message, begging for her forgiveness.

On the brink of tears by the time I hung up, I suggested to Gavin that we finish unloading the truck.

It took a great deal of grunting and a couple of minor back spasms to get the job done, but eventually everything was inside the house. I drove the U-Haul to the nearest rental center and Gavin drove me back to Ida's.

"Do you want me to stay for a bit and help you unpack?" he asked, when he pulled into the driveway.

"No, you've helped enough, and god only knows what horrible things I'd say to you if you stayed."

"Good point," he said, with a wry smile. "Hey, do you want to maybe catch a movie on Tuesday night?" His smile widened and for a brief moment I wished I could just fall in love with him.

"Tuesday, huh?" I asked.

"I'd even see a girly one, if you wanted to."

"Is that right?"

"Well, girly movies mean . . ." he cocked his eyebrows and waited for me to finish.

"*Girlies,*" I said, with a roll of the eyes. "Okay, I'll pick you up, just e-mail me the times or something."

"Hey, Laur," he said, softly. "Are you sure you'll be okay if I leave you?"

"I'm sure," I lied, attempting a smile of my own. "I probably need the time alone to figure out how to make things right with her."

He offered a sympathetic pat on the back and I not only willingly accepted it, but leaned in to rest my head against his shoulder and hugged him.

"I know," he said, quietly. "It's been a shitty few months."

I felt the tears welling and rushed to say good-bye and get him out of the house before they fell.

Exhausted by both the labor and events of the day, it was all I could do to climb the stairs and fall onto the guest bed for a nap and I spent the next couple of hours thrashing back and forth, twisting the sheets around my legs and dreaming I was stuck to a wall-sized swatch of Ida's sticky flypaper.

I WAS AWAKENED by the insipid tune of my cell phone, and in the moments it took to unravel myself from the death grip of

Ida's sheets and find the damn thing, I hoped with all my heart it was Rachel, returning my call.

I couldn't afford to lose her.

When I checked the ID screen, the words *Mom and Dad* flashed with each ring.

"All settled in?" Mom asked, when I answered.

"Ha!" I barked, envisioning the boxes piled in the living room.

"It'll take some time," she said.

"Everything seems to," I said, voice still thick and raspy with sleep.

"We really think it would be a good idea for us to come out. This move was so . . . *spontaneous.*"

"You say that like it's a bad thing. I'm okay, Mom."

"That may be true, but we'd like to help get you settled. You've had a lot going on."

"Hey, I'm finally starting my new life. I'm keeping busy with work, and unpacking and everything. Why don't you wait until I've got myself organized and come out then, for a real visit?"

"I don't know . . . we worry about you."

"Just enjoy yourselves, Mom. That's what retirement's for."

"Well," she hesitated. "We *do* have that doubles ping-pong tournament coming up, and your dad has been pretty excited about that."

"See?"

"And the cooking classes are continuing for a couple more weeks—"

Thankfully, the doorbell interrupted the conversation before they could mention the dance classes, water aerobics, or trivia tournaments. Their jam-packed social life put me to shame.

"Mom, there's someone at the door. I'll talk to you later."

"Don't forget your pepper spray," she warned.

"It's probably Rachel," I told her, hoping I was right.

I glanced at the box of linens at my feet and envisioned a bed-sheet turned cape, perfect for my new role as an antihero: the Alienator.

The bell rang again.

"I'd better go," I told Mom.

"Okay, we'll talk to you later, then," she said. "I'm serious about the spray, honey, and it wouldn't hurt to look into an alarm system as well," she added, before hanging up the phone.

"Pepper spray," I muttered, shaking my head with disbelief, rushing downstairs and across through the maze of boxes on the living room floor to open the front door.

Little did I know, life was about to get a bit salty.

Eleven

ON MY FRONT step stood a tiny, wrinkled, and wild-haired woman in gigantic overalls, giving me what could only be called a suspicious look.

"You moving in here?" she asked, her voice low and gravelly as she looked me over, from greasy hair to grubby sneakers.

"Yes," I said, smiling politely.

Who the hell are you?

"You're Lisa," she announced.

"Lauren," I corrected, brightening the smile a watt or two with the hope that she'd crack one herself.

No dice.

"We met when you were a little girl, visiting." She buried her hands in her denim pockets and tipped her head to one side. "I live next door."

"Really? I'm sorry, I don't remember . . . it was a long time ago."

"Yes, it was." She sniffed loudly and frowned at me before speaking again. "Where did you come from?"

The smart aleck in me was tempted to mention my dear mother's uterus, but since my big mouth was only bringing me grief, it seemed wise to steer clear of that sort of thing, so I simply stated, "Beaverton."

"Beaverton, *Oregon*?" she asked, dark eyes widening with surprise.

"Yes."

She shook her head. "So, what stopped you from visiting her?"

"Who, Ida?"

"Yes, *Ida.*" Her eyes flashed angrily and I almost stepped back.

"I don't know . . . I guess I just—"

"Do you know what it's like being an old woman, alone?"

I'd certainly learned a bit about being a young woman alone, which sucked. I was pretty sure that throwing a few decades into the mix would only make it worse.

"Well, not from direct experience, but I—"

"Do you know what it would have meant to have family come by?" she growled. "She always acted like it didn't make a difference to her, but you know what? It did."

I didn't know what to say as the guilt slowly washed over me. "I'm sorry."

"Don't apologize to *me*," she said, scowling and digging even further into her pockets, toying with what I assumed were keys. The fabric threatened to swallow her up to the elbows.

"I wasn't. I mean, I . . ."

"I saw you at the funeral," she said, squinting. It sounded like an accusation.

"I didn't see you."

"I didn't go," she said, dismissing the idea with a wave of her hand.

Huh?

"I don't think I'm following—"

She sighed. "Too emotional, you know? I had every dang intention of going, but when I got to the cemetery, I couldn't do it. I watched from the car for a minute or two, turned right around, and came home."

"You were close," I said, nodding in understanding.

She glared at me. "I *just* told you I got as far as the parking lot."

"I meant close to Ida."

Her nostrils flared. "*Of course* we were close. Hell, we were neighbors for almost forty years. We were like family." Her eyes hardened as she looked me over again. "Closer than family, when it really comes down to it."

Ouch.

"I should have visited her," I murmured.

"Damn straight," she snapped.

I thought of my mother and tried to imagine what she would do to smooth things over. "Would you like to come in? Maybe have something to drink?"

She paused long enough to make me wonder if the offer had offended her before nodding and voicing a gruff, "Thank you."

I held the door open as she moved past me and into the living room.

"It's a bit of a mess," I said, wincing.

"It sure is."

Taken aback, I decided to view her rudeness as . . . candor.

I walked toward the kitchen. "I've got water, Coke, or beer."

"Beer's good," she said. "But only if it's bottled."

Returning with one in each hand, I tried another smile, and this time she looked a little less stern.

Maybe it's a matter of baby steps.

"Here you go," I said, handing her a bottle.

She twisted off the cap and took a quick sip, then licked her lips. "I'm not trying to be the crotchety old bitch next door, you know."

Unsure of how to respond, I motioned for her to sit down on the couch and settled in next to her.

"Ida was a real good friend," she continued, and suddenly there were tears glistening in her eyes. Her lids fluttered to blink them away. "A good woman. She was always there when I needed her, and I think she felt the same way about me."

"I'm sure she did," I whispered, sensing it was true.

"She deserved the good things in life. I don't have much family either, so we kind of watched out for each other."

"That was very kind of you," I said, then sipped my beer awkwardly.

"You and the boy were real bright spots for her when you were kids," she said, shaking her head sadly.

"The boy? Oh, my brother, Tim."

"I don't think I saw him at the cemetery."

"He was there," I told her. "He's balding." I couldn't resist adding, "Rapidly."

"She would have liked that." She paused and shook her head, then clarified, "Not the balding, but him being there. It wouldn't have meant as much as a drop-in when she was alive, of course." The ferocity returned in a flash, but died down again.

"Of course," I repeated, wondering how long she was planning to spend running me through the wringer.

We sat in silence for a couple of minutes, sipping from our bottles.

"You know—" I began, but she cut me off.

"I don't want to start on a sour note with you, Lisa."

"Lauren." Afraid the correction could not only annoy but *enrage* her, I hastily added, "And I don't either."

"Don't what?"

"Want to start on a sour note."

Are we not speaking the same language?

She moistened her lips. "Well, I just felt like I had to say my piece. You know, for Ida's sake."

"I understand," I told her. "You have every right to be angry on her behalf."

I was amazed by my diplomacy. Why couldn't I be agreeable and hold my tongue all the time?

Because it's a slippery little SOB.

The woman lifted her bottle and smiled, two rows of perfect teeth exposed. "You know what? You're okay." Clinking her bottle against mine, she said, "It's nice to meet you. Well, re-meet you."

"You too, uh . . ." I waited for her to fill in the blank.

"Patty," she said, sniffing hard enough to clear not only her sinus passages, but mine as well. "They call me Patty Melt."

"Why?" I asked, sipping my beer.

She squinted at me and spoke very slowly. "Because my name's *Patty*, and there's a grilled sandwich called—"

"Yeah, I know. I was just wondering what the connection—"

She cackled with apparent delight. "It's a *nickname*, for Christ's sake. Shit like that ain't rocket science."

"Right," I mumbled, then bit my lip like a chastised kid.

She nudged me with her elbow. "I'm just giving you a hard time."

"Sure." My chuckle was tepid, at best.

"Did anyone ever mention that you could stand to relax?"

"I actually just woke up from a nap."

"In the middle of the day? A young thing like you? Jesus Christ!"

"Well, I've had a lot going on lately and it felt good to—"

"Sleeping in the middle of the day is a sign of depression."

"Well, I don't think—"

"Then again, it's also a sign of tired." She cackled and slapped her knee.

"I suppose."

I was starting to wish she'd mosey back home.

She surveyed the room, slowly, her gaze ultimately resting on the stack of real estate flyers from Rachel. "Some folks thought you might just sell the place."

"Nope." I shrugged. "Here I am."

"Ida would be happy you're here," she said, eyes welling up again. She blew her nose into a hanky she pulled from the bib pocket of her overalls and cleared her throat. "I'm sure a youngster like you can spruce it up a bit." She paused to look me over again. "Tired or not."

"I hope so."

She cast me a sidelong glance. "You're alone, huh?"

"Yes, I just separated from—"

"Oh, for Christ's sake. *Cream* separates. *People* get divorced."

"We weren't actually married, yet. Just engaged."

Just?

Who am I kidding?

"He cheat on you?" she asked, leaning toward me at the prospect of dirt.

"No, we just—"

"My Walter cheated on me, the son of a bitch."

"I'm sorry to hear that," I said.

"Not as sorry as I was," she replied, with a grim laugh. "Sometimes life surprises you, and sometimes it just kicks the crap out of you." She finished off her beer and placed the empty bottle on the real estate flyers. "So it'll be just you rattling around in this old place?"

Not quite the way I want to look at it.

"I guess so," I mumbled.

"Just like Ida."

"I guess so."

As I'd moved from room to room during that first inspection with Gavin, admiring items like the bird's-eye maple chest of drawers and a small collection of filigree bracelets, a small voice in the back of my mind kept whispering, "It's all mine." But when I peered inside cupboards and drawers, a larger voice hissed, "at least two years' worth of cotton balls, an economy-sized package of Ex-Lax, almost three dozen boxes of Rice-A-Roni, a dripping faucet, a mothball in every drawer, and a life of utter loneliness."

It's all mine.

And mine, alone.

"So, if you don't mind me asking," Patty continued, "how come you're still wearing your ring?"

I glanced at my hand, and at the sparkly diamond I'd slipped onto my finger before my nap. There was something unnerving about that vulnerable strip of pale, unengaged, lonely skin being exposed to the world and I'd wanted to cover it up, even for a moment. It was silly, but wearing the ring had briefly helped. "I don't know. Security, I guess."

"Security comes from here," she said, reaching over to poke my sternum with a bony finger, while staring me straight in the eye.

"I suppose," I sighed.

She looked me over again, then at the sea of cardboard before speaking. "You know, it's one thing to have everything out of the truck and into the house," she said, wiping her hands on her overalls, "but organizing it's another matter."

"I know." I was thoroughly dreading it.

"Want a hand?"

"What?"

"Geez," she muttered, shaking her head. "You young people can't follow the thread of a conversation. I think it's those damn video games."

"Video games?"

"All that flashing addles your brains or something."

"Uh . . . thanks."

"So, what I want to know is if you want help getting your stuff moved into the right rooms."

I stared at her as the offer sunk in. "What, you mean *you?*"

"Yes, me!" she barked, smacking her forehead. "Jesus! Try to keep up."

I looked at her, skeptically. "Um . . . I don't know."

It kind of seems like child labor, but geriatric.

She looked me right in the eye. "I'm old, not dead."

"It *would* be a huge help," I admitted.

"Then let's get to it."

For the next hour and a half, we worked with surprising efficiency, chatting as we went. I learned that Patty had retired from a career as a law enforcement officer, a fact that caused my jaw to drop.

"I can't believe it," I told her.

"Now I work a couple of nights a week at the movie theater concession at Lloyd Center, just to keep busy."

"You were a *cop*?" I asked, still trying to wrap my head around it. "That's such a dangerous job."

"Oh yeah?" Patty snorted. "Try upselling overpriced popcorn."

As we carried hangers loaded with clothing to the spare bedroom, she asked me about my work, so I gave her a brief overview, which sounded even duller than the job itself.

"Why do you do it?"

"What, work there?" I laughed. "Money, Patty. Money makes the world go around."

"You're too young to be settling for something that doesn't satisfy you."

"You sound like my brother."

Except that he would have cushioned the criticism in an insult.

"What do you *want* to do?" she asked, handing me a number of dresses I never wore.

"I don't know." It was the truth.

"Come on, there must be *something*."

Of course there had to be. I just didn't know what it was. I'd fallen into the insurance business after seeing an ad in the paper almost two years earlier, not that I'd ever dreamed, or even *thought,* of doing clerical work forever. "I'm sure there is."

"Don't let life pass you by, Lauren."

"What can I tell you?" I asked. "I'm doing my best to keep up, but every now and then I have a flat tire."

"So get out and walk," she said, matter-of-factly. "Hop a bus, catch a ride, pull your bike out of storage and keep the pace."

"Sure." I was getting tired just *listening* to her.

"Say, I saw some fella up on the roof earlier, checking things out," Patty said, raising a white eyebrow at me.

"My friend, Steven," I explained, though I doubted the accuracy of the statement in the aftermath of recent events. "He says there's a lot of work to be done here."

"Aw hell, all it needs is a little TLC, and you can handle that."

I frowned, skeptical. "You really think so?"

"I've lived next to this house forever, and I saw how well Ida took care of it. Sure, it may need some surface touches, but that's about it. No need to break the bank."

A wave of relief washed over me, warm and welcome.

"Thank you, Patty. You have no idea how much that helps."

We walked downstairs for what felt like the hundredth time, and Patty lifted the last remaining box from the floor. In black marker I'd scrawled "Daniel photos, etc."

"That your guy?"

I looked at the name and wondered how many times I'd written it inside cards and on notes.

"Ex-guy, yeah," I sighed.

She grunted. "Ditch it."

"I don't think I can," I told her.

She dropped the box on the floor with a resounding thud. "There's no reason to keep this."

I started to reach for it. "But they're memories—"

"Make new ones," she said, moving in front of the box to block me.

She's spry, this one.

"But Patty—"

"Look," she said, shaking her head and loosening her bun in the process. "Do you keep dead batteries?"

"No."

"Because they're useless, right?"

"I guess so."

Her nearly black eyes pierced me again. "Are you picking up what I'm laying down?"

Maybe she had a point. I didn't have to keep *everything*. Why did I want to cling to the past, anyway? What was the point of leaving the relationship if I was only going to wallow in it?

"I'll get rid of them," I said softly, reaching for the box.

"This is a fresh start, kid. Don't blow it by dragging your ass."

I sighed as I carried the box through the front door and to the side of the house. I laid it on top of Ida's garbage cans.

When I stepped back inside the house, Patty Melt was preparing to leave.

"Thanks for all of your help," I told her.

She shrugged and looked a bit embarrassed. "You like jam?"

"Jam?"

She rolled her eyes and sighed. "Preserved berries you spread on toast. *Goddamn,* it's like a whole generation's brains have short-circuited."

"I know what jam—"

She pulled a small jar from a voluminous pocket and handed it to me. "Marionberry," she grinned. "Welcome to the neighborhood."

With that, she turned on her sneakered heel and was gone.

Twelve

I SPENT SUNDAY morning unpacking and leaving countless messages for Rachel, who never responded.

Granted, my big mouth had led the way to rather pedestrian trouble in the past, but it had never done quite so much damage in one damnable breath. I could only hope that I hadn't sabotaged her relationship with Steven completely, and that he'd given her the opportunity to explain the relationship she'd had, emphasizing her foolishness at the time and her immense regret afterwards.

Of course, I also hoped she'd give me the opportunity to redeem myself on Monday morning.

I took a quick break for lunch, got both my satellite radio and computer up and running, then started seriously scrubbing Ida's kitchen and bathrooms. It was tough work, but it felt good, especially when my elbow grease revealed sparkling taps and shining countertops. I didn't even mind the pink toilet, once it was gleaming.

By mid-afternoon I was physically tired but mentally raring to go, so I showered and checked the phone book for the nearest Home Depot, which happened to be just minutes away, right by the airport. I made a list of some of the simple sprucing-up projects I could handle, like interior painting, and zipped onto 205 to do a little shopping.

I wandered the wide aisles, admiring everything from floor tiles to shower doors, slowly filling my cart with unplanned items, like a new set of numbers for the front of the house, featuring bold, black type surrounded by tiny purple and yellow flowers, as well as a wel-come mat for the front door, some colorful light-switch covers, ce-ramic planters, the plants to inhabit them, and a couple of rolls of shelf liner.

Since Patty Melt's comment about the house being in good shape, I'd felt like I could be a little loose with my credit card.

Every now and then an employee, decked out in an orange apron and a tool belt, would offer me assistance, and while I asked a question or two, I handled most of the product selection myself. It was a refreshing kind of alone time, where I felt in control of my life, as though choosing the right area rug or faucet would somehow guarantee me a happy and fruitful existence.

By the time I reached the paint section, I had a full cart, which I leaned against while perusing the wall of color cards.

I spent close to an hour comparing shades and trying to visual-ize the rooms in my new home before settling on a color palette that Daniel, the reigning King of Beige, would have forbidden.

Welcome to *my* new life.

I chose a cheery yellow for the living room, and a deep, almost crimson red for a couple of walls in the kitchen, planning to leave the other two neutral. I found a lovely shade of green for the down-stairs bathroom and decided to paint Ida's room a rich purple, since my ultimate plan was to make it my own.

When I held the paint cards in my hand, my choices looked like those of a small child, random and bright, but I didn't care.

It was my place, dammit.

Thank god Patty knew more about the lack of necessary house repairs than Steven, and I could spend freely.

I loaded the car with my fabulous purchases and stopped by the house to unload before deciding that a new coffee table was in order. Ida's wouldn't match the new look I suddenly had in mind for the living room.

In mere moments, I was on the road again, searching for furniture stores. I couldn't resist pulling over in front of a lighting shop on Sandy Boulevard, and soon found myself carrying a beautiful stained-glass floor lamp out to the car.

I found a furniture mecca off Interstate 205 and spent a couple more hours admiring dining room sets and entertainment centers before buying not only the simple wood coffee table I'd come in for, but a new Mission-style bedroom set, complete with the armoire I'd fallen for but didn't really *need*, a nice, solid bookcase for the guest room, which I planned to use as a home office in between visitors and, splurge of all splurges, a new leather couch.

It was a warm dark brown, long enough to lie down on—which I knew from testing it out on the showroom floor while a bemused saleswoman took down my address for delivery—and in the style of countless couches I'd seen in the law offices of old black-and-white movies.

Now, all I need are a couple of chairs and an ottoman.

Figuring those purchases could wait until another day, I made my way to the register and handed over my credit card.

Spontaneous shopping had proven to be exhilarating, exciting and, when I was handed my bill . . . pretty damn expensive.

I gulped and, after the card had been violated, tucked it back into the safety of my wallet.

To my utter amazement, the furniture was delivered that very evening. A Sunday, no less!

Everything's going my way.

Once two burly guys had wrangled the couch in the front door and carried the rest of the goods inside as though they weighed nothing, I tried to enjoy the satisfaction of seeing how fabulous it all looked in the house, even with Ida's stuff piled haphazardly around it, but I was already dreading my mailbox's next missive from Visa.

Just pay off what you can, when you can.

A little interest won't kill you.

As I sat on my brand-spanking-new couch, I surveyed the packed room and tried to decide which pieces of Ida's furniture I'd like to part with. Right off the bat, there was a footstool I knew I'd never use, tucked in one corner, next to a wooden magazine rack I could do without.

Rising from the couch, I figured I might as well clear the space of the unwanted items I could carry.

I moved five pieces into the basement before I saw it, and when I did, I couldn't help smiling. It was tucked in a corner, covered in dust, and boxed in by an old love seat, but there it was.

A sewing machine.

I wrestled it out of its hiding place and dragged it upstairs to set it on Ida's dining table.

Perfect.

I zipped back down to the basement, knowing full well that anyone with that kind of equipment was sure to have scraps. Sure enough, I found a box of fabric and a Peg-Board loaded with spools of thread, and underneath that, a Tupperware box crammed with all the tools I needed, from scissors to fabric markers.

"Hot diggity," I whispered, carrying the load upstairs.

It took a good twenty minutes and some elbow grease to get the Singer somewhat cleaned up and threaded. I plugged it in and grinned when I pressed the foot pedal and heard a lovely whirring sound.

Standing with my arms folded, I admired my find, and that was when the idea struck me, right out of the blue.

I'll make the couture outfit Candace adored.

Cackling, I imagined how good it would feel to watch her eat crow. A subtle yet satisfying comeback to her fashion snub.

I dug through the material until I found a substantial piece of black satin that would do for the skirt and what I estimated to be enough of a pale green knit for the top.

Not precisely what I would have chosen, but well suited to my impromptu project.

"She said I couldn't make it," I murmured, pins and scissors flying. "A simple skirt and blouse. Ha! You'd better believe I can do this."

As I worked, I was amazed at how quickly all the sewing tricks I used to know came back to me, and while the machine hummed, I felt both relaxed and happy. Soon enough, I was enjoying the process so much, it stopped mattering to me how Candace reacted.

I even temporarily forgot about the mess I'd made with Rachel.

Of course, the sewing wasn't entirely smooth sailing, and in the space of a couple of hours I'd stitched, torn apart, and restitched more times than I cared to count, but when I finally tried on the outfit for the final time and climbed the creaky stairs to the full-length mirror in Ida's bedroom, it was all worth it.

While I didn't look like the glamorous, waiflike ingénue from the magazine clipping, I looked darn tootin' *good*. The top clung in all the right places, and I'd even managed to pull off a more flattering, slightly squared neckline than what I'd remembered from the clipping. The pale green shade made my eyes look vivid and the skirt had wonderful movement when I spun around.

Giddiness set in and when it was finally time to crawl into bed, I was still grinning like a fool.

I felt like I'd found a part of me that had been lost for a long, long time.

IN THE MORNING, I dressed in my new outfit, slipping a light cardigan over my bare shoulders and headed for work, terribly pleased with myself. For the first time I could remember, I actually had time to stop at Starbuck's.

I arrived at the office on time, for once, only to discover that I'd forgotten about the early meeting I'd reminded the staff about via a late Thursday e-mail flagged "urgent."

Lovely.

Thankfully, I received no more than a raised eyebrow from Knutsen, who apparently didn't expect much more than tardiness from me. Praising the gods of low expectations for the favor, I sat between Susan, an adjuster who always smelled like coconut, and Michael, who looked like my Uncle Gene and was after me to join his trivia team for battle at some skeezy bar.

Rachel was seated directly across from me, but refused to acknowledge my presence in any way.

Candace, on the other hand, wouldn't stop staring, her brow furrowed in confusion.

The meeting was almost as dry as the bagels provided for our dining pleasure, but we were released to return to our desks about twenty minutes after I arrived.

As I left the conference room, I was tapped on the shoulder.

I turned to see Candace and Lucy.

"Where did you get this?" Candace asked, bending to touch the silky softness of the skirt.

"I made it," I told her, nonchalantly.

She straightened like a startled animal. "No," she said, hesitation in her voice.

"Yeah, last night," I told her. "In a couple of hours."

Her eyes widened and she unzipped her purse to rifle around until she found her crumpled photo. "It doesn't match," she said, with a hint of triumph.

Lucy plucked the clipping from her hand and scrutinized it before giving me a careful once-over. "No, Lauren's looks *better*."

Candace winced.

I blushed with delight and thanked Lucy, just as Rachel walked by.

Okay, you had your fashion fun, now take care of the business at hand.

I followed her back to our work area, again trying to find the right words to patch things up with her, but failing miserably.

"Hey," I said, hopefully.

She glared at me as she took her seat, then turned away to start her computer.

"Rachel?" I cleared my throat. "Rachel, I'm so sorry about Saturday."

She said nothing.

"I was a complete ass, and you have no idea how bad I feel about it."

Still nothing.

I pulled the slightly crumpled Starbuck's paper bag from my purse and placed it next to her.

"I don't want it," she said, pushing it away.

"It's a muffin."

She swiveled in her seat. "A muffin," she scoffed.

"Yeah. Blueberry-lemon. I know you like the cranberry, but—"

"A *muffin*," she repeated, this time with venom.

"Yes," I nodded, meekly.

She cocked her head and hair cascaded down her shoulder in a beautiful blonde wave. "You think *baked goods* are going to fix this?"

I bit my lip. "Uh . . . no?"

Yes.

Wouldn't they help?

Just a little bit?

She made a very obvious effort to move her chair as far away from me as possible and turned away.

"Rachel, I—"

"Grow up, Peterson."

That was the last thing she said to me all day.

I spent hours sorting through my in-box, responding to company e-mails and wishing like hell I'd taken the shock-collar idea seriously.

Blurt Alert.

I spent the lunch hour alone, wallowing in self-pity and eating mediocre tandoori at Indian Palace.

The afternoon was equally dismal, despite my efforts to engage with other employees. Lucy and Candace were no substitute for my best friend, even when they regaled me with karaoke tales from Saturday night.

I tried to focus on the positive elements of my life, but had a hard time coming up with much.

You still have your health.

Aside from a stomachache, courtesy of my lunch.

You have a home.

Which is in need of cosmetic help.

You have a family who loves you.

Not Tim.

You have *parents* who love you.

When they aren't too busy with beach volleyball and cocktail hour.

You have friends.

I have Gavin.

I glanced at Rachel, who was reorganizing her already organized desk in utter silence and thought back to the night we became friends.

AT THE FIRST company Christmas party I ever attended (before they started calling it a "holiday get-together," then changed it to a "winter gathering"), with just under two months of service, Rachel and I were the newest employees there.

We grabbed a couple of drinks from a passing tray and stood back to peruse the crowd and chat. An older man appeared next to me, introducing himself as Martin from the corporate headquarters. He was pretty nondescript, aside from the silvery tufts of hair attempting to escape from his ears, and he seemed to enjoy our girly banter.

As we guzzled booze and flagged down the waitstaff for countless coconut prawns and stuffed mushroom caps, our lips became looser than recommended and, soon enough, we were voicing our opinions to our anonymous audience of one, on everything from the bland selection in the break room vending machine ("I mean, where are the peanut M&M's?" Rachel repeatedly whined) to the company's choice of unusually rough toilet paper and the sorry state of our salaries.

I'd had enough drinks that I barely registered the coworkers who joined us, listened for a moment or two, then quickly left, sporting winces and mortified looks. I even brushed off Lucy when she gave me a firm elbow to the ribs.

When the evening wound down and our companion left, Nick from Purchasing approached us with a vaguely worried expression.

He *always* looked vaguely worried.

And well he should, considering he was the supplier of the shoddy toilet paper.

"How did things go with Martin?" he asked.

"He wasn't much of a talker," I told him, "but we filled in the blanks, didn't we, Rachel?"

"We sure did," she nodded.

"He looked kind of pissed off when he left, you guys."

"No, he didn't," Rachel said, with a wave of her hand.

"And what would he have to be pissed off about, anyway?" I asked, teetering slightly in my heels before righting myself. "We were engaging conv . . . conversationa . . . con . . ." I sighed, frustrated with my errant tongue. "We were engaging."

"More like *enraging*," Nick said, shaking his head.

"What's that supposed to mean?" Rachel asked, taking a sip from an abandoned glass, half full of red wine.

"Lucy said you were complaining about your Christmas bonus."

"*Holiday* bonus," I corrected.

"*Winter* bonus." Rachel grinned, exposing pinkish teeth.

"Whatever," Nick sighed. "She said you were ranting about the vending machine, and—"

"Where are the peanut M&M's?" Rachel moaned, yet again. "I have *never* seen a machine without them. And who the hell eats *Skittles*, anyway?"

"I can't believe you complained to Martin about the freaking—"

"Don't say 'freaking'," I begged. "I hate it when people do that. It's the lamest cover-up move on the planet. Everyone knows you really mean *fucking*, so just be a man and say it."

Nick blinked rapidly as his face reddened. "I don't think masculinity should be judged by a willingness to use profanity."

"And I don't think vending machines should be without peanut M&M's," Rachel murmured.

"I'll be surprised if you two have jobs on Monday," he said, stalking toward the coat check area.

We shrugged at each other and I didn't give it another thought until I arrived at work on Monday morning and saw that Rachel wore a grim expression on a grey face.

"What's wrong?" I asked her, dropping my bag on the seat of my chair.

She closed her eyes and said, "Martin."

"What?"

Rachel rose from her chair and crooked a finger at me to follow her. We walked past the conference room and stopped in front of the wall of old-man head shots I usually ignored.

She pointed at a photo, and my jaw dropped.

It was him.

Or, more accurately, it was Martin Ray Powers, our vice president.

"Shit on a stick," I muttered.

Was it me or Rachel who complained about the bonus?

"A FedEx package came this morning, addressed to both of us," she gulped.

"Already?"

"Well, you're late, Lauren."

"What's in it?"

"I was waiting for you to get here, so we'd find out together. The sender is Mr. Powers."

"Crap," I whispered, leading the way back to our work space.

Sure enough, there was a box.

Rachel cut through the tape and we each held our breath as she opened the flaps.

I'd heard about a company that packaged and shipped cow pies as "gifts" and couldn't help noting the size of the box seemed about right.

Rachel sifted through the foam packing shells until we spotted something bright yellow.

"What the . . ." she murmured.

"Peanut M&M's!" I announced, thoroughly relieved and *loving* the fact that we worked for a guy with a sense of humor.

"Not quite," she said, her skin fading to a ghostly white.

At the bottom of the box was a piece of bright yellow paper, and on it were two words: "You're fired."

"No fucking way," I whispered, heart pounding.

"This can't be serious," Rachel asked me. "Can it?"

It was, but lucky for us, what was more serious was the embezzlement charge against Mr. Powers.

Uncertain of our fate, Rachel and I spent the next two weeks nervously showing up for work and waiting for the bomb to drop, but it never did.

The bastard had been picked up before he had the chance to file our walking papers.

I glanced at my cohort and sighed.

I missed her.

ON THE WAY home, traffic was unbelievable, and it took me fifteen minutes longer to reach my exit than it had to get to work that morning. The commute was going to kill me, if nothing else did first.

I made two more calls to Rachel's cell phone, and left messages that were solemn, serious, and desperate as I told her, yet again, how sorry I was.

I stopped for some orange juice and deli chicken fingers from Safeway, too tired to even contemplate cooking. As I waited at the checkout, irritated by the man in front of me counting out eleven dollars in small change, I thought of my beautiful new couch and how good it would feel to lounge on it in front of the television for a few blissful hours of oblivion.

When I pulled into my driveway, I knew I was mere seconds away from peace and quiet: an evening of reality TV and reheated comfort food.

What I found instead was a little boy on my doorstep.

Thirteen

I STEPPED OUT of the car and cast a quick glance up and down the street, searching for signs of an adult, but saw no one. Slipping my purse onto my shoulder and grabbing my two grocery bags, I cautiously approached the boy, worried that the sudden appearance of a stranger might startle him.

Hell, he'd startled *me*.

He looked to be of school age, but what grade, I could only speculate. Despite Daniel's career as a teacher, I didn't see much of the children beyond his annual class photo.

The boy could have been old enough to tie his shoelaces and maybe ride a bike.

Was that six?

Seven?

His dark brown hair was nicely trimmed, but tousled, and an unruly cowlick dominated his forehead.

He stared at me as I walked closer, attempting a smile.

He didn't smile in return, but looked at me with doleful eyes of a deep, dark brown. Freckles weren't the only marks on his pale skin; a scab the size of a strawberry and almost the same shade swallowed most of his chin and a smudge of dirt ran from the tip of his nose across his left cheek. His red T-shirt featured a cartoon rendition of a monster truck, partially covered by a zippered hoodie.

He sat cross-legged, leaning against my path to a relaxed evening.

"Hi there," I said, my false cheer echoing down the empty street as I lifted a foot to the bottom step and stopped there.

"Hi," he said, in a surprisingly deep voice.

I waited for more, but he said nothing. He continued to stare at me while slowly rubbing the knees of his corduroy pants with a dimpled hand.

"Nice weather, huh?" I asked, stunned by the stupidity of the question.

"Sixty-eight degrees," he said, the flash of a pink tongue visible through a dark gap.

One of my favorite parts of childhood was the temporary lisp that accompanied a lost tooth. I'd tried to adopt a permanent one in the second grade, but by then it was too late. I strove for a sibilant *s,* but even that was difficult to maintain.

"Sixty-eight degrees," I repeated slowly, for no apparent reason.

"It was seventy before," he said, solemnly.

Before what?

My head hurt.

All I want is my couch and my chicken strips, not a weather report.

Granted, I'd asked for it, but that was beside the point.

I climbed another step, and then another, but the boy showed no sign of moving from his position as a human doorstop. He simply clutched a pale blue flannel blanket, ratty around the edges, and stared at me.

"Who are you?" I asked, growing exasperated.

"Thomas."

I waited for more, but was disappointed.

What kind of idiot parents let their kid roam the neighborhood unsupervised?

Wasn't this supposed to be an age of vigilance when it came to speeding motorists and pedophiles?

"How old are you?" I asked, amazed that no one was watching out for him.

He released one knee long enough to display the five fingers of a grubby hand.

"I was four, but now I'm five."

"Five," I murmured. I climbed the rest of the steps and perused the street again, seeing no one beyond an aggravated looking tabby two doors down. "Where's your mom, Thomas?" I asked, ready to tear a piece off of her.

"In Heaven," he said, quietly.

Oh, shit.

"What about your . . . uh . . . dad?" I asked, swallowing hard. "Where's he?"

"In Heaven, too," he said, matter-of-factly. "They caught on fire."

I felt my heart constrict.

"I'm sorry to hear that," I said, knowing the words were woefully inadequate. "Where do you live?"

"At home, silly!"

I ground my teeth, but maintained a friendly tone. "So, where's home?"

"Next to my friend Max."

Now we're getting somewhere.

"Max?" I asked.

"He's a dog," Thomas explained.

I rubbed my forehead. "Where does Max live?"

"Next to me," he said, giggling.

"I had a feeling," I sighed. "What's your address?"

"Guess!"

"I'm not a very good guesser," I said.

"Then you should practice," he informed me. "I wasn't good at soccer until I practiced."

I had to put one of the grocery bags down so I could search my key chain for the front door key. Prepared to call the police and report him missing, I couldn't help envisioning his face on a milk carton.

"Do you live here?" Thomas asked.

"Yes, and it's time for me to go inside. Can you please move out of the way for a second?"

"No," he said, apologetically.

"No what?"

"Uh . . ." He paused to lick his lips while apparently looking for the right response. "No, thank you?"

"I'm serious, Thomas."

His smooth brow furrowed with concern. "Grandma said stay right here, don't move."

Eureka!

"Who is your grandma?" I asked, hoping we were finally making headway.

"My daddy's mommy. He used to be little like me."

I closed my eyes briefly and took a deep, irritated breath.

"Oh, good," a voice said, from behind me. "You're home."

I spun around to see Patty Melt, smiling brightly from the bottom of the steps.

"He's yours?" I asked.

"Yup, that's my boy." She climbed the steps, waving a bony hand to direct him away from the door.

"Cute kid," I told her, shoving the key into the lock, anticipating solitude and salvation.

"Go inside for a second, okay, buddy?" Patty said, shooing him through *my* doorway.

I froze, stunned. "Hold on a second. I don't want—"

"It's just for a minute or two," Patty assured me.

"Patty, I—"

"Christ! Take a breath. *Chill out.*"

"What are you—" I began.

She shushed me with a wrinkled finger raised to her lips and closed the door behind him. "I've got a problem."

"And I've got a whole stinking stack of them," I groaned. "All I want to do is lie down and—"

"My friend Gloria was just admitted to the hospital for emergency heart surgery."

Okay, she has a bigger problem than rapidly cooling chicken fingers.

"I'm sorry to hear that." But more sorry that I wasn't inside, lying on my new leather couch.

"Anyway, he really likes Gloria and I had to make some phone calls I didn't want him to hear. That's why I had him sit over here, in case you were wondering."

"I was," I assured her.

"The kid's been through too much already."

"He was telling me," I said, suddenly realizing that it was either Patty's son or daughter who'd died. "I'm sorry, Patty."

"That's okay," she said, not meeting my eyes. "Things happen and we move on, right?"

"I suppose," I said, though I wasn't so sure. Hell, I'd barely moved on from a dead relationship.

"Anyway," she continued, "we work together, Gloria and me."

"Look, Patty, I'm sorry about your friend, but—"

"I have to cover her shift tonight."

"And?" I asked, my heart sinking.

"I need you to watch Thomas for a couple of hours."

"What?" I gasped, although I'd somehow known it was coming.

"I'll be back by ten at the latest."

"Patty, he doesn't even *know* me!"

"He's *five*! Hell, if you have a TV, you're golden."

"You'd actually leave your grandson with a complete stranger?" I asked, hoping guilt would stop her in her tracks.

She tilted her head, causing her bun to bob, and smiled. "You're Ida's niece, so you're okay with me."

"That isn't even a legitimate argument. I can't just . . . I don't even . . . I haven't been around little . . . I'm tired, I've got all kinds of stuff going on." I groaned in sheer frustration. "This really isn't a good time."

Her smile faded and she looked at me with the most disappointed expression I'd ever seen. "I get it," she said, her tone icy.

"Patty, I just—"

"Don't explain," she said, holding up one hand.

"Surely there's someone else who could—"

"You think I'd be asking if I had folks lined up to do it?" She let out a harsh laugh. "Most of my friends are over eighty, and dropping like flies. And the ones who are okay? Well, dumping a kid on them is B.S. Even a good kid."

"Look, maybe if—"

"Never mind," she said, brushing me off. "I'll figure something out."

"I'll do it," I mumbled, feeling like the most selfish, rotten person on earth.

Before I knew what hit me, I found myself in a tight embrace.

"Thank you," Patty said, voice muffled by my sweater.

I patted her back, awkwardly. "It's no problem, really," I lied.

When she released me, she grinned. "I'll make it up to you."

"Maybe you could let me complete a sentence every now and then," I suggested.

"We'll see," she said, descending the steps. "I'll give it a shot. In the meantime, I'll be back by ten."

I took a deep breath and opened the front door, hoping I

wasn't in over my head. It had been a long time since I'd done any babysitting, and I had no idea what kids were interested in or what to talk to a five-year-old about.

I found Thomas sitting on the couch, hands clasped in his lap.

"I'm going to look after you for a bit until your grandma gets back, okay?" I said, my tone saccharine-coated. "I'm Lauren."

"Do you have a PlayStation?" he asked.

"No, I don't."

"Xbox?"

"No."

He frowned, deep in thought for a moment. "iPod?"

"No."

"Do you have—"

"Look, I've got chicken strips, Jo-Jo's, and basic cable, okay?"

"Okay," he said, cheerfully, leading the way to the kitchen.

I unloaded the groceries, popped dinner onto one plate, and microwaved it for a couple of minutes. While we waited for the food to heat up, I poured us each a glass of orange juice and set the table.

"I'm supposed to have milk," he said, gravely.

"Not tonight," I told him.

"But Grandma says."

I spun around, searching the room. "Grandma's not here, is she?"

"No," he said, biting his lip.

"Juice, it is."

When we were both seated and ready to eat, he lifted a limp but golden chicken strip and asked, "Do you have honey mustard?"

"No."

"Do you have ranch?"

"No."

"Do you have sweet and sour?"

"No. Do you have any idea how many questions you ask?"

"Lots. Do you have barbeque?"

"I've got *ketchup,* Thomas," I told him, pointing at the lone condiment bottle gracing the table.

"Okay," he shrugged, lifting it and pouring a large enough puddle of Heinz that I suddenly understood the popularity of large-volume generic brands.

It was strange to sit across from such a small person. Between soggy bites, I marveled at the dexterity of his teeny fingers and the look of deep concentration on his face when he double-dipped in the ketchup.

I kept waiting for him to spill something, or make a mess, but he was a very controlled and tidy eater.

"Taste okay?" I asked.

"Yum City," he said, smiling broadly.

We ate in silence for a couple of minutes. Well, *I* was silent while Thomas hummed an unfamiliar song consisting of only three notes, repeated.

And repeated.

And repeated.

"Why don't you tell me a bit about yourself?" I finally asked, when I couldn't take it anymore.

He stared at me, blankly.

"Do you like sports?" I asked.

"I like monster trucks," he said, pointing to his T-shirt with a Jo-Jo and dropping a big glob of ketchup onto his lap in the process.

"Neat," I lied, lifting a wilted chicken strip to my lips.

This is grueling.

Ten o'clock might as well be a week from now.

"Where's your mister?" he asked, wiping his nose with the back of his free hand.

"My what?" I asked, baffled.

He pointed at my ring. "Your mister."

"Oh," I said, quietly. I needed to take the damn thing off and get rid of it, security or not. I'd tried to give it back to Daniel but he'd refused to take it. "He doesn't live here."

"Is he in Heaven?" he asked, conversationally, as he reached for his juice.

"No, he lives in another house."

"Why?" His freckled nose crinkled as he took a sip.

"Because we broke up."

He lowered the glass to the table. "Why?"

Why hadn't I just taken the fucking ring off?

"It's complicated," I said, pulling it off my finger and tucking it into my pocket.

"Because you fighted?"

"Fought? No." By the end, we barely even spoke.

"So, how come?"

"*I don't know*," I told him, tired of the interrogation. "We just grew apart."

Then he surprised me by slowly nodding with a look of such complete understanding and maturity that it was hard to believe he was a five-year-old boy.

That is, until he grabbed a piece of chicken, smiled, and said, "My friend Max the dog eats cat poo."

Fourteen

THE NEXT MORNING I went in to work determined to at least have a conversation with Rachel. It didn't have to be a *good* one, but we had to get past the silent treatment.

"Rachel, I need to talk to you," I said, placing my hands on her side of the desk to brace myself.

"So talk," she said, sliding her letter opener under the flap of an envelope and not looking at me.

"I need you to listen."

"Well, sometimes it's not about what *you* need," she said, pulling out an invoice.

"What?"

"You heard me."

I started again. "Look, I'm feeling—"

Rachel dropped the opener on her desk with a clatter and looked me in the eye. "Hey, would it be okay if we had *one day* that wasn't all about you and your feelings?"

"Excuse me?"

"When was the last time you asked me how *I* was doing, Lauren?"

"Well, I—"

"Or better yet, when was the last time you made it through a day without mentioning your *new life*?" she sneered.

I took a deep and shaky breath. "Okay, I deserve that, but you know I've been going through a hard time, Rachel, and—"

"Your hard time has lasted for *months,* Lauren. Gina in Purchasing has gone through a whole round of chemo and had a fucking double *mastectomy* in the time it's taken you to get it together."

Really?

"Yeah, but—"

"Sam Parker's wife *died* and I never hear him carrying on like you do."

"*Carrying on?* I hardly think—"

"I listen to you and offer support. When you need help, I do what I can and when I need something, you blow me off." She paused. "And your mouth—"

"Look, I didn't mean to say anything about that married—"

She raised a hand to stop me. "Just don't talk to me right now, okay?"

"Can't we—"

"Do *not* talk to me, Lauren."

"But—"

"I'm serious." She turned back to her computer screen.

"Can't we just talk about this?" I asked, meekly.

"*No.*"

WHEN I RETURNED home from work, frustrated, sad, and *still* tired, I was tempted to call Gavin and cancel our movie plans, but figured it would do me good to disappear in a dark theater for a bit. God knew I wouldn't make any headway on housework, anyway.

Patty Melt approached me on my front steps before I even had my key in the lock.

I'm not up for this today.

"Uh, hi," I said.

"I've got an idea I wanted to run by you," she said, hands resting on the hips of another pair of overalls.

I didn't say anything, but waited for her to continue.

"Okay, so here's my idea. We're both living alone, right?"

Did she have to remind me?

"Yes."

"And I don't know about you, but I don't create that much waste."

"Waste?"

"*Garbage,*" she said, with a note of impatience. "What would you say to sharing a can and going halves on pickup? It would save us both a bit of money and cut into the profits of those racketeers."

"That's a great idea," I told her. "Count me in."

Just as I was about to mentally deduct the cost from the monthly budget I'd been working on during my lunch break, I realized that I'd failed to factor it in.

Typical.

"A penny saved is a penny earned," Patty said. "Not that a penny can get you Jack these days."

"I know what you mean." I thought about Gavin's passing comment about selling the dead animals. "I was thinking about having a garage sale, to clear the place out a bit. What do you think?"

"Depends," she said, shrugging. "If you're talking lace doilies and old magazines, you're better off donating them. They'll give you a ticket for a tax write-off, you know."

"Actually, I was thinking about the . . . uh . . . dead stuff."

"Dead?" She paused, her brow wrinkled in confusion before she smiled. "Oh, you mean the animals."

"Yeah."

"Wait a second." She frowned. "You don't want them?"

"No way."

"But what about Murph?" she asked, hands on her hips.

"Who?"

"I'll show you." She pulled the key from my hand and unlocked my door for me, then led me to the raccoon.

"Murph?" I asked.

"He won't answer you."

I sighed. "I'm asking *you,* Patty."

"Yes, that's him. Ida's baby."

I stared at the creature, and thought of the others I'd had Gavin transport to the basement.

"This might be a weird question, but why didn't she just have pets?"

"These *were* her pets," Patty said.

"Okay, let me rephrase this. Why did Ida only have dead pets?"

She looked at me for a long moment. "Because they don't leave. She never had to say good-bye."

"But surely—"

Patty shrugged. "She was a lonely woman, Lauren."

I didn't want to feel guilt over ridding myself of the damn things, but what else could I do with them?

"JT might buy some back. You know, on consignment."

"Who's JT?" I asked.

"He owns the taxidermy shop where Ida got most of her critters."

"Really? You think he'd want them?" I found it hard to believe there was a market for used stuffed animals.

"I'm actually heading over there right now to look at a Volkswagen he's selling."

"For you?"

"The way gas prices are going, I need a cheaper rig," she said, with a shrug. "Anyway, I can take you over there and introduce you. In fact, we could load up my van with some of them so he can have a look."

"That would be *great*," I said, wondering how on earth I'd reached the point where a plan that started with loading dead animals into a van could be considered "great." Remembering my movie with Gavin, I added, "Provided I'm back here by six-thirty or so."

"Can do," she said, with a brisk nod.

The phone rang and when I saw that it was Tim, I figured I'd better answer it and get the conversation over with.

"This will just take a second," I told Patty as I picked it up. "Hi."

"Hey, Laur. Just checking in. How's everything going?"

"Fine," I said, amused as Patty made no effort to hide the fact that she was listening. In fact, she stared at me with undisguised interest. "I'm settling in."

"*Settling*, you mean."

"What's that supposed to— god, can you just drop this whole house thing?"

"Lauren."

"Look, if you called to make me feel bad—"

"I didn't," he sighed.

"Well, you're doing a bang-up job of it."

"I'm sorry, okay?" He paused, and I could hear his fingers tapping a computer keyboard. "I'm just worried about you."

"There's nothing to worry about."

"I've got some vacation time stored up. I was thinking I might come and visit."

"I'm *fine*," I nearly whined. The last thing I needed was him strolling into my new life to try talking me out of it.

"I'd like to see that for myself."

"How about I e-mail you a photo?" I offered.

After a couple of awkward minutes and a handful of deflected questions, I managed to hustle him off the phone.

Patty waited a grand total of three seconds before asking, "Was that your boyfriend?"

"No, my brother."

"Got a boyfriend?" she asked.

"No."

"If you don't mind me asking, what sunk your engagement?"

"It's hard to describe," I said. For what seemed like the millionth time, I wished there was a one-sentence answer that would sum it all up. People wanted a very specific reason, like abuse or cheating, but it wasn't that simple. I told Patty the same thing I'd told everyone else. The truth. "We just grew apart."

"Ha!" she whooped, slapping her knee. "Of course you did. Hell, Lauren, the only couples who don't grow apart are Siamese twins."

I winced and murmured, "Conjoined."

"What?"

"They're called *conjoined twins* now."

"Oh brother," she said, rolling her eyes. "You aren't one of those P.C. freaks, are you?"

"I don't—"

"Because if there's one thing I can't stand, it's hoity-toity lingo and putting on airs. Call a spade a spade, for crying out loud. Why use a thousand-dollar word when a nickel makes your point?"

I nodded in response. "Right."

"Sorry, that was a bit of a rant. Sometimes I get fired up."

"Don't we all."

"Okay, so we're good on the garbage, right?"

"Right."

"Perfect. Let me grab Thomas from in front of that dang TV and we'll scoot over to JT's."

As Patty, Thomas, and myself carried a small collection of mounted animals out to her minivan, a lovely neighborhood lab started retrieving waterfowl from the open tailgate.

"Son of a bitch," Patty cried, chasing the dog, who dropped a mallard in her front yard and took off running.

Thomas collected the bird and once we'd packed all we could, he raced back into the house for his frayed blue blanket and we all climbed into the minivan.

The first thing I noticed, after the initial shock of an overwhelming scent of vanilla, courtesy of not one but *three* cardboard air fresheners hanging from the rearview mirror, was the number of crocheted items surrounding me. The seats were covered with stitched blankets, two tissue boxes had their own crocheted cases, and even the gearshift had a knitted cozy, which seemed not only insanely tacky, but dangerous.

Patty caught me checking out the merchandise and answered all of my questions with one word. "Ida."

"It looks like she kept pretty busy," I said.

Patty threw the car into gear and accelerated before I had a chance to fasten my seat belt. As we zipped down her driveway and careened onto the main drag, narrowly missing what Thomas announced was a 1974 Lincoln Town Car, I found myself hoping she had air bags.

We drove east on Sandy, past tire stores, gritty-looking pubs, and a Kmart before she pulled onto a side street boasting a Plaid Pantry and a Burger King, screeching into a parking lot in a cloud of gravel and dust.

"This is it," she said, hopping from the van and helping Thomas out of the backseat.

The boy and I followed Patty Melt into JT's, which she informed me was the premier taxidermy shop in the area, not that I believed anyone gauged such things.

I held my breath as she opened the front door, prepared for visions of carnage and fully expecting to have nightmares that very evening.

To my surprise, the front room looked rather tasteful, even to a fan of plated rather than preserved salmon, and moose on the loose. The walls were cedar planks, and care had been taken to add enough foliage to make the room feel like the great outdoors. I could have done without the country music, but I didn't mind the mounted antlers, or the shellacked trophy fish, and I was amazed at how natural some of the waterfowl looked. I idly wondered how much time had to be spent watching birds in the wild in order to make them realistic in death.

Beautiful, really.

That said, I had to look away from the cougar with bared teeth and the small black bear standing on its hind legs. There was something very tragic about the combination of glassy eyes and lively poses.

A guy in his mid-forties, with a tired face and a whiskery beard, appeared in a doorway that led to the back, where I could hear a number of men's voices.

"Patty, how goes it?" he asked, speaking to her, but giving me my third thorough once-over in as many days.

"It goes, JT," she said, leaning against the countertop next to an antique cash register. "It always goes."

"And who's this?" he asked her, rubbing his substantial belly with a free hand while smoothing his thinning black hair with the other.

"Ida's niece."

"Ida's niece," he murmured, rubbing his chin thoughtfully. "She has some nice stuff."

I blushed and crossed my arms over my chest, mortified at the pseudo-compliment.

"He's talking about Ida's collection," Patty didn't whisper, but *announced*.

"Oh." My face got a couple of degrees warmer.

"She wants to *unload* that collection," Patty told him.

"For real?" he asked.

"Definitely," I said, with a nod.

"And you're interested in the car?" JT asked Patty, hopefully.

"I'd like to take a look at it," she told him.

"Come on," he said, beckoning us toward the back room.

I looked to Patty for reassurance, and she nudged me with her elbow. Thomas quietly followed close behind me.

We stepped into a workshop, where four tables were topped by carcasses in various stages of rebirth, but what caught my attention wasn't the bizarre display of unfortunate creatures, but the man among them.

A bona fide giant stood behind a dead skunk and lifted his hand to tip his cap, his eyes on me for a split second before he looked downward. There was something about the old-world charm of the action that made me smile.

"Meet Stump," Patty said.

It was clear where the nickname came from. He was thick like an oak, with a wide chest and bulging arms that looked like something out of a Marvel comic book. He was probably in his mid to late seventies, but appeared to be in better physical condition than a college football player.

He popped the last bite of a donut in his mouth and swallowed it without chewing as he stepped toward me and offered a huge paw. Pink and yellow sprinkles clung to his lips.

"Nice to meet you," I squeaked, my hand disappearing inside his warm and surprisingly gentle grip.

"Pleasure's mine," he said, deep blue eyes shying away as soon as they met mine. His free hand lifted his cap in greeting again before he returned to his work.

"He's a big softie," Patty whispered.

I watched Stump pull a package of cigarettes from his jacket pocket. He gave the box a quick upward shake and pulled a single smoke out with his lips, then struck a match, his hands cupping the flame as he inhaled deeply. Every movement was precise and cautious. I could tell by the way he kept his elbows in close that he was well aware of his size and the damage a broad gesture could do to those around him. He was a bull, and JT's was his china shop.

"Is he married?" I asked, imagining a delicate twig of a woman Stump could carry under one arm.

"*Jesus!* He's old enough to be your grandfather," Patty hissed.

"I'm not asking for—"

"But I won't deny he's got the bod. Don't think I haven't given old Stump the once-over from time to time."

I cringed. "I really don't need to know—"

"Buns of steel, kid. I wouldn't mind getting my hands on those biscuits."

"Patty, I don't think—"

"My Walter was built like a goddamned Girl Scout. Scrawny, pasty white, and a chest hollowed out like a sugar bowl. I told you he cheated on me, right?"

"Yes, you mentioned that."

"With a woman the size of Texas, thank you very much. Now, I'm no small thing, but that gal was *enormous*." She walked to Stump's worktable. "Who in the hell wants a skunk in their living room?" Patty demanded, circling him and his work.

"Earl Carter," JT answered for him, continuing toward the back door of the shop. "Car's out here."

As we followed him, we passed the only other occupied table, where a large grey rabbit was being tended to by a rather sweet-looking guy near my age. His expression was terribly serious as he gazed from the animal to a book propped on his lap and back again.

He had dark brown hair in need of a trim, unless he was moonlighting as the bass player for a local garage band, in which case it was perfect. Then again, he would have been a welcome addition to any café, bar, or bookstore in town.

"Ethan, be social, would ya?" Patty said, from behind me.

He looked up and adjusted his glasses, then gave me a quick smile and a quiet "Hello."

"I thought we put the kibosh on gushing and carrying on," Patty teased. "For Christ's sake, the woman is going to drown in your tidal wave of charm."

Ethan rolled his eyes.

"Nice to meet you," I said, as I walked by, but he only cleared his throat and nodded in response.

That is, until Thomas made an approach.

"What's that?" he asked, resting the tip of his pink nose on the table.

"A rabbit," Ethan answered.

"Dead?"

"Well . . ." He looked at me before answering. "Yes."

"My mom's dead."

Ethan's eyebrows shot upwards. "She is?"

"Yes. She's in Heaven, with my dad and my turtle, Gus."

"I'm sorry," Ethan said, resting a hand on the boy's shoulder.

It was a gesture that made my heart push against the confines of my chest.

"It's a nice place," Thomas told him. "You can have an ice cream cone with all the scoops you want and it never falls over."

"In Heaven?" Ethan asked.

"Yup, ten million scoops . . . an *infinity* scoops. And there are baby bunnies everywhere. And kitties. And baby everything. My mom and dad have a campfire every night and they cook hot dogs and they don't need bug spray because there's no bugs, and there's no snakes, and when their tooth comes out sometimes a whole dollar is under their pillow."

He grinned, showing the gap in his own front teeth.

"My grandson, Thomas," Patty said, proudly ruffling his hair. "He's been living with me for the past few months."

"Nice to meet you, Tom," Ethan said, sticking out his hand.

"Thomas," the boy said, sternly, but allowed the handshake.

"Thomas," Ethan repeated, with the hint of a smile.

Just as JT called us to the back door, a bell chimed out front. He cursed and spun on one heel, pushing past us and making his way toward what I doubted was stellar customer service. He grunted that he'd be right back and disappeared to the land of the cash register.

"That's enough out of you, Chatty Cathy," Patty said to Ethan, who blushed in response. She sighed and folded her arms across her chest, leaning against a countertop to wait for JT.

After nearly a minute of silence, he poked his head into the back room. "Mrs. Canton's here to pick up her poodle."

"Bichon," Ethan corrected, without looking up. No one appeared to hear him, or if they did, they didn't care.

JT sighed. "Where is it?"

"Behind the register," Stump said.

"Nope, I already checked."

"Well, that's where I last saw it."

"Him," Ethan said softly, still focused on his work.

"Her, him, it, whatever," JT snapped, stepping toward Ethan to grab the rabbit and move it to another table. Ethan frowned slightly, but said nothing as he stood to retrieve it. JT watched him. "What's the matter, Bookworm? You got a hare outta place?" He cackled at his own joke, then shook his head at Ethan's lack of response. "You got no sense of humor, buddy. Anyone ever told you that?"

"Maybe Gary's working on it," Stump said, with a shrug.

"What, Bookworm's sense of humor, or early retirement?" JT asked, guffawing as he slapped his knee. He'd definitely missed his calling on the laugh track circuit.

"I heard that," a balding man I assumed was Gary said, the back door swinging shut behind him. He carried a tray of Styrofoam coffee cups in one hand and jangled a set of car keys with the other.

"Weren't you working on Mrs. Canton's poodle?" Stump asked him.

"Bichon," Ethan repeated.

"What the hell are you saying, Bookworm?" JT asked.

"It's not a poodle, it's a Bichon."

"Okay, okay," JT said, raising his hands to stop him. "It's a fuckin' Bichon."

Gary laughed and said, "If she brought it here, it ain't fuckin' anymore." His words were welcomed by a collection of snorts and chuckles from everyone but Ethan, who glanced at me with apparent embarrassment. "And no, I haven't been working on it. You know I don't do pets."

"I know, but—" JT began.

"*But nothing.* I'd rather stuff a trunkload of rotting opossums than a lapdog. I mean, what's she gonna do with it?" he asked the room. "Dress it up and park it in front of the fireplace? Cram it into holiday sweaters so she can stare at it while she sips hot cocoa and remembers the good old days?"

"I know," JT agreed. "What's the point of keeping it? It's dead."

"He," Ethan said.

"Huh?" JT asked.

"He."

"Huh?"

"Jesus, you two sound like a retarded donkey," Gary said.

"There are little ears in here," Patty reminded them, pointing at Thomas, who was too sidetracked by a jar filled with fake eyes to notice the conversation around him.

"I said 'he' because the Bichon is a *male*," Ethan explained, laying down a scraping tool. "His *name* is Teddy."

"Can you hear yourself?" JT asked. "Look, the missus is waiting for the damn dog, and I have no idea where *he* is."

"Well, he didn't walk out of here," Gary laughed. "That's for sure."

"Then where is he?" JT asked.

"I don't know, yappy dog heaven?"

"Very funny, but I'm serious. Maybe someone stole him?"

"Why would *anyone* steal a dead dog?" Stump asked.

"Why would *anyone* stuff one?" Gary countered.

"Good point," JT said. "But when was the last time a crime was committed around here?"

Gary looked him over, from head to toe. "This morning, when you left the house in that fucking getup."

JT cleared his throat awkwardly and glanced at Patty, then me. I was doing my best not to snicker, but my best fell short of the mark. As the person closest to my age in the near vicinity, I looked to Ethan, hoping he might offer a smile of camaraderie, and I was rewarded with a flash of friendliness, which lit up his whole face, until his attention returned to the rabbit in front of him.

"Stump, can you take care of her?" JT asked, and Stump nodded. "Okay, the car," JT continued, clearing his throat again and moving toward the back door.

"Is it okay if he stays in here for a minute?" Patty asked, resting a hand on Thomas's shoulder.

"No problem," Ethan assured her.

As we walked toward the door, I heard him ask Thomas, "What do you want to be when you grow up?"

"Six-foot-two."

"No, I mean—"

"That's seventy-four inches," my little buddy explained. "I have a big ruler on my wall."

I heard Ethan chuckle.

Patty and I followed JT out into a small alleyway where a pair of Dumpsters sat on either end of an orange Rabbit, at least 40 percent of which was scabbed over with rust.

"Ugly," Patty clucked, shaking her head, hair bun bobbing.

"Damn straight," JT said as he picked something from between his teeth with a grubby fingernail. "Runs good, though. Probably needs an oil change, but other than that, she's fine." He looked at me, eyebrows raised. "Wanna take a peek under the hood?"

I wouldn't even know what I was looking at. I'd once paid over two hundred dollars for countless unnecessary parts and services at Quik Lube. Those jumpsuit-sporting jackasses had soaked me for everything from brake fluid to an overpriced air filter just by pointing at my dirty engine and frowning.

"Thanks, but no."

"Your call." JT shrugged.

"How much are you wanting?" Patty asked.

"Four grand," JT said, casually slipping his thumbs into the belt loops of his jeans.

"Ha!" Patty barked. "This car's got more blemishes than Britney Spears' fan club."

"Okay, three," JT conceded, looking slightly sheepish.

"*Thousand?*" Patty laughed even harder. Hard enough to cause a coughing fit, which quickly subsided when I slapped her back a couple of times.

"This is a quality vehicle," JT assured us, "just perfect for a lady. Reliable, easy to park—"

I almost stopped him there with a feminist shriek, but the truth was that I left the parallel parking to professionals, preferring to circle my destination in ever widening sweeps until I found something I could nose into.

"Is it automatic?" Patty asked.

"Nope, stick," he said.

"Can I take it for a test drive?" Patty asked.

Concern shadowed JT's face. "What, *now*?"

"Yeah," she said, stepping toward him, her hand reaching for the keys.

"I'm not sure that's—"

"You wanna sell the car, or not?" Patty asked. "Just give me the keys."

I half expected the key chain to be made from a dried, hardened badger's paw or something equally creepy, so when he handed her a standard-issue brown leather swatch with a key dangling from it, I was more than slightly relieved.

With a little finagling, she managed to get the door open, and when I climbed into the passenger seat I made a mental note to buy Patty some air freshener. Lots of air freshener. It smelled like every scrap of roadkill in the vicinity had done time in the backseat of the poor little shitbox.

"Quite the aroma," I said, through the open door.

"It just needs airing out," JT assured me, though he didn't even sound like *he* believed it.

Patty shoved the key in the ignition, lowered her foot on the clutch, and attempted to start the engine.

Nothing happened, beyond a pitiful click.

"Try again," JT suggested.

She did, with the same results, or lack thereof.

"One more time," he begged, so she gave it another shot, with no luck.

Patty climbed out of the car and handed the keys back to him. "I'll think about it."

"It's just the battery."

"I know," she said, nodding sympathetically. "I'll think about it. In the meantime, we've got some stuffed stuff you'll want to look at."

We reentered the shop, where Thomas was regaling the ever-cuter Ethan with tales of the dust bunnies under *my* furniture.

"I think that's probably enough," I told him, taking his hand to drag him away.

Ethan's dark eyes twinkled with amusement. "It was nice meeting you," he called after us.

I blushed like a pro, all the way to Patty's van.

"What's wrong?" Thomas asked, squeezing my hand.

"Nothing," I assured him.

"You're red," he said.

"I'm hot."

"And bothered," Patty snickered.

"What does that mean?" Thomas asked.

"It means your grandma's being silly," I told him.

He looked at me intently, and I knew there were questions zipping through his little brain. He must have seen that I didn't want to answer them, however, because he simply said, "Okay," shrugged, then wiped his nose with the back of his free hand.

Patty hoisted the back door and JT perused the dead stock. In short order he made a substantial offer.

"Or we could trade for the car," he said.

"I don't think so," I told him. "You pay cash?"

"Sure do," he said, and started unloading the beasts.

"You know, I have more at the house that I'd like to get rid of."

"Give me the address and I'll have one of the guys come check it out."

My heart skipped.

Ethan?

"That sounds great," I said.

WHEN WE LEFT JT's, I had a nice chunk of change in my purse *and* the promise of more.

Not bad.

We cinched Thomas in with his seat belt and as Patty went to buckle her own, she let out a short whoop of laughter.

"What?" I asked, smiling without knowing why.

"The car."

Baffled, I asked, "What about it?"

"I don't know what made me think a goddamn taxidermist would try to sell me anything *but* a dead Rabbit."

Fifteen

WHEN PATTY DROPPED me off, Thomas asked if he could come in for a visit before I left to pick up Gavin for the movie.

"I had fun last time," he said, grinning.

"You did?" I asked, kind of flattered. The last time anyone had fun with me involved booze and strippers.

I wanna be the pole.

"Yeah. We had chicken strips and watched TV."

"I remember," I told him.

"It was fun."

"Well, you can stay for a bit, but I'm warning you that I won't be as much fun tonight. I'm just going to be tidying up the house."

"That's okay." He shrugged, leading the way toward the front door.

"You've got a fan," Patty said, gently slapping my back. "Just send him home when you need to."

When I got inside, I offered the kid a glass of juice, fully expecting him to park himself on the couch, cartoons blasting. Instead, he took a big gulp of the drink, placed the glass *on a coaster,* and started following me around.

"What are you tidying?" he asked.

"It's not so much tidying as deciding what to change or add to make this place my own."

"Like this couch?" he asked, pointing to the sales tags that were still hanging from it.

"Yes." I surveyed the room. "You see those curtains?" I pointed at the floral monstrosities hanging on the far windows.

"Uh-huh."

"They're on their way out."

I grabbed a kitchen chair and got to work unhooking the clips and letting the fabric bunch at my feet, a rolling sea of chintz.

"Do you like the sound of music?" Thomas asked.

"Sure. Most music. I'm not a big fan of country." I glanced downward and saw he wore a rather perplexed expression. "What's wrong?"

"The *movie.*"

"Movie? Oh, *The Sound of Music.* Sure, sure I liked it."

"They maked clothes from curtains."

"*Made,* and yes they did."

"Can you?"

"Can I what?" I asked.

"Make clothes from curtains."

"I suppose I could," I said, glancing at the sewing machine.

"For me?"

"Well, yeah." I looked at him again, bewildered. "Wait, you mean from *these* curtains?"

"Yeah."

"I could, but don't you think it would be better to pick material from a fabric store? You know, something with . . ." I grasped for an image. "Robots or dinosaurs, or something?"

"Nope," he said, fingering the cloth.

"Thomas, it's covered with *flowers.*"

"I like it."

"But flowers are for . . ." I stopped myself, figuring that stifling the unbridled enthusiasm of a little boy wasn't high on my list of priorities. "I guess we could make sort of a Hawaiian shirt."

He grinned, flashing the gap in his teeth. "Cool!"

"Or some shorts?" I suggested, visions of surfers dancing in my head. "Maybe black with a strip of the curtain fabric down one side?"

He stood with his legs spread wide, and gave me two solid thumbs-up. "Awesome!"

If nothing else, the kid's easy to please.

We spent just over half an hour together, during which time I learned that Thomas was allergic to bees, liked Emma Bradley but not her sister Jane, loved LEGO, Hot Wheels, and Blue's Clues, disliked lamb chops and Vespa scooters, and wanted to be a scientist when he grew up.

"Why?" I asked.

"So I can figure stuff out."

"Good idea," I told him. "Someone needs to figure it out."

"I will," he announced.

"I like your style, kid."

He gave me a solemn look. "Thanks."

I laughed. "Hey, I'm pretty hungry. Do you want a grilled cheese sandwich?"

"Awesome!" he nearly screamed.

I shook my head and laughed some more.

Later that evening, I spent the drive over to Gavin's growing increasingly enthusiastic about sewing. I had some great ideas pop into my head, like bottle rockets of creativity. I tried to remember when I'd been as keen on anything other than tarting up Ida's house, and couldn't.

I turned up the radio, bobbing my head to the beat as I drove, barely registering the amused looks I received from my fellow drivers.

While I wouldn't have admitted it to anyone, in addition to the sewing, my mind was occupied with thoughts of a certain taxidermist.

I pulled into Gavin's right on time, but he was back to his usual pattern of being two steps shy of ready.

"Give me ten minutes," he called from the bathroom.

"Seven," I countered.

As I waited for him to style himself, I slowly wandered around his living room, admiring how the garish, lime green vinyl couch was somehow a perfect match for the multicolored striped rug under his Asia-inspired black coffee table. Three star-shaped lamps hung asymmetrically in the room, one red and the others two shades of blue, and a turquoise La-Z-Boy recliner sat directly in front of his flat screen TV, an Xbox resting next to it.

On his bookcase, amid the tomes he'd never read, I spotted the photo of us at Disneyland just after high school graduation, when we drove a bleating, shaking, reluctant Ford Fiesta to Los Angeles in one stretch, hopped up on caffeine and countless mixed tapes. We'd stayed for the day, racing from one lineup to the next, from the moment the gates opened until they shooed us back to the real world. The picture was taken in front of the Matterhorn, our exhausted, sunburned faces grinning at whatever stranger we'd asked to take the shot.

Smiling, I glanced at the other solid wood and pewter frames surrounding glossy images of Gavin and his mom at the beach, their noses coated with yellow and green zinc, a shot of Gav and his pal Jeff posing next to a giant dinosaur somewhere near Palm Springs, and a group shot of ten of us during a camping trip on the Olympic Peninsula.

It was the final day, when we were all greasy, grimy, and hungover, having packed in several cases of beer, but no water. I shook my head, chuckling at the memory of our horrific singing around the campfire on the last night and falling asleep in a tent to the sound of small, soothing waves.

I paused at a picture of the mixed breed hound, Buzzard, who was hit by a car and killed when we were in eighth grade. I could still remember Gavin showing up at my back door, tearstained and gasping for breath as he told me what had happened. I felt a lump in my throat. He never had another dog.

"What do you think?" he asked, from behind me.

I turned to see him decked out in a pair of perfectly distressed Levi's, an emerald green "Kiss me, I'm Irish" T-shirt and a pair of Vans. His blond hair was carefully sculpted into a careless mop and on his bony wrist was a frighteningly sporty yellow watch.

"You're not Irish," I reminded him.

"So? What about the rest of it?"

"Aren't we going to be sitting in the dark, staring at a big screen?"

"Not on the way in and out of the theater," he said, with a cheeky grin. "Opportunities are everywhere, Laur."

"What's with the timepiece?" I asked, pointing to his wrist.

"Oh, it's *incredible*," he said. "It's a diver's watch."

"You aren't a diver."

"Yeah, but it works up to like a mile underwater."

"When are *you* going to be a mile underwater?"

"I don't know, but I could schedule a time to be there on this thing." He grinned.

"What is wrong with you?"

"I enjoy life." He shrugged. "You should try it sometime, Laur." He posed in front of me, hands on his hips. "So, will the ladies like it?"

Yes, the ladies would like it.

The ladies always did.

"I'm guessing that if you spent as much time toiling for clients as you spend trolling for chicks—"

He rolled his eyes. "I work my ass off, and you know it."

I peered at his backside. "You certainly do, Buttless Wonder."

He tried to check the rear view out himself. "Actually, I was thinking about implants."

"You've got to be—"

"I am," he assured me, laughing. "I'm not *that* bad."

I peered at his right earlobe, which was a different color than the rest of him. "Are you using tanning cream?"

"No," he said, quickly, but his darting eyes told me otherwise.

"You are!"

"Maybe just a little." He shrugged. "I'm so pasty, Laur. It makes me look healthier."

"Gav, it makes you look *orange*."

"Well, oranges are healthy, right?" He laughed.

"Let's get you sorted out," I said, leading him into the bathroom by one arm and cleaning him up with a damp facecloth. "You know, people always ask me if you're gay."

"I'm not."

"I know. I think if you were gay you'd do a better job applying the damn tanning cream."

"You might be right," he said, laughing. "So, is it gay men who ask if I'm gay?"

"No, why?"

"I just wondered if they were asking out of personal interest, like maybe they thought I was cute." He paused for a moment. "So, it's straight women asking?"

"I don't know. It's a variety of people."

"Are the straight women relieved or excited when they find out I'm not?"

I stared at him. "Can we get going?"

"What? I'm not allowed to gauge my curb appeal?"

"We're going to be late, you goon."

I drove to the theater and we had a hell of a time finding parking. By the time we'd bought our tickets, I desperately wanted to get seated, but my bronzed companion was more concerned with the concession stand.

"I should have eaten first," he said, rubbing his stomach.

"I did."

"Maybe a hot dog . . . or popcorn."

I pushed past him to the counter, where I bought him a hot dog, a drink for each of us, and large popcorn to share. The total rivaled my car payment.

"They should have a loan officer stationed near the front door," I muttered, leading him toward the theater.

"Thanks, Laur," Gavin said. "I'll get it next time."

Of course, he wouldn't.

Thankfully, the previews hadn't started but the theater was packed, and with Gavin preoccupied with the task of girl-watching, it was up to me to find seats.

I scanned the crowd quickly, spotting two vacant spots a couple of rows from the top, and grabbed him by the arm to drag him along.

As we climbed the stairs, he hesitated and waved at someone.

"Uh, Lauren?" he murmured.

"What?"

"Daniel."

"Daniel what?" I asked, turning to face him.

"He's here," he said, through a false smile.

"So?" I didn't want to look, fearing it would be too obvious.

"*With someone.*"

"I don't . . . oh!" I gasped. "Do you mean a woman?"

"I mean a hottie."

I pinched him, hard, then searched the row for Daniel's face.

And there it was, next to the face of Jane Something-or-other who taught fourth grade, a petite brunette with lovely almond eyes and flawless skin.

I smiled tightly and waved, relieved when they both waved back in a perfectly friendly manner.

"Okay, let's get to those seats," I said, my mouth dry.

"Are you all right?" Gavin asked, once we'd reached our destination.

"I'm fine," I told him, taking some popcorn from his bag. "Totally fine."

"Are you sure?"

"I'm sure."

"Because you're staring at the backs of their heads."

"Well, what do you *expect* me to do, you idiot?" I snapped, causing the woman in front of us to shush me.

"Don't make a scene," Gavin whispered.

"I *won't*." I grabbed another handful of popcorn and shoved it in the general direction of my mouth.

"You wanted the split, right?"

"Of course, I did."

"And I know you've said you'd like him to meet someone."

"I didn't say I wanted it to happen this fast."

Who was I to judge? I'd spent the afternoon enamored with a virtual stranger.

Ethan.

I hadn't expected to feel the current of attraction, but there it was. At the first moment of eye contact there'd been a *ding-ding-ding* in my head.

So why shouldn't Daniel have the right to the same feelings?

Because he's acting on them first.

But if you'd acted on them first, you'd feel guilty.

Whose side are you on, anyway?

"Do you want to leave?" Gavin asked.

"No," I sighed. "We're here, we're seated. Let's just enjoy the stupid movie."

"Hey," he teased, nudging me with an elbow. "With an attitude like that, how can we do anything but?"

I did my best to watch the film, but it was too distracting, knowing that Daniel was out there in the darkness with dainty Jane.

You're jealous.

I wasn't, though. I didn't want Daniel for myself, but it was strange to see him with someone else.

You're afraid no one is going to want you.

Yes, I am.

AFTER THE MOVIE, the best bet seemed to be avoiding an encounter, but we accidentally walked right into Daniel and Jane outside the theater.

"Hey," I said, raising one hand in a floppy wave.

"Uh, hi," he said, smiling awkwardly as Jane tensed next to him.

"Good movie, huh?" Gavin asked, full of false cheer.

"Decent," Daniel said, with a nod.

I carefully looked him over, from the curly red hair that was always a bit unruly to the ruddy pink cheeks that always looked sunburned and the lips I'd kissed thousands of times.

Oddly enough, he seemed no closer to me than someone I'd played baseball with as a child, or worked next to at a part-time job years earlier. I'd known this man more intimately than anyone else on earth and I couldn't read the expression in his pale blue eyes. Even his voice didn't sound the way I remembered it. He was wearing a shirt I'd given him for his birthday, but that was the only article of his clothing I recognized.

He even smelled different.

He wasn't mine anymore.

He looked at me for a second, with a slightly baffled expression that likely mirrored my own. I wondered if he was assessing me and my appearance in the same manner.

"Well, we'd better get going," I said. "Nice to see you both."

"You too," Daniel said, visibly relaxing as he realized the conversation was already over.

Jane offered a tight smile as they turned to leave.

"Well," I said, exhaling. "I survived it."

"You did, indeed," Gavin said, giving me a quick squeeze.

We walked to Imperial Palace for Chinese takeout and drove back to his place to enjoy it.

"So, I've been thinking about Internet dating," he said, once we were seated on his living room floor, open cartons and heaping plates in front of us.

"I thought that wasn't your bag," I said, trying to snag a piece of almond chicken with my chopsticks.

"I meant for you."

"No, no, *no*." I laughed. "Not a chance."

"Have you even looked?"

"No."

"Come here," he said, standing to carry his plate into his home office.

As he started his computer, I admired the work adorning the walls. Posters for skateboard companies vied for space with restaurant menus, featuring bold splashes of color, and seven or eight calendars advertising a variety of pharmaceutical companies and hotels.

"This is all *your* stuff?" I asked.

"Yup," he said, biting into an egg roll. "Here's what I've been working on this week." He opened a file and a series of logos for Lakeside Health Bars popped up.

"You're doing Lakeside?"

"Yeah." He grinned. "Cool, huh?"

"They're huge! That's a major corporation."

I glanced from one design to the next, marveling at how they were very distinct, yet clearly connected. They had a retro style, like something out of the Fifties. Smooth lines and delicate touches, using unusual color combinations that really worked together, like aqua and tan, or orange and maroon.

"They are, but they want to look very Mom 'n' Pop," he said. "So . . . you like them?"

"Gav, they're incredible. They look . . . I don't know . . . *real.*"

He laughed. "They *are* real."

"No, I mean, they look so professional. Like they're already on the shelf."

"You think so?" he asked.

"Definitely. At the risk of sounding like we're still in seventh grade, they're *awesome,* Gav."

"Thanks," he murmured, closing the file.

Even under the orange skin, I could see he was pink with delight, but he'd already moved on to the next item of business.

"Check this out," he said, opening a Web page with a gigantic pair of puckered pink lips as a background.

"Do I have to?"

"Just give it a chance, would you?"

The next thing I knew, I was seated in his chair while he stood behind me, directing me through the site. When we reached a personality questionnaire, he made me start answering.

I had to grade my responses to countless questions on a scale of one to five. Was I a drinker, a smoker, a nudist, a Christian, an "educated" person? Was I smart, funny, quiet, boisterous, silly, or superstitious?

"This is crazy. What if I'm a smoker who wants to meet a non-smoker?"

"Just keep answering."

"Do they set you up with your opposite, or someone exactly like you? I don't want to meet someone just like me."

"Lauren."

"Am I bothered by loud noises? What kind of question is that?"

After almost an hour, the bar at the top of the screen indicated that I had completed 14 percent of the questionnaire.

"You've got to be kidding," I groaned.

"Keep going," Gavin said, taking a sip of the Fat Tire I'd been nursing between questions.

"Is physical attractiveness important to me? Of course, it is. I have to be attracted to someone if I'm going to be involved with them. But do they mean attractive to *me,* or in a broad sense, like Hollywood attractive?"

"I think you're reading too much into the question."

"Of course I am! Geez, one minute they ask if insignificant things bother me, and two minutes later I come across the question, 'Are you easily irritated?' "

"I think you're easily irritated," Gav said, laughing. "I'd give you a four on that."

"I mean, how many times can they pose the same damn question?"

"Can I bump that up to a five on irritation?"

"Oh my god," I groaned, rubbing my eyes. "I can't do this anymore."

"That's okay," he said, reaching for the mouse to sign off. "The site will save your answers so you can finish another time."

"Great," I said, stretching as I rolled my eyes. "Listen, I better get going. I've got work tomorrow, featuring another round of Rachel, and—"

"How's that going?"

"It isn't." I shrugged. "I mean, I've tried to approach her so many times, in person and on the phone. She won't listen to me, and even though I know I said something really stupid, it was *one lousy comment,* you know?"

"Laur, how many times have you mistakenly thought women were pregnant?"

"What's that got to do with—"

"How many times?"

"Not that many," I told him.

"And then asked them about their due dates?"

"Maybe . . ." I counted in my head, "four?"

"More like six, and all were *thoroughly* offended."

"What's your point?"

"You know," he said, quietly, "sometimes the stuff you say really hurts people's feelings."

"I know," I agreed, "but it's not *deliberate*."

"That doesn't really matter, Laur."

"Well, I've never hurt *your* feelings."

He took a breath and his eyes met mine for a split second before shying away. "Sure, you have."

"When?" I gasped.

"Geez." He leaned back against the cushions. "Let's see . . . the time you told me Jocelyn Fields was totally out of my league."

"That was fifteen years ago!" I paused. "And she *was*. Come on, Gav."

"And that camping trip when you blabbed that I'd been a bed wetter until I was six."

"But—"

"Every time you called me an idiot or a dork, every time you call me a slacker instead of a freelancer, or make fun of the women I date."

"Oh." I frowned. "But—"

"And the time you said it would be impossible to kiss me without laughing."

"It's true, though. You're like my brother, or something."

"Hey, I never wanted to be anything else. But the reasoning behind it doesn't matter. It's what you actually *say* that counts."

"I'm sorry, Gav," I said, placing one hand on his knee. "I never meant to say anything to hurt you. You know that was never my intention, right?"

"I know, but sometimes—"

"I know," I interrupted, biting my lip. "It's like this Rachel thing. My mouth got away from me, and now I've lost my best friend."

He looked at the floor, took a breath, then looked me straight in the eye. "You see, Laur? You just did it again."

"What?" I asked, genuinely confused. "What did I do?"

"All this time," he said, softly. "All this time . . ." His voice trailed off.

"What is it?" I asked, growing impatient.

"All this time I thought . . . I thought your best friend was *me.*"

The pain in his eyes made me feel like I'd been punched in the stomach.

"Gav," I murmured, reaching toward him.

He brushed me away and left the room.

"Gav?" I called after him, then followed. "Gav?"

"I'll talk to you later, okay?" he said, from the top of the stairs.

"But, Gavin—"

He held up his hand to stop me. "I'll talk to you later."

By the time I buckled my seat belt, I was crying.

As if it wasn't bad enough to have lost one best friend, I'd managed to lose *two.*

Sixteen

WHEN I ARRIVED back at the house, eyes puffy and nose red and raw from crying, I climbed the front steps and tried to soothe myself with thoughts of a long, hot bath.

Opening the front door, I flipped the light switch, but instead of a soft glow, I got a flash of brightness, a popping sound, and utter darkness.

"Get out of town," I muttered, squinting toward the glass fixture above me, then dropping my bag and making my way into the kitchen to search for a new bulb. Thankfully, it was only a matter of moments before I located a box of bulbs in a bottom drawer, next to the kitchen sink.

I dragged a dining chair to the center of the living room, using the shaft of light from the kitchen to see my path, pulled a bulb from the box, removed the cushion from the chair, and stepped up onto the seat.

Reaching to unscrew the expired unit, it became apparent that my arm was about a foot too short for the job.

"Son of a monkey," I grunted, returning to the floor.

I glanced around the room, looking for anything that could give me a bit more height while cursing my ladderless state.

Sighing, I cleared the mail and papers from the dining table, then carefully deposited Ida's sewing machine on the floor and pushed the table with my hip. The behemoth didn't budge. I placed both hands on the edge of it and tried to lift and push at the same time. It moved less than two inches. Bending at the waist and knees, I took a deep breath and pushed with all of my might, and finally got the monster moving.

I used most of my remaining energy to shove it across the floor, and the screeching resistance of wood on wood acted as my personal sound track as I got the furniture perfectly situated below the fixture. Just as I was about to climb aboard, I remembered to cross the room to turn off the switch and avoid electrocution, only to bash my shin against my new coffee table in the process.

After I'd released a stream of profanity, full of four- and five-letter word combinations I'd never before considered and would probably be unable to recreate, I grabbed the bulb and stepped onto the chair. I carefully tested the table with one foot before determining it was built like a tank and putting all my weight upon it. It was so solid, it didn't even waver or creak, and I silently praised Ida's choice of furniture. I carefully unscrewed the old bulb, and once it was free, I gave it a little shake, so I could enjoy the satisfying tinkle of the broken filament.

Unfortunately, my shake was more forceful than intended and the bulb slipped from my grasp.

The light tinkle turned into a shattering against the wood floor.

"Come *on*," I groaned, staring at the sea of broken glass beneath me, glittering in the glow of the kitchen light.

Swearing under my breath, I reached upward to screw in the new bulb, only to discover it was too small for the fixture.

On top of everything else going wrong in my life?

You've got to be shitting me.

Defeated, I climbed down to floor level and surveyed the mess. Deciding the cleanup could wait until morning, I turned off the kitchen light and started up the stairs, flipping the hallway switch as I went.

Another flash, pop, and darkness.

Gritting my teeth, I climbed the stairs in utter darkness, feeling my way along the railing and wall. When I reached the upstairs landing, I flipped another switch.

Flash, pop, darkness.

"No fucking way," I groaned. I could hear Steven's voice reverberating in my head. Two words, over and over.

Amateur wiring.

Making my way down the hall, I was overcome with exhaustion, and it was all I could do to cling to the hope of my hot bath. I stopped at the linen cupboard to pick up a couple of candles, just in case, and when I reached the bathroom, I took a deep breath before flipping the switch.

The room was illuminated, from toilet to tub, and I almost giggled with relief.

I put the plug in the drain, cranked on the hot water, and started peeling off my clothes, pleased that one small yet gigantic thing was going my way. Reassured by the splashing roar of steaming water, I felt my shoulders relax and let out a reasonably contented sigh.

Flash, pop, darkness.

"Oh, for crying out loud," I muttered, rubbing my forehead.

Screw the candles, screw the bath. I'm going to bed.

The bedroom light was working, but I didn't press my luck by trying the small lamp on my nightstand. Instead, I slipped into a pair of flannel pajamas, pulled back the comforter, and climbed into my downy nest. Certain that I was safe from the world for a few hours, I settled into a deep and dreamless sleep.

Until four a.m., anyway.

I was awakened by a loud cracking sound and sat bolt upright in bed. My first thought was that one of the tree branches in the front yard had broken, and I immediately began worrying if it had landed on my poor car.

I'll have to pay the stinking deductible.

I briefly considered my anorexic bank account.

I shouldn't have bought the couch.

Or even the cushions for it.

My feel-good purchases were going to bite me in the ass, using all of their teeth.

I slipped into a robe and charged down the pitch dark stairway, my gaze focused on the front door. Unlocking the bolt, I whipped the door open and peered into my front yard. From what I could see by streetlight, the trees and my car appeared intact.

I stood on the front step, hands on my terry cloth–covered hips, and wondered what on earth I'd heard. The light sprinkling of rain ruled out the clap and roar of foul weather, and there were no crunched vehicles nearby, or sounds of approaching sirens in the distance.

What the hell had been loud enough to jolt me out of slumber?

I slowly closed the door and turned to grab a glass of water from the kitchen.

That was when I saw the faint shadow of the dining table, tilted as though two of its legs were broken.

My hands reached for the slight bulge of my stomach, though I knew there was no way my weight had broken the damn thing. I took a couple of steps closer, wondering how on earth it had spontaneously collapsed, and gasped.

It wasn't the table, it was the *floor.*

The hardwood had splintered and broken, the effect like fangs devouring the carved table legs.

It looked like something out of fucking *Poltergeist.*

Steven's voice echoed again.

Dry rot.

I stood, frozen, for several minutes, unsure of what to do. There was no way I could lift the table to safety by myself, but I was afraid the hole in the floor would grow if I didn't. I couldn't tell if it was safe to walk to the kitchen, thanks to both the sink-hole *and* the sprinkling of broken glass surrounding it.

Shit.

If I went back to bed, would I awake to find the whole living room had relocated to the basement?

Was there anyone on earth I could call at four in the morning to ask?

My heart leapt.

It's past seven in Florida!

It sunk again.

What could Mom and Dad do over the phone?

I slowly climbed the stairs and crawled back into bed, hoping everything would be okay by morning.

Yeah, right.

BY DAYLIGHT, THE floor looked about ten times worse, and when I stepped around it to slip into the kitchen after my shower, I winced at the thought of what it would cost to repair. I leaned against the door frame, nursing a cup of coffee as I con-templated the possibility that the whole floor would have to be replaced.

How much would *that* cost?

Near tears by the time I left the house, I decided to plead my case to Rachel, with the hope that Steven could help me out him-self or refer me to someone who could do the work inexpensively.

Why did I buy all that fucking furniture?

I arrived at the office, ready to turn on the charm, only to dis-cover that Rachel had called in sick.

Shit.

The day dragged on forever, silent and lonely. I sent off a couple of apologetic e-mails to Gavin, hoping I could mend that partic-ular fence, and spent my lunch hour considering calling contractors, but not actually doing it. The truth was, I didn't want to know how bad it was.

WHEN THE TIME finally came to go home, I couldn't get out the front door fast enough. In fact, I accidentally hip-checked Tonya from Claims into the hall closet on the way out. Though I apologized profusely, I was relieved that for once it wasn't my mouth, but another body part, that was getting me into trouble.

I tried calling Gavin a couple of times on the drive home, but, like the e-mails I'd sent him earlier in the day, he didn't respond.

Dreading the thought of entering my house, I stopped in at a Fabric Depot for a few moments of procrastination.

Thirty minutes later, I was carrying two bags filled with material, thread, and patterns to modify.

Nothing like piling on the debt.

When I arrived home, I pointedly ignored the gaping black hole in the middle of my living room and concentrated instead on something I *could* handle. The first thing I did, after changing from my work clothes, was move the sewing machine to the coffee table and plug it in.

House *and* relationship repairs were looming large in my life but both could be put on hold for an evening while I completed one small project. I needed to feel the satisfaction of getting something done.

Feeling a sense of purpose, I used quick, confident movements to cut the floral curtains down to a manageable size in a matter of minutes.

I whipped out a pattern and set to work, cutting and pinning the tissue paper pieces to the heavy-duty black fabric I'd chosen for Thomas's shorts.

Once I'd cut out all of the components, I threaded the machine and started sewing them together. The hum and whir was soothing to me, and for a time I didn't think about anything but even stitches and following directions.

When I checked the clock it was almost seven and the shorts were finished. To my surprise and delight, the floral accent stripes down the sides looked even better than I'd imagined.

Thomas would be thrilled, I was sure.

By the time the doorbell rang, I was downright chipper, despite the chaos in my life.

I threw the door open, expecting to find Patty or Thomas, but there stood Ethan.

I'd forgotten JT was sending someone over to check out the critters, and my heart did a little jig.

"Oh, hi," I said, wishing I was wearing anything but the striped pajama bottoms and navy blue T-shirt I'd thrown on when I arrived at home. And why was I still clutching the tiny shorts?

"Hi," he said, smiling.

He tucked a chained wallet into the back pocket of his baggy grey jeans and slipped his hands into the front pockets of his dark blue hoodie. I could imagine Thomas wearing the same outfit and the thought tickled my fancy.

"Hi," I repeated, like some kind of an idiot.

"I'm Ethan," he reminded me, though I certainly didn't need the help.

"I know. From the taxidermy shop. JT sent you."

Nothing like stating the obvious.

"He did," Ethan said, stepping into the living room when I widened the door for him. "Well, I volunteered, actually."

"Oh." I blushed, clasping my hands behind my back.

"Nice place," he said, glancing around the room, then catching sight of a certain feature and exclaiming, "Holy shit!"

"Yeah," I said, nonchalantly turning to survey the damage.

"What *happened*?" He moved closer to peer down the hole.

"I guess it's dry rot," I said, with a shrug.

"Holy *shit*," he repeated.

"It's no big deal," I lied.

"You've got someone coming to take care of it?" he asked, turning to face me.

"Not exactly . . . I'm going to hold off for now," I explained, hoping the plan sounded more sane than it was.

Why did I spend all that money?

"What?" he gasped.

"It's *fine*," I assured him. "You know, when I was a kid, my Dad decided to convert the downstairs bathtub into a shower. It turned out to be a bigger project than he'd expected, and we couldn't use that bathroom for six months." My laugh was hollow. "We just kind of worked around it."

He stared at me in apparent disbelief. "You're going to *work around* a crater in your living room?"

"Sure," I said, smiling brightly. "It'll be fine. It's not as bad as it looks."

"It *looks* really dangerous." He squinted at the disaster site. "Is that broken glass?"

Could we maybe change the subject? "Technically, yes."

"Technically?" he asked, eyes widening.

"Well, yes. Look, can we talk about something else?"

"What, pretend the hole isn't there?"

"Please," I said, quietly.

There must have been something in my voice that made his expression soften. He looked into my eyes for several seconds, and I felt a blush fill my cheeks. When he did break eye contact, he glanced at the garment in my hand. "What have you got there?"

"Oh, that's . . . I'm making some clothing for Thomas."

"Nice," he said, his smile making my hands sweat a bit. "*Hip* clothing, by the looks of it."

"That's the idea."

"You know, I'm pretty good with a needle and thread myself."

"Sure you are," I said, rolling my eyes.

"I'm serious. My work is actually pretty intricate." He coughed self-consciously. "Speaking of work, I should probably take a look at those pieces while we chat."

He wants to chat?

"They're, uh . . . in the basement," I said, with a wince.

"Is it safe?" he asked.

"Yup," I blurted. "Follow me."

I led him to the stairs, hoping I was right, and flipped the light switch.

Flash, pop, darkness.

"Have you got a spare bulb?" he asked. He was close enough that I could feel the faintest touch of warm breath against the back of my neck.

The boy's giving me goose bumps.

"We'll be fine," I said, taking a step.

He rested a hand on my shoulder. "Let me just replace the bulb."

"Don't worry about it," I said, reluctantly taking another step, knowing it would mean losing physical contact with him.

"Lauren," he said. "Let me do this one small thing. Where are the bulbs?"

I sighed and stopped on the second step. "I think it's a bigger problem, actually," I confessed, looking into the darkness. "They're all kind of burning out."

He rubbed his forehead. "Geez, you've got a wiring problem too?"

"It'll be fine," I said, quickly.

"So, you plan to work around this as well?" he asked.

"It'll be *fine*," I repeated, all false cheer as I continued down the steps.

He followed me without another word, and when we reached the basement, fairly well lit, thanks to a gaping hole in the ceiling, I led him to the far wall, where the creatures were stored on window ledges, the washing machine, and an old worktable.

"She was a collector, all right," Ethan laughed.

My shoulders relaxed at the sound, and I watched as he gently handled a rooster, peering at it from every angle.

"If you don't mind me asking," I said, as he moved on to a pheasant, "what got you into the taxidermy business?"

"I was in art school—"

"Really?" Not what I expected.

"*Really*," he said, chuckling. "May I go on?"

"You may," I said, blushing.

"I was focusing on sculpture, mostly clay, and enjoying but not loving it."

I couldn't help interrupting. "Just out of curiosity, what were you planning to do with a degree in clay sculpture?"

"I was going to *sculpt clay*," he said, dryly.

"Right," I said. "Gotcha."

Can I file a restraining order against my own mouth, legally requiring it to stay two hundred yards away from me?

"So, I spent a summer working at the Burke Museum in Seattle."

"I've been there!" I shrieked, recalling a trip with Dad and Tim when I was in elementary school.

"I worked at a McDonald's during high school. Have you been there, too?"

"I have!" I said, laughing. "I'm a big proponent of the Mc-Chicken."

"A bold statement in an era when Ronald McDonald is viewed by many as the devil incarnate. But I digress," he continued. "So,

I worked at the museum and became intrigued by the animal exhibits, particularly the birds, and the head of the ornithological collection took me under his wing, if you'll pardon the pun."

"I don't think I will," I said, shaking my head as I chuckled. "That was pretty weak."

"A lame duck?" he asked.

"Please stop."

"I will, but only because you asked nicely."

I smiled, full of the irrational hope that he'd stay for a bit. Aside from my visits with Thomas, the house was a lonely place. "So, you left art school, and—"

"No, I got my degree but decided to pursue the taxidermy."

"To work with JT? He seemed like such a jackass."

"He is, but he's a very *knowledgeable* jackass, and working for him has meant gaining all kinds of museum contacts, and museums are the direction I want to go in."

"Very interesting," I told him.

"What about you? What do you do?"

"Well, I started out as a fry girl at Burger King, so my path was a bit different from yours."

"Of course," he said, nodding solemnly, "the competition."

"I got an English degree and—"

"Just out of curiosity," he said, with a twinkle in his eye, "what were you planning to do with a degree in English?"

"*Speak English.*"

"Mission accomplished," he said, tapping his rather lovely hands together in silent applause.

"Anyway, now I work in insurance."

"Because you *love* insurance?" he asked, eyebrow cocked.

"Nope."

"What do you love?" he asked, quietly.

"I don't really know."

He looked at me for a full ten seconds before saying, "You'll figure it out."

And I believed him.

WHEN ETHAN HAD finished his animal inspection, I walked him to the door.

"I think this place is going to look great," he said, with forced confidence.

"Well, I think I'll start painting tomorrow night."

He stopped to stare at the hole for a long moment, then at me, concern in his eyes. "I'm not sure painting is the most logical starting point."

"Logic is overrated," I said, cheerily.

"Okay," he said, hesitating at the door. "Uh, good luck with it," he said, stepping onto the welcome mat. "It was nice talking to you."

"You too," I told him.

Very, very nice.

As he drove away, I waved, and was probably wearing a goofy grin as Gavin pulled into my driveway.

I was thrilled to see him, considering the events of the previous night.

I was decidedly less thrilled to see Lucy climb out of the passenger side of his car.

"Hey," I said, as they climbed the front steps.

"How's it going?" Lucy asked.

"Fine."

I glanced at Gavin, who explained, "I was on my way over to see you when Lucy called."

"Oh?"

I must have looked as confused as I felt, because he continued, "We exchanged numbers that night we all went out."

"*I wanna be the pole!*" Lucy crowed.

I grimaced. "Do you want to come in?"

"Sure," Lucy said, stepping inside. "I wanted to see your new place."

I smiled tentatively at Gavin, who leaned in and whispered, "We're okay, Laur."

"For sure?" I asked, hopefully.

He shrugged. "I can't stay mad at you."

What have I done to deserve him?

Absolutely nothing.

At that moment, Lucy gasped, "Holy fuck!"

"What?" Gavin asked, pushing past me. "Oh, my *god*!"

"Dry rot," I murmured.

"Unbelievable," Gav said, circling the hole. "You're gonna need someone to fix this, Laur."

"Great tip, Gav."

"I mean, it's like a swimming pool," he continued.

"It's only a couple of feet wide," I snapped.

"A Jacuzzi, then," Lucy offered.

"Aside from the lack of cement, water, and intent, you mean?" I asked.

"Have you got a contractor?" Gav asked.

"Can we talk about something else?"

"Maybe Steven could—" Gav began.

"Rachel's not talking to me," I reminded him.

"Maybe if you just called him—"

"I can't," I said, shaking my head. "New subject?"

Gavin glanced at Lucy. "I wonder what's holding up your little sidekick."

"My what?" she asked.

"Your cohort," he said. "The Daphne to your Velma."

"What?" she frowned.

"It's a *Scooby-Doo* reference," I explained, though I wasn't sure who we were talking about.

Lucy turned to stare at Gav. "Oh, you mean Daphne the very attractive yet ditzy woman who makes Velma look like a Cyclops in comparison?"

"I didn't mean it like that," he said, frowning. After a moment, he offered, "How about the Chrissy to your Janet?"

She stared at him. "Once again, it's beauty and the beast," she snapped.

"Hold the phone, here," Gav said, raising a hand to stop her. "*Janet* was the cute one."

"No, Janet was the dark-haired one."

"Well yeah, the cute one," he nodded.

They both were silent and I thought that if the hole didn't do it, the sexual tension would suck all of the oxygen out of the room.

Very interesting.

"You mean," Lucy said, glancing at me, then back at Gavin, "you think *I'm* the cute one?"

"Yeah. The cute, smart one."

"Hello?" Candace called from the front door.

"You *found* the place," said, his tone indicating that the feat was nothing short of miraculous.

"Your car's parked right outside," she said, then turned to me. "They dropped me off on the corner so I could get some Gatorade."

"It was an emergency of sorts," Gavin smirked.

"What's all this?" Candace asked, oblivious to the hole as she walked toward the sewing machine and fabric on the coffee table.

I lifted up the shorts to show the group.

"Oh my god, where did you get those?" Candace squawked.

I pointedly stared at the sewing machine, then at the scraps of fabric I'd trimmed away. "I *made* them."

"Very funny," Candace scoffed.

"I'm serious."

"She's always been into sewing," Gavin explained.

"I used to make some pretty cool stuff," I told the girls. I wasn't normally one to brag, but I was still enjoying the adrenaline rush I'd received from Ethan's visit, making the shorts, *and* Gav's forgiveness.

"Everyone used to do things they thought were cool," Lucy said. "I played the clarinet in a freaking *marching band* and thought it was cool."

"No," Gavin said. "She really did make cool stuff. Remember you made me that jacket thing?"

"It was a *poncho*," I said, with a roll of the eyes.

"It had no sleeves," he said to Lucy, miming sleevelessness.

"I guess that's what made it a poncho," she said, sarcastically.

"Anyway," he said, shrugging, "I loved that thing and wore it forever."

"Which was about three months, until you left it at Darren Fraser's house and someone swiped it."

"I still think it was Sean O'Dell, and I plan to confront him at our next reunion."

"Good luck with that," I laughed. "He's an NFL linebacker, now."

Gavin pretended to ponder it, then suggested, "Maybe you can just make me another one."

"We'll see."

"So," Lucy said, a gleam in her eye. "Who was the cute guy leaving when we pulled up?"

"Yeah!" Candace chimed in. "He *was* cute."

"I'm glad you asked," Gavin said, "because I'm very curious, myself. Did you finish your online profile before hitting the hay last night?"

"Online profile?" Lucy and Candace asked, in unison.

"*No,* I didn't. He's a guy from the local taxidermy shop."

"Ooh!" Candace clapped her hands. "An accountant."

Dear god.

"No, a *taxidermist.* He stuffs dead animals."

"You mean with herbs and stuff?" Candace asked. "Is he a chef?"

Gavin let out a low whistle. "Holy smokes."

"No, like *that,*" I said, pointing at Murph the raccoon, the only critter still on the main floor.

Candace's gaze followed my finger and she let out a bloodcurdling scream.

"Anyway," I continued, when she regained control of herself, "he was checking out some of Ida's things and we ended up having a really nice conversation."

"About what?" Gavin asked, his interest clearly piqued.

"Oh, you know. Work, and all that. He was asking me about what I'd really love to do, and I didn't really have an answer."

"Why not?" Lucy asked.

A thought that always tickled my fancy came to mind.

"This will sound kind of stupid, but I never was a 'natural' at anything I tried, so I've always had this idea that buried deep within me is some deluxe skill or talent I've never tapped."

"Like what?" Lucy asked, lips forming a smile.

"I don't know. Minigolf, maybe. Or pottery."

"Why don't you try them out?" she asked.

I laughed, amused at just how preposterous the idea was.

"I *can't.* If I find out I'm no good at it, I'll be killing my own dream. I mean, maybe I'm really good at shot put."

"I can't think of too many track and field job opportunities I've come across," Gav murmured.

"I can juggle," Candace said, hopefully.

"I guess I like the idea that if I tried chess, I'd be a prodigy or something, and tour the globe, beating champions and signing endorsement deals."

"Not dozens of items or anything," Candace said. "I don't think I could handle more than four or five at a time."

"Who knows, I might be an expert at breaking spy codes, or I could be a human divining rod."

"Good grief," Gavin sighed.

"Nothing *sharp,* of course," Candace murmured, "and certainly nothing *flaming.*"

"Maybe I'm really good at Latin, and I don't even know it. Or chemistry."

"Didn't we take that together in high school?" Gavin asked.

"Well, yeah, and I only got a C, but I might be a late bloomer or something."

Candace continued to mumble. "Nothing *alive,* I don't think. Unless it was something that didn't wiggle around too much. No, nothing that might put up a fight."

"What the hell are you talking about?" Lucy asked her.

"Juggling," Candace said, with a shrug.

"Somehow, I doubt I'm the only one seeing this," Gavin said, folding his arms across his chest, "but you *do* have an untapped talent, Laur."

"I do?"

He held up the shorts. "You *do.*"

"Oh, come on. That's just fooling around."

"People would *pay* for these," he insisted.

"No, they wouldn't," I laughed. He was being ridiculous.

"I would," Lucy said. "I have two nephews who'd be all over these."

"I just spent almost sixty bucks on two outfits for baby showers," Candace added. "And they had nothing on those shorts. Could you make shirts to match?"

"Well, yeah. I mean, I bought some patterns I was planning to alter and—"

"Could you make infant sizes, too?" Lucy asked.

"Sure," I blurted, though I hadn't given it any thought.

"You know, there's a huge craft fair next month at my nephew's school," Lucy said. "Why don't you register, get some stuff together, and just see how people respond?"

"Because that's *insane.*"

"Why?" Gavin asked. "You could totally do it."

"No, no," I said, shaking my head. "This is just an old hobby of mine, and I'm pretty rusty."

"I know clothes," Candace said, "and there's nothing rusty about these." She looked at me sheepishly. "I loved the outfit you wore to work that day. I was just jealous that you'd managed to make it."

"Just do the freakin' craft fair," Lucy urged.

It was all happening a bit too fast for me. I'd only sewn a couple of articles of clothing in the past five years.

But you had fun doing it.

How many items would I have to make for a craft fair?

Find out.

I looked from one friend's face to the next before I quietly asked, "Do you really think—"

"Yes," they all agreed.

"I'll think about it," I said, my mind already racing with possibilities.

At that precise moment, Candace finally spotted the hole and stared at the precariously balanced table.

"You're going to have to eat off your lap," she said, shaking her head.

Certainly the least of my worries.

Seventeen

RACHEL CALLED IN sick again on Thursday, and I couldn't resist phoning her house to see if she was okay.

Unfortunately, she *could* resist answering my call, so I left yet another message.

Lucy and Candace had suggested I whip up a little shirt to turn the shorts into an ensemble I could bring to work in an effort to test the water on my sewing project. I figured it couldn't hurt to try, so I'd stayed up an hour later than usual and managed to complete two outfits, the second being a tank top and shorts in hot pink with silver and black trim to cover the girl angle.

My desk was a hive of activity for the first part of the morning, as various coworkers stopped by for a look and to offer feedback. With no children of my own, I was oblivious to the latest trends in kids' wear, and that seemed to have served me well. Numerous people told me the outfits were different and unique, and even more asked where they could buy them.

When I explained that I'd made them, at least four people asked me what on earth I was doing working at Knutsen Insurance.

Just before my morning break, Lucy gave me the contact information for the craft fair, which turned out to be at none other than Daniel's school.

Needless to say, that put a damper on the plan.

But not enough to snuff it out.

During lunch I called the school and was told that an information packet would be mailed, the registration fee had to be
received no later than the fifteenth, and the school was entitled to
20 percent of my sales.

Give it a shot.

WHEN I ARRIVED home that afternoon, I completely ignored the
hole, which was stupid and juvenile, but it was also all I could do.
I had no money for repairs, my card was almost maxed out, and
I certainly couldn't fix it myself.

I knew that if I didn't start painting right away, I never would,
and my gorgeous cans of color would sit in the basement until the
estate sale that followed my death. At the same time, I knew I
should be at least coming up with a plan of sorts for the craft fair.

I glanced at the hole.

*Yeah, you're screwed. Just concentrate on painting and sewing for
now.*

I'd just changed into a pair of sweatpants and a T-shirt for
painting and turned the radio on to an Eighties station when
there was a knock on the door.

"Coming," I called, making my way down the stairs.

"Hi, Lauren," Thomas said, when I opened the door and
found him and his blue blanket before me.

"How are you, buddy?" I asked, genuinely pleased to see his
little face.

"Good. I made this for you." He offered me a miniature muffin, lightly glazed with a sugary coating.

Starving, I admired it for only a split second before shoving it
in my mouth while he gasped, "No!"

The glaze turned out to be shellac.

He groaned. "It was for *show.*"

"I see," I told him, sputtering.

"To make the house yours, like you said."

I looked at his earnest expression and felt a tightening in my chest, wondering if this was a gift the other kids were making for their mothers.

"Thank you, Thomas," I said, through the sudden lump in my throat.

I invited him inside and he stopped short, gaping at the hole. He took several hurried steps backwards, bumping into the couch in the process. All of the color had left his little face and he whispered, "What's in your basement?"

I would have laughed if he hadn't looked so terrified. "Nothing, Thomas. The wood just rotted and the floor broke."

"Are you sure?" His voice was barely audible.

"I'm sure. Do you want to come downstairs and see?"

"No!" he gulped, parking his rump on the couch, where he could keep an eye on the hole.

I rinsed my mouth with cold water, and when my taste buds were almost back to normal, I showed him the shorts outfit.

"Awesome!" he shouted. "Can I try them on?"

"Go for it."

Forgetting he was a child, I assumed he'd change in the bathroom, but he peeled down to his skivvies right in front of me while I made a concerted effort to act natural.

"Can you do my buttons?" he asked after a minute or two. He stood in front of me with his shirt open, exposing a strip of ghostly white skin.

Once he was completely put together, I directed him to the full-length bathroom mirror, where he posed and danced around, strutting his minuscule stuff.

"Thank you, Lauren!" he gushed, reaching up to hug me around the waist.

"You're very welcome."

He cautiously pointed at the hole. "Is that going to be there tomorrow?"

"Probably," I admitted.

"The next day?" he asked, with a wince.

"I'm betting so, yeah."

He bit his lip and I could almost hear the wheels turning in his mind. "Can your daddy fix it?"

"My daddy's in Florida." And his last woodworking project was a set of bookcases with only one level shelf.

"My daddy's in Heaven."

"I know, Thomas." The lump returned to my throat. He was so young, and he'd already been through so much.

He stared at the hole and very softly said, "Sometimes I want to go to Heaven."

"You will," I assured him, eyes stinging.

"I mean *now*."

I rested my hand on his shoulder. "You can't go yet, Thomas. Without you, who would figure stuff out?"

He turned to look at me for a second. I returned his gaze, with every scrap of sincerity I possessed. Eventually, his lips formed a smile. "You need me."

"Yeah," I said, heart tightening another notch. "I need you."

WHEN THOMAS LEFT for Patty's, sporting his new look and carrying his old duds in a plastic grocery bag, I took on the task of transforming my living room with paint.

After about an hour, my phone rang.

Mom and Dad.

"Hello?"

"Honey, it's Dad."

"Hi, I was—"

"Here's your mother."

He was gone before I could say good-bye and after a brief pause, during which I could visualize Mom plucking the clip-on pearls from her phone ear, her voice came through.

"Darling? Are you all right?"

"I'm fine. I just got in and—"

"Have you eaten?"

"Dinner? No, I—"

"You've got to eat *something*, Lauren. My god, all of these changes are starving the life out of you."

"Okay, I haven't eaten dinner because I just got home from work, Mom. I'll heat up a frozen meal or something, and I'm going to start painting."

"Wonderful!" she gushed. "I guess it's only six there, isn't it? It's nine here. We had the Prushkovs over for an early dinner."

"The who?"

"The couple from down the way. They're Ukrainian or something." There was a brief pause and I could hear Dad in the background. "*Estonian?*" Mom's voice was rich with incredulity. "No, Estonians don't play Boggle, dear. Anyway, Lauren, they're lovely people, although I must say I don't like her tendency to reach rather than requesting that dishes be passed her way. Maybe it's an Eastern European thing, but I'm not a fan. Oh, your father wants a word."

I waited for the phone to be passed over.

"Lauren?"

"Yes, Dad."

"Did you see that *60 Minutes* piece on alkaline batteries?"

"No," I sighed.

"Lay off them. I can't emphasize that enough."

"Thanks."

"And make sure you check the expiration dates on your groceries.

Particularly the canned stuff. There's no telling how long a can of beets might sit on the shelf."

"Good point."

How could a man so concerned with death by food staples be comfortable hurling lawn darts through the air every Sunday?

And what would he think about the death trap in my living room?

"Okay, then. By the way, I've mailed you a screwdriver with multiple heads."

"What? Why?"

"It saves you buying a set."

"Dad, there *are* hardware stores around here."

"I know, but I wanted you to have a good one." He cleared his throat. "Oh! James and Edith are just pulling into the driveway, honey. Cocktail hour, you know. I'll put your Mom back on to say good-bye."

"But speaking of repairs—"

Before I could finish, he was gone.

"Honey?"

"Hey, Mom, I was just going to tell Dad that it seems the house *does* need some work." I was hoping he could recommend a reasonably priced contractor. Maybe the guy they'd hired to put the kitchen back together after Dad had "renovated" it.

"You said you bought some paint the other day. It sounds like it's going to be lovely—" Mom began.

"Yeah, I know, but it turned out that my pal Patty was just being optimistic when she said the place was in good shape. When I say there's work to do, I mean"—I started reading from the steno pad on the coffee table, where I'd listed Steven's original findings—"replace furnace filters, which I think I can do, but then I need to clean the furnace burners and ductwork, cover the asbestos, reseal the upstairs toilet, and unplug the shower drain, repair the back screen door and garage door, rewire the circuit breaker, take care of the dry rot in the basement"—I glanced at the hole and cringed—"fix the leak on the kitchen faucet, reattach the gutter pipes at the back, repair the chimney mortar—"

"Enough," Mom said. "I'm sending your father."

"What?"

"Give him a week and he'll get you all sorted out."

"But Mom, Dad's not exactly an expert on—"

"He's a *wonderful* handyman."

"You don't remember the dishwasher installation at the old house? Or the 'repairs' he made to the back deck? We never used those stairs again, Mom. And the tiling project in the guest bathroom?"

"He's learned a lot since then."

"Mom, he—"

"Lauren, honey, he has a *tool belt* now."

"That doesn't mean—"

The doorbell cut me off.

"Maybe we'll both come out. Make a little holiday of it," she offered.

"A well-deserved break from retirement?" I asked, as the doorbell rang again. "I've got to go, Mom. We'll talk about this later."

I answered the door, fully expecting the return of Thomas, but it was Ethan who stood before me, carrying a paper bag and a six-pack of Mirror Pond.

"Uh, hi," I said, self-conscious about not only my appearance, but my Eighties sound track.

"I thought you might want some help with the painting," he said.

"Seriously?" I said, stunned.

"Yeah, I was supposed to see a show with a buddy of mine tonight but the band broke down somewhere in Idaho, so . . ." He shrugged.

"That's great! I mean, not about the band, but you being . . . I guess what I'm trying to . . ." I stepped back from the doorway to let him in. "Thank you, Ethan."

I darted over to the satellite radio for a new music selection, cringing as Bonnie Tyler's raspy voice sang the chorus to "Total Eclipse of the Heart."

"I love that song," Ethan said, setting the six-pack on the over-loaded coffee table and offering me a beer.

"You do?" I gasped.

"No." He laughed, and dimples very like my own punctured his cheeks.

"Very funny," I said, moving to the Nineties instead.

"Better," Ethan said as Michael Stipe's voice filled the room. He rested his hands on the worn leather belt that held up his faded jeans and surveyed the walls. "Okay, I'll make a point of ignoring the very disturbing issue at floor level and tell you that you've chosen a nice color for the walls."

"Thank you. I think the yellow is a bit more 'me' than the blue."

"Definitely," he said, meeting my eyes for a moment with a quick nod. "Nice and sunny." He cleared his throat and looked away. "I see you're skipping the tape." He pointed to the windows.

"Well, I'm leaving the trim white, and I figured it would be faster to just—"

He faced me again. "Do you want to do it fast, or right?"

If Lucy and Candace were here, they'd turn this into a bedroom conversation.

"Well, I—"

"Let's do it right," he said. "Have you got any masking tape?"

I led him into the kitchen and opened the drawer beneath the silverware, forgetting until it was too late that it also housed the "hard candy" condom my Mom had found in my purse.

"Oh!" I gulped.

He cleared his throat. "Interesting storage place."

In a panic, I tried to make light of it. "Well, you know . . . pizza delivery guys, UPS, the mailman. You never know when you might need one."

He frowned, and pulled the roll of tape from the drawer. "I guess you're right."

"I was just . . ."

Why are you such an idiot?

"I mean . . . so," I continued, scrambling for a topic, "what's in the bag?" I asked, stupidly pointing at it.

"What?"

"What's in the—"

"No, I heard what you said, I just . . ." He looked at me for a moment and sighed. "I brought some sandwiches."

We sat on opposite sides of Ida's farmhouse table, and when he opened the bag, he gave me a choice between turkey and roast beef.

"Meat or meat. Good thing I'm not a vegetarian," I said.

"Yeah, I guess it is lucky," he said, rubbing his forehead with the back of his hand. "Do you always do that?"

"What?" I asked, fearing I'd already dripped mayo on myself.

"Blurt whatever's on your mind."

"No . . . well, kind of."

Idiot! Idiot! Idiot!

Are you really this socially inept?

"Just curious," he said.

"I'm working on it."

He stared at me in apparent disbelief. "Like you're trying to do it more?"

"No, less. It gets me into trouble."

He chuckled, grimly. "I'm sure it does."

How did you ruin this so damn fast?

"Look," I said, trying to keep the pleading tone from my voice, even though that's exactly what I was doing. "Can we just start over for today?"

"Meaning?"

I rose from the table and mimed opening the door. "Ethan! What a nice surprise!"

He looked at me, his arms folded across his chest for a moment before he stood as well. "I, uh . . . came to help you paint."

"You did?" I gasped.

The ghost of a smile tickled his lips. "Yup, and I brought us some sandwiches and beer to *enjoy* while we're at it."

"You've got to be kidding! Oh my gosh, I hope they're *meat* sandwiches."

The smile bloomed, along with a chuckle. "As luck would have it, they are."

"Ethan, this is the nicest thing anyone has done for me in a long time." I couldn't hide the fact that I was serious.

"Really?" he asked, breaking out of the game and cocking an eyebrow.

"Really," I assured him, blushing. "Thank you very much for thinking of me."

"Well, it's something that seems to come naturally," he said, smiling.

"Hey, Ethan?"

"Yes?"

"What I said before, about the . . . pharmaceuticals—"

He interrupted with a puzzled, "Pharma . . . *oh,* the condoms."

"Uh, yes." I winced. "I was kidding, about that. I mean," I stammered, "I haven't used any . . . I don't mean *ever,* but *recently.* I mean, I haven't—"

"I think I get it," he said, quietly. "Good," he added, with a very gentle smile that made me tingle to my toes. "That's good."

When we got to work, him with the tape and me, the paint, I dipped my roller and ran it up and down the wall, enjoying the process of brightening the room one stripe at a time. As I got closer to the window where Ethan was working, I caught a clean, woodsy scent over the smell of the paint and inhaled deeply.

In a couple of minutes, I was right next to him, staring at the wall in front of me, spreading my paint while breathing him in.

I leaned over to pull my tray closer and when I straightened, he was even closer to me, and no longer taping.

I felt his warm breath against my ear, and goose bumps rioted all over my skin. He very gently stroked my cheek with the back of his fingers, and I could barely breathe.

That is, until I tuned in to our sound track.

"Is our first kiss really going to be to Nine Inch Nails?" I whispered.

I felt his whole body tense.

"Maybe not," he said, pulling away from me.

Why is he stopping?

All we have to do is change the station.

"No, I didn't mean—"

"I know," he sighed, shaking his head.

"It's just that when I think of—"

"Hey, Lauren, isn't *thinking* supposed to be *silent?*"

"Well, yes, but . . ." I looked into his eyes and saw something more important than what song was on the radio. I swallowed, hard. "I'm ruining this, aren't I?"

He looked me right in the eyes and softly said, "Yes."

"I always—"

"It seems to me that this would be an excellent time to practice *not* blurting."

"You're probably right," I said, reaching for his arm with my free hand and pulling him against me, amazed by my own aggressiveness.

I looped my arm around his neck while his circled my waist.

Thankfully, the song ended just in time and a gentle sound came through the speakers. It took me a second or two to think of the band.

The Cranberries.

Much better.

And the song is "Dreams."

Perfect.

He tilted his head toward me, and I rose onto tiptoes to greet his lips with mine.

His breath was warm, his lips perfectly damp and soft.

Really perfect.

My sigh was barely audible, but he heard it, and pulled me closer.

I lifted my other arm from my side, to wrap it around his neck. Unfortunately, I was too enthralled to remember I was still holding my roller, until I hit the back of his head with it.

"What the—" he cried, pulling back.

"Sorry!" I winced, noting the trickle of yellow paint coursing down his neck. "I forgot about this," I told him, dropping the roller onto the paint tray and stepping toward him with a paper towel to tidy him up.

"You're smooth, aren't you?" he chuckled.

"I guess clumsy is how I . . . operate."

"Then we should thank our lucky stars you aren't a surgeon," he murmured, taking the soiled paper towel from my hand and dropping it onto the newspaper.

"I don't normally do this," I murmured.

"Ruin moments?"

"No, I do that. I meant I don't usually do *this*."

"Neither do I."

I looked into his warm eyes for a second before smiling. "Good."

"Okay, so let's try that again."

"If you insist," I said, getting back into position.

"Oh, I insist," he murmured.

Through the course of the evening I was delighted to discover that he was very consistent with his insistence.

Eighteen

AFTER EXTENSIVE PRODDING from Ethan, I called three contractors and made appointments for them to stop by the house
with estimates.

I was informed by the first guy that my problem wasn't dry
rot, but carpenter ants. While my mind entertained the thought
of a small army of bugs carrying teeny hammers and toolboxes,
he set to work tallying up the damages.

When he quoted me, I could barely speak. "That's for the floor
and the wiring, right?" I asked, hopefully.

"What wiring?" he asked. "I don't do electrical."

"But—"

"My brother-in-law does."

"Really?"

"Yeah, but he's spendy."

"And you're . . . not?" I asked, meekly.

"Hell, no. You're not going to get a cheaper quote than I just
gave you for this floor." He paused for a moment. "I should tell
you I'm booked solid for the next month, so I wouldn't be able to
get to you for a while."

The second guy wanted almost double the money, and couldn't
start for two weeks.

"Do you take Visa?" I asked, as if my card could actually with-
stand more charges.

His lip curled with distaste. "I take cash."

By the time my doorbell rang a third time, I was afraid that simply answering it was going to cost me.

In a way, it did.

"Tim," I said, frowning at the sight of my brother. "What are you doing here?"

"Nice to see you too, Laur," he said, smiling.

"Seriously, what are you doing here?"

He self-consciously patted the thinning hair on top of his head back into place and cleared his throat. "Can I come in?"

I stepped back to let him enter, and braced myself for his reaction to the floor.

He let out a low whistle and slowly circled the table, just as Gavin and Ethan had done. "Dry rot?"

"Carpenter ants, but I'll get it taken care of," I said, defensively. "It's no big deal."

"It kind of looks like a big deal, Laur." He shook his head and settled on the couch.

"I didn't know you were coming back to town so soon."

I remained standing, hoping the visit would be brief.

"Business," he said, with a casual wave of the hand. He looked from one end of the room to the other, gaze settling on the light switch. "Any chance we could brighten things up a bit in here?"

"I like it like this," I lied.

"That's ridiculous," he said, starting to move toward the switch.

"It doesn't work, okay?" I snapped. "I've got some wiring issues to deal with, and I'm going to . . . deal with them."

He stared at me. "Do you know what an electrician costs?"

"A lot."

He frowned. "How much of a *wiring issue* have you got?"

"You couldn't have come all the way from Idaho to talk to me about this, Tim, mainly because you didn't know any of it was going on." I paused, doing my best to stare him down. "Is there something I can do for you?"

"Well, I did want to talk to you about something."

"Go for it," I snapped.

"You're in over your head, here."

My entire body tensed. "Meaning?" I asked, through gritted teeth.

"You've got big expenses and a small budget. This house is too much for you right now." He raised a hand to stop me from responding. "Hey, I commend you for giving this a shot. It was a gutsy undertaking, but sometimes gutsy just doesn't do it."

"I can handle it, Tim."

He shook his head. "I don't think you can, Laur. And that's nothing to be ashamed of. You just bit off a little more than you could chew, just like that fruit punch stand when we were kids. That was a flop, but you *tried*."

My fists clenched. "It *flopped* because you made me charge a dollar a cup instead of the twenty-five cents I wanted to. I couldn't sell anything."

"I was just looking out for you. I'm your big brother."

I stared at him, looking for any sign of the brother I'd known.

"That's the weird thing, Tim. I remember the kid who watched *Family Feud* with me in this very room, the kid who proofread my Christmas list and taught me how to peel the stickers off a Rubik's Cube and reattach them so it would look like I'd solved the damn thing." I took a breath. "I want that kid to come over and hang out with me in this house sometime."

"Lauren," he sighed, shaking his head. "You can't live in the past. Jesus, you're going to need a fortune to fix this place, when you could just sell it, make some bank and buy a loft, or a condo or something."

"The only thing is, I don't want a loft."

"You're not listening to what I'm saying. You're sitting on all this money—"

"It was *left to me,* Tim."

"Just think of all the ways you could reinvest even half of what you'd make on this place."

That stopped me cold. "And why would I only be reinvesting *half?*"

"Well," he said, with a nervous smile. "I figured that after we last spoke you'd want to split the proceeds with me."

"What?" My head was spinning.

"Like I said before, Lauren. It's the *fair* thing."

He reached down to tug his pant leg over his black sock, then continued to fiddle with the hem.

"Tim?"

He released the fabric but kept his head bowed.

"Tim?" I asked again.

"I just think it's the right thing, the *fair* thing to do."

"I don't see it that way. I mean, she left you the—"

He raised his head, and there was a look of panicked anger in his eyes. "I need the fucking money, Lauren!"

Shocked, I could barely speak. "Tim, I—"

"I'm sorry," he said, his voice shaking. "I just . . . I just need the money. If you could just sell the house, I—"

"What's going on?" I interrupted. "Why do you need the money?"

"It doesn't matter—"

"Yes, it does. Are you in some kind of trouble?"

"I just need the money. For Christ's sake, Lauren. I'm your only brother."

It was true.

A silent slide show played in my head. Tim helping me tie my shoelaces, accompanying me to the classroom on my first day of school . . . making me steal cookies from Mom's cooling rack. We'd spent an entire childhood together, and while it had been filled with ups and downs and our adult relationship wasn't quite what I may have wanted it to be . . . he was my only brother. He was right about the inheritance not being fair, and he was right about how far the money could go for both of us.

I could feel the words on the tip of my tongue, the blurt that would save me from mounting debt and make him extremely happy. I could just give it all up to help him out of whatever trouble he was in.

It was the right thing to do.

The words were right there, waiting, but just as I opened my mouth to give him what he wanted, I glanced at the vulnerable patch of skin on the top of his head and remembered the games of hide and seek we'd played in that very house. I remembered cracking walnuts in front of the television and watching the fly-paper fill with victims.

I thought of my parents' Beaverton house, sold so they could make their Florida move, leaving us no family home, no gathering place, in Portland.

I needed this house, but more importantly, *we* needed this house.

"I'm sorry, Tim," I said, quietly.

"You're what?" he asked, lifting his head.

"I'm sorry. I can't sell the place."

He started at me in stony silence for a full ten seconds before speaking. "You're kidding."

I shook my head. "No."

His jaw was flushed as he stood. "I can't believe you're doing this to me."

I thought of the boy in the Halloween Underoos, and imagined his kids trick-or-treating on this very street. I thought of holiday dinners and backyard barbeques.

Keeping the house in the family was the right decision.

"I'm sorry," I said, biting my lip.

"You," he growled, nostrils flaring as his face turned a deeper shade of red.

"Tim," I said, hoping to reason with him.

His hands curled into tight fists. "I can't believe you."

"Tim, I—"

"*You selfish little bitch,*" he spat.

I watched in stunned silence as he turned his back on me, stepped through the door, and slammed it behind him.

THE REST OF the week passed by in slow motion. Work was the same drab place it had always been, but without Rachel it was several shades worse. I couldn't stop thinking about Tim's outburst and the fact that no matter what I said, I was constantly pissing people off. I'd alienated, angered, saddened, and frustrated people for my whole life, and I was tired of it.

Sick and tired.

ASIDE FROM THOMAS'S visits, the only saving grace that week was Ethan, and we talked a lot.

It was refreshing to hear his opinion on any topic, but extremely helpful when it came to the situation with Rachel, who had returned to work as silent as ever.

Ethan and I were lying in bed one night, following an energetic and enjoyable romp on my newly christened couch, when I mentioned how much I missed her friendship.

"She means enough to you that you can't go on like this, right?"

"Yes."

"I think you need to confront her," he said.

"I *have*."

"No, you've tried to talk to her at work, and you've left her phone messages, but you've never really *confronted* her."

"I tried—"

"I mean to the point of *resolution*. Lauren, if *you* don't get it resolved, it will never *be* resolved."

"You sound resolute," I said, resting my hand on his bare chest.

"I am, my dear. I am."

WHEN SATURDAY MORNING rolled around, I was beyond frustrated that Rachel could hold a grudge like it was welded to her palm and decided to take Ethan's advice, drive to her place, and get things sorted out, face to face.

When I arrived, I saw her green Beetle, but no sign of Steven's Honda. Hoping they hadn't left together, I climbed the front steps and rang her doorbell.

"Coming," she called from inside.

I took a deep breath to prepare myself. We'd gone so long without speaking to each other, I had no idea where to start.

"Hi," I said, lifting one hand in a meek wave when she opened the door.

Instead of a smile or a greeting she looked mildly irritated and said, "What do *you* want?"

This won't be a cakewalk.

"I was hoping you might have a minute to talk," I said, smile wavering but still present.

"Actually, I was just on my way out."

I pointedly looked her over, from her slippered feet to her flannel pajama bottoms and ratty T-shirt combination, one hand clutching a bowl of popcorn, and the other a DVD.

"Is that right?" I asked.

She glared at me for a moment before speaking. "No, but you should have called first."

"I did call," I assured her, pulling Exhibit A from my purse. I unfolded my cell phone bill, where every occurrence of her number was highlighted in hot pink. "Twenty-seven times."

She gave it a cursory glance. "Come in," she sighed.

"Thank you."

I stepped into the living room, which always smelled like incense and dried my mouth to the point of tasting like parchment.

Opting for the wooden rocking chair, I sat and waited for her to return from the kitchen with the Coke she'd offered. Her cat, Gouda, a flat-faced Persian with a superiority complex, sat at my feet and glared at me, as though she was a stand-in and Rachel was hating me by proxy.

"Hey, Gouda," I whispered, then rubbed my fingers together in an effort to lure her into some petting.

She wasn't having it, and opted to clean her ears instead of acknowledging my efforts. I could only hope that Rachel would prove an easier target.

"Here," she said, handing me an opened can.

Under normal circumstances there would have been a glass.

And ice.

Maybe even a curly straw.

"So," I said, sipping the Coke to buy some time. I'd had ample time to come up with an approach, but I was still struggling. "I wanted to talk to you about—"

"Betraying my trust and sabotaging my relationship with Steven just because your own life isn't turning out how you planned and being too selfish to care about anyone else, despite the fact that your yo-yoing drama has gone on for months while the earth has continued to spin, and you don't appear to notice because you're so damn busy navel-gazing and obsessing about yourself?"

Yikes.

"Uh . . . that wasn't quite the angle I was going for," I mumbled.

"Really?" Rachel snapped, her eyes flashing. "I'd *love* to know what other angle there could possibly be."

"First of all, I don't think I sabotaged your relationship, by—"

"Telling the guy I love that I'd been involved with a married man?"

"Telling him the *truth,*" I reminded her.

"Yeah, *my* truth, Lauren. *I'm* the one who gets to decide when, how, or if I share personal details with someone."

"Still, I—"

She shook her head with disgust. "And to think I thought you came here to apologize."

"I did, but—"

"But *what?* You forgot the words? It's a short and simple statement, Lauren, but it can pack a wallop. *I'm sorry.*"

"Me too."

I was relieved that the sentiment was out there, until I saw the look of stunned disbelief on her face.

"*You too?*" she choked. "I'm not apologizing to you, Lauren. I have done absolutely nothing to you."

"Well, you stopped talking to me."

"With good reason! My god, are you really this out of touch with reality?"

"Look," I snapped. "It's been a hell of a few months, okay?"

"Do you know how many people split up, Lauren? Hundreds of thousands. Maybe even millions every year. Some of those are *divorces* that involve cheating, children, debt, abuse, and who knows what else, but people get through it. Your split was a Caribbean cruise in comparison to most of what's out there."

"How can you—" I gasped, but she cut me off with a raised hand.

"I know it was sad, and I know it was hard, but now it's all in the past. It's time to get on with your life."

"I *am* getting on with it," I snapped. "I'm trying to tell you that I want *you* to be a part of it."

"You know, I'm not trying to be a bitch here, but I'm kind of at the end of my rope."

"I know, I—"

"I think I've been incredibly supportive of you over the past few months. I've done everything I can think of to make things easier for you, and half the time, you haven't recognized the effort."

"I have, though. I just neglected to—"

"Yup," she said, nodding. "You neglected to."

"But I'm trying to—"

"I miss you, Lauren. I kept waiting for you to snap out of it and start being the fun person I used to know, or someone even better, but the waiting continued, and then that whole thing with Steven at your place. Oh my god."

"I'm sorry," I murmured. "Really, truly sorry."

"Are you, though?"

When I looked at her, there were tears in my eyes.

"Yes. You're the best friend I have, Rach, and I absolutely hate how things are between us, thanks to my big, fat mouth. I am more sorry than you'll ever know."

She watched me for a brutally long moment, then quietly said, "Thank you for that," and moved to hug me.

When we released each other, I wiped my eyes and cleared my throat. "Can I ask you something?"

"What?"

"Were you ever going to tell me that you're getting married?"

She turned to look at me, frowning slightly. "You were in the middle of calling things off when we got engaged."

"So?"

"So, it didn't seem like the most tactful announcement."

"Since when did you think I required tact?" I smiled, cautiously. "I haven't exactly been using any, myself."

"No," she chuckled, "you haven't."

"I'm going to be totally honest with you, Rachel," I said, taking a deep breath. "It hurt my feelings to hear it from Lucy."

"I'm sorry," she said. "I didn't mean for it to happen that way."

"You know I'm happy for you, right?"

"Are you?" she asked, peering into my eyes.

"Absolutely. I think you and Steven are a great match."

"You do?" she asked, a hint of skepticism in her voice.

"*Yes.*"

"You truly do?"

"Yes."

"Because I wanted to ask you to be my maid of honor."

"I'd love to, Rach!" I told her, forcing the words past the lump in my throat.

"Well, I love *you*, Laur."

"Even when I'm an idiot?"

"I have to," she said, sighing dramatically, "because that's most of the time."

WHEN I ARRIVED back at the house, Ethan was waiting on my doorstep.

"How did it go?" he asked.

"Really well," I said, reaching up to hug him. "We're back on track."

"Excellent," he said, giving me a tight squeeze then taking my hand to lead me into the house. Once inside, he gently kissed my neck. "What do you feel like?"

"This," I sighed, running my fingers through his hair.

"You know I've never jumped into anything this quickly before, right?" he murmured into my neck.

I tensed, immediately worried that he was trying to tell me something I didn't want to hear. "Neither have I."

"We're moving pretty fast," he said, his voice muffled by my skin.

I pulled away from him.

"Hey, it wasn't my idea to jump into bed when we did," I told him, defensively. "And I already told you that isn't my usual M.O."

"What's wrong?" he asked, eyes meeting mine.

"If you want to go—" I began, heart pounding with dread.

"Go where?" he asked, brow furrowed.

"It just sounds like you're . . . wanting some breathing room."

He frowned. "When did it sound like that?"

I stared at him. "You just said we were moving too fast."

"No, I didn't."

"I *heard* you, Ethan."

He shook his head. "I just said it was *fast,* not too fast. And I'm telling you that because I don't want you to think I just do . . . *this.*"

"But you think *I* do?"

"Man," he said, chuckling. "You don't make it easy on a guy, do you?"

"What are you talking about?"

"I'm trying to tell you how much I care about you, Lauren." He cupped my chin in his hands. "It's a good kind of fast, because I love being around you and feeling like I've known you for ages."

I grinned. "You do?"

"Yes," he said, lips curling into a smile. "You're good for me."

"Oh," I said, biting my lip and blushing.

"That's all you can say?" he asked, wryly. "I've silenced the mouth with a few choice words?"

Before I could answer with a nice deep kiss, there was a knock at the door.

"Don't get it," he whispered in my ear, but I was already moving to answer it.

"My blanky!" a tear-streaked Thomas howled when I opened it.

"What happened?" I asked, pulling him inside so he could sob in my living room.

"It's gone!" he wailed. "I lost it and I don't know where."

"We'll find it, Thomas," I said, with as much authority as I could muster.

"We looked all day." His shoulders heaved.

"I'm sure you did."

"For *hours*," he sniffled. "Grandma says she's tired and we have to give up."

"Hey, Thomas," Ethan said, stepping toward him. "I think I know where it might be."

"You do?" the boy gasped, wiping his runny nose with the back of his hand.

"Come here for a second," Ethan said, sitting on the couch and patting the cushion next to him. "I'm going to tell you something that not many people know about."

That was all it took to get my favorite little boy to have a seat.

"What?" he asked, leaning toward Ethan, eyes still shining with tears.

"Have you ever heard of . . ." Ethan glanced over both shoulders to ensure privacy, "the blanket circus?"

Thomas turned to look at me, so I just shrugged and waited for more.

"No." His tone was hesitant.

"Well, some blankets want more out of life than just cuddling, you know?" Ethan didn't wait for an answer. "They have big dreams, about riding the trapeze or being shot from a cannon."

Thomas turned to check with me again, then quietly asked Ethan, "They do?"

"Yes." He glanced upward and gave me a quick wink. "For a long time they have this dream, then one day, the blanket caravan comes through town, calling for them, and the blankets that want a taste of the Big Top join them, leaving their old lives behind."

"But—" Thomas began.

"Do you think your blanket dreamed of being a circus clown?"

"I don't know," Thomas said, biting his lip, brow furrowed.

"Or maybe a lion tamer?"

"Maybe," Thomas said, with the glimmer of a smile. "He could make them fall asleep!"

"Like he did for you?"

"Yeah!" The boy's voice was louder, his enthusiasm building. "Maybe he was practicing on me."

"And now?" Ethan asked.

"Now he's in the circus!" He jumped off the couch and ran toward the front door. "I gotta tell Grandma!"

"That was something," I said, closing the door behind Thomas. "Thank you."

Ethan bowed, dramatically. "My pleasure."

"And now for my pleasure," I said, taking his hand and pulling him off the couch, "I've got some unruly blankets I'm hoping you can help me with."

"Are they in cahoots with some sheets?" he asked, moving toward the stairs. "Because if they are, getting them straightened out will definitely take two of us."

"Then two it is," I chortled, leading the way.

"Hey, I meant to tell you that at work the other day I asked Stump about checking your place out. He used to build houses, before he worked at JT's full time."

I sighed. "Ethan, I don't have the money to pay for repairs."

"Look, you can't keep relying on flashlights and fancy footwork."

I stopped midway up the stairs as what he was saying sunk in. "When you say you asked him about it, do you mean he already agreed to come here?"

"Yes."

"Crap, Ethan!" I groaned. "You didn't think to ask me first?"

"I figured you'd say no," he responded, pointedly.

Why can't anyone just leave it alone?

"With good reason. I'm doing just fine and—"

"You're not doing fine, Lauren. I worry about you living here. Geez, between the lights and that damn excavation site—"

"Hey," I barked. "It's *my* excavation site, okay?"

"I'm just saying that I hate to come over when—"

"So don't come over," I snarled, before I could stop the words.

His beautiful lips thinned and he gave me a long stare. "I was trying to help."

As much as I wanted to smooth things over, I couldn't back down. "Well, don't."

"Gotcha," he said, coldly.

In a split second, he'd descended the stairs and before I could stop him, he'd walked out.

Overwhelmed by it all, I sat down on the stairs and wept.

Nineteen

SINCE THE DAY we'd met, Thomas had slowly adopted the habit of stopping by my place when I returned from work, and I looked forward to the visits more than I could have ever imagined.

He was a clever, entertaining character who made me laugh more than anyone else.

Anyone but Ethan, actually.

Why had I blown everything with Ethan?

Because you're a complete idiot.

A complete idiot with no skills when it came to biting the bullet and tackling the task of winning him back.

In the days that followed the fight, Patty was feeling under the weather, so Thomas and I ran errands together. Since he had an innate interest in how virtually everything on the planet worked, he asked a lot of questions, and we both enjoyed the simplified explanations he received from various strangers.

In the seafood department at Safeway, we learned about the life span of the lobster, and how best to enjoy him when his time was up. He charmed the produce lady, who gave us little samples of mangoes and pears while explaining the regimented schedule of the veggie sprinkler.

Thomas couldn't walk past a car without stating make, model, and often year. I took him for a haircut late one afternoon and the barber was able, at the boy's urging, to estimate the weight of the hair he swept from the floor on a monthly basis.

"Why do you want to know all this stuff?" I eventually asked

him, after he'd drilled a neighbor on the mechanics of a tree
pruner.

"It's interesting," he shrugged.

"All of it?" I asked.

"Yup."

Patty seemed content with the arrangement, but would stop by to
pick him up on the days she thought he might be overstaying his
welcome. Some nights, the two of them traipsed back to their place,
and other times they had dinner with me before heading home.

"You've been pretty busy feathering your nest," Patty said one
afternoon, admiring the completed paint job in the living room.

"It's coming along," I said, with a smile.

"You know, birds use more than feathers and moss."

"They use twigs," Thomas chirped.

"Yeah, they do," Patty Melt said, gaze fixated on the hole.
"Twigs, branches, and sticks."

"I get it," I sighed. "And by the way, you're the one who told
me the place was in great shape."

Patty cackled. "What am I, a home inspector?" She nudged me
with her elbow. "So, are you going the get the dang thing fixed, or
what?"

"I've got some, uh, financial issues."

"I hear you, loud and clear," she said, nodding solemnly. "Hey,
I'd loan you the cash, but—"

"I wouldn't borrow it," I told her. "But thank you."

"You'd think my social security would go farther than it does,"
she said, with a shrug. "I worked my whole goddamn life and I'm
still working."

"Grandma makes movies," Thomas said, patting her knee.

"I'm no Spielberg, kiddo. I just make the popcorn." She sighed.
"I'm tired, you know? I used to have all this energy, but now I just
feel old."

"You're not old," I told her.

"Ha!"

Before she could say any more, there was a loud knock at the door.

"Expecting anyone?" she asked.

"Nope," I said, moving to answer it.

"Jesus. You get more drop-ins than a VD clinic."

"That's . . . colorful," I said, opening the door.

On my front step stood Stump, complete with a toolbox.

"Ethan asked me to come by," he said, quietly.

"Hey, that's very nice of you, Stump, but I'm okay. I don't really need—"

"Get in here," Patty said, yanking the door open from behind me. "The whole damn place is falling apart."

"Is this okay?" Stump asked me, tipping back his hat.

"Come on in," I sighed. "I guess an estimate wouldn't hurt."

Without wasting a second, he flipped the light switch and asked, "Lights working upstairs?"

"Yeah, the bedroom's fine."

"What about the bathroom?"

"Nope." I paused for a moment, confused. "How did you know there was one upstairs?"

His lashes lowered. "Standard blueprint on a house like this."

"But I'm pretty sure it wasn't built with bathrooms. They were added on and—" I would have continued, but he was already on his way downstairs.

"What gives?" I asked Patty, who merely shrugged.

"Can I play upstairs?" Thomas asked.

Knowing he was fond of the nooks, crannies, and closets overhead, I told him it was fine.

"Got a beer?" Patty asked, settling on the couch.

"Indeed, I do," I told her, grabbing one for both of us.

"I haven't seen Ethan around much in the past few days."

"We kind of had a fight," I said, quietly.

She peered closely at me. "You mean you mouthed off."

"No!" I thought about it for a second. "Well, yes."

"That seems to be the thing you do best."

"You know you're not helping, right?" I asked her.

"The hell I'm not," she said, leaning toward me. "You only go through this life once, and if you want to go through it pissing people off, that's your choice."

"Thank you," I said, sarcastically.

"But it's a *stupid* choice."

"Look, he barged into my business by—"

"You *welcomed* him into your business, honey."

I blushed. "Okay, but—"

"He's a good guy. Thomas loves him, and that kid is a great judge of character."

"He's *five*, Patty."

"He likes *you*." She chuckled. "Just give Ethan another chance, would you?"

Stump appeared in the doorway. "You've got some wiring trouble."

"That's what I figured."

"You always going to keep this much stuff running?"

"This much stuff?" I asked, incredulously. "Stump, I've only got a computer and the fridge going right now, so yes, I'm always going to keep *this much stuff* running."

Patty called from the couch, "Hey, Lippy, watch yourself."

"I wasn't—"

"Just watch it," she warned.

Stump continued, "It looks like too much of the heavy-load stuff got wired to one circuit."

"Am I going to have to rewire the whole place?" I asked, bracing myself for the worst.

"Nope, I can just reconfigure it."

"What do you mean?"

"Right now your dryer is on the same circuit as your stove and fridge, which is too much for that small gauge wire. All you need to do is plug in an alarm clock or flip a light switch and it's overloaded. I can mix things up a bit so they're more evenly distributed."

"Seriously?" I asked, amazed at my good fortune.

"Yup, and I can do it tomorrow."

Embarrassed, I looked at my feet instead of into his eyes as I told him, "I can't pay you, Stump."

He smiled. "You can patch things up with Ethan. He's been a bear to work with."

"Is that a taxidermist joke?" I asked, chuckling.

Stump frowned. "No." He glanced toward the living room. "As for the floor, I've got a buddy who owes me a pretty big favor and that job would just about cover it."

"Stump, I can't let you do that."

"Talk to the boy," he said, with a smile. "Just talk to the boy."

Once he'd left, I hugged Patty with glee.

"Lauren," Thomas said, from the stairway. "Look what I found."

I turned to see him clutching a blue shoebox, bound with white string.

"Where did you get that?"

"In the little door."

"In the hallway up there?" I asked.

"Uh-huh."

Puzzled, I stepped into the kitchen for a pair of scissors, curious about what Ida would have tied so tightly. Thomas handed me the box and I snipped through the string so I could lift the lid.

A musty scent wafted toward me as I saw a small stack of envelopes, neatly tied with a ribbon.

"Letters?" Patty asked.

I nodded. "Should I open them?"

"It's up to you."

"It feels like a violation of her privacy," I said, cringing.

"Then don't."

"But I'm curious."

"Then do," she shrugged. "Nothing you find is going to hurt her now."

Weighing her words, I untied the bow, opened the top envelope, and pulled a folded piece of paper free. As I unfolded it, I saw sure strokes of dark blue ink. "It's a letter," I said, then looked to the top of the page. " 'My Sweet Ida.' "

"No!" Patty gasped with glee.

I nodded as I scanned the letter, which was full of loving words and *longing*. When I reached the bottom, I was blushing.

It was signed with only the letter *J*.

"Who's J?" I asked.

"No idea," Patty said. "Open another one."

I opened three more, all of which were beautifully written love letters in the same hand. It wasn't until I read the fourth that I found a full name. "It's James."

"James who?" she asked.

"I can't make out the name too well. Fallow?"

"Fellow?" Patty asked.

"Yeah, maybe that's it."

"Well, god love a duck," Patty said, shaking her head.

"What?"

"James Fellow," she murmured, with a smile.

"Yes. Who is it?"

She grinned. "Our man Stump."

"No!" I gasped. "You're kidding, right?"

"That would explain today's visit," she said.

"I guess it would," I murmured.

"Oh, Ida," Patty chortled. "You little minx."

ONCE I KNEW the letters were from Stump, I didn't read any more. He was such a private, gentle man that I couldn't intrude in his personal life. Instead, once Patty and Thomas had left, I carefully wrapped them in their ribbon and was about to put them in the box when more folded papers in the bottom of the box caught my eye.

Thinking they were more letters, I lifted them from the box to add them to the bundle, but to my surprise, the pages weren't stationery like the others. They were thick and coarse, like construction paper.

I slowly unfolded the first one, noting the wear at the edges. Bright orange and red crayon lines were slowly revealed, and when I had the page fully opened, my jaw dropped.

It was my drawing.

Ida had kept my illustrated insult for all those years.

My heart sunk in my chest as I thought about how it must have made her feel. I lifted the next page, expecting to see one of Tim's drawings, but when I unfolded it, I saw my name scrawled in the bottom corner.

I couldn't remember creating it, but there was a field of yellow flowers with two figures, one large and one small, walking hand in hand.

I exhaled, relieved at the sweetness of the picture.

When I turned the page over, my breath caught in my throat.

In childish print, complete with backward letters, were the words, "I love Ida."

Tears pricked my eyes, as I opened the final two drawings and saw more of the same. Butterflies, birds shaped like the letter *m*, and the word *love* in bold black print.

I left the letters from Stump in the box and carried the drawings into the bedroom, where I laid them on my bedside table— *Ida's* bedside table—and smiled.

AFTER WORK THE following day, I drove to JT's with the shoebox on my passenger seat and hope in my heart.

When I entered the shop, the bell rang and JT himself came to greet me.

"Ethan filled me in on Ida's collection. Are you ready to sell?" he asked.

"Yeah," I told him. "All but one. I'm keeping the raccoon."

He named a price and I told him I'd bring the creatures by later in the week.

"Is there any chance I might be able to speak to Ethan?" I asked, when our business was complete.

"Bookworm!" JT shouted, in the general direction of the workshop.

My palms were sweating by the time he appeared in the doorway. Rather than looking delighted to see me, as I'd secretly hoped, he didn't even smile.

"Hey," I said, my own wavering.

"Hey," he responded, with a nod.

Dead silence.

"Freakin' *Masterpiece Theatre* out here," JT groaned, slipping into the back.

"Can you talk?" I asked, once he was gone.

"I can listen," Ethan said, shoving his hands into the front pockets of his cords.

"Okay, that's good, because I wanted to tell you how sorry I am." I waited for a response, but there was none. "I was rude to you when all you tried to do was help me." Still nothing. "And you *did* help. Stump fixed the wiring issue and he's got someone coming to handle the floor on the weekend."

"Great," Ethan said, dryly.

"I don't know what to say," I stammered. "I miss you, Ethan."

He started to move toward me, but apparently changed his mind.

"I know we haven't known each other long," I continued, "but the time we've spent together has meant a lot to me and . . . well, what I'm trying to say is," I cleared my throat, nervously. "I'm trying to tell you that . . . the thing is . . . can you please give me another chance?"

He looked at me for several seconds before his lips curled into a smile. "Of course, I can."

I stepped behind the counter to give him a hug and a fast smooch, but once I caught a whiff of his clean, soapy smell, I was in it for more than a quick peck on the cheek.

His lips met mine and he tasted so familiar and so sweet that I never wanted to stop kissing him. Our tongues chased each other and I murmured his name, totally caught up in the moment.

That is, until JT's voice interrupted us. "Jesus Christ."

Ethan and I leapt apart as though there were flames between us. I could only guess that I was a deeper shade of red than he was, and he was *crimson*. He shoved his hands in his pockets and JT rolled his eyes at both of us before heading for the back room.

"Hey, JT?" I asked. "Could I see Stump for a second?"

He smirked. "For some of that, I'm sure he'll be right out."

"I just meant—" I began, but he was gone. I turned to face Ethan. "I really have missed you, you know."

"So have I."

When Stump entered the room, I wasn't sure how to handle my delivery. I didn't want to embarrass him, so half of me regretted that I'd brought the letters in at all. I smiled as gently as I could and stepped toward him, box extended in my hand.

"What's this?" he asked, raising an eyebrow as he took the box.

"Something I found that belongs to you. Something that seems to have been treasured for many years," I said, softly.

As he lifted the lid, I saw a glimmer of recognition in his face.

"Ethan, will you walk me out?" I asked, turning away to allow Stump some privacy.

"Sure," he said, following me, only asking what was going on when we were safely outside the shop. When I told him about the letters, he leaned in close to my ear and whispered, "You'll have a box of your own. I'll make sure of it."

Goose bumps ran rampant all over my body.

"Who are you?" I asked, my voice filled with wonder.

He smiled at me. "I'm your guy."

Twenty

I FOUND MYSELF in front of the sewing machine a lot in the following days, hunched over bits and pieces of fabric that gradually became a mini wardrobe, and the closer the craft fair deadline got, the more excited I became.

And when I wasn't sewing, there was other work to be done. Painting the upstairs was a breeze, as I had help from Ethan one night, Thomas another, and when the stars aligned I had time with both. We laughed and joked a lot, the three of us, and the sound made Ida's house feel like a home.

IT TURNED OUT that Mom and Dad had been serious about flying in to help, and while the big issues had already been taken care of, there were lots of little details for Dad to attack.

The Saturday they were due to arrive, Ethan, Thomas, Patty, and I had decided to take a day trip to Astoria, but at the last minute, Patty backed out in favor of a quiet day at home.

The remaining three of us left Portland and drove north to Longview, where Ethan pulled off the interstate and through town. Within minutes, we were crossing a sprawling bridge that took us over endless stacks of logs and lumber, then cruising up a long hill, complete with a scenic viewpoint pullout. He stopped the car and we got out to admire the beauty below us.

"How are pulp mills scenic?" I asked, frowning at the pipe stacks and smoke dominating the landscape.

"The smoke looks like clouds," Thomas explained, patiently. "Clouds from a machine."

"It does, doesn't it?" Ethan said, lifting him up for a better view. "Beauty is just a matter of perspective." He looked at me and grinned. "It's all about recognizing it." He winked. "And I have a pretty good eye."

"Are you going to kiss her?" Thomas asked.

"Yup," he said.

"Again?" Thomas covered his eyes.

"*Always,*" Ethan laughed before pressing his lips against mine.

"Oh, brother," Thomas groaned, then broke into a fit of giggles.

Thankfully, our exuberant audience of one wasn't enough to stop Ethan, whose lips lingered, making my toes curl in their boots.

We drove onward, winding through greenery until we reached the scenic little town with the towering bridge and parked the car at Safeway so Ethan could show Thomas the local marine life.

"Seals!" Thomas shrieked, running toward the pier and losing his hat in the process.

Ethan chased it down in the wind and we caught up with the kid, who was mesmerized by the barking beasts scattered and sunbathing.

"Actually, they're sea lions," Ethan told him, crouching down to Thomas's level.

I stood back to watch them and a middle-aged woman joined me.

"It's nice to see a young family out enjoying themselves," she said, smiling. "It reminds me of when Bill and I just had our oldest, Shelley."

I was too stunned to respond.

We look like a family?

"Boys certainly do look up to their fathers," she continued, watching them.

I started to tell her that Ethan and Thomas weren't related, that none of us were, but then it seemed pointless to correct her. I'd never see her again, and what difference did it really make?

"They do," I agreed. "That little guy can't get enough of him." *True enough.* Thomas was always delighted to be around Ethan.

Why does that make me so damn happy?

Because you're delighted to be around both of them.

I could feel my cheeks flush with color.

"You'd better get some sunscreen," the woman said. "You're already a bit pink. It doesn't take much around here."

"I will," I murmured, lifting my hand to the heated skin as I watched the guys and grinned.

We stopped for lunch at Andrew and Steve's Diner, and got cozy in an old brown booth.

"I'll have the fish and chips," Ethan said, when the waitress came to take our order.

"Me too," Thomas chimed in. "Please."

"With tartar sauce?" she asked him.

Thomas looked to Ethan for an answer.

"Do you *like* tartar sauce?" Ethan asked.

"Do *you*?" Thomas countered.

"I love it."

Thomas turned to the waitress, smiling as he said, *"I love it."*

Ethan shot me a little smile and my heart fluttered in response.

WE LEFT THE coast in mid-afternoon, and made the drive back to the city. I was keen to see my folks, but nervous about them meeting Ethan. He'd come to mean so much to me in such a short period of time that I could only hope they'd understand and adore him like I did.

Thomas fell asleep in the backseat, so Ethan and I spoke softly all the way home. He rested his hand on my knee while I drove, reminding me of the way my dad showed affection for my mom.

Everything about him, and about us, felt right.

"I love you," he whispered, and my heart swelled in my chest, to the point that I thought it would burst.

"I love you, too."

Somehow, the moment was only made sweeter when I heard a tiny sigh of contentment from the backseat.

WE ARRIVED BACK at the house thirty minutes before my folks' flight would land and woke Thomas up.

"Did you have a good day?" I asked as I opened my car door.

"The best day *ever*," Thomas announced.

Before I could get out, he was standing on the driveway next to me, with a shy smile on his face.

"What is it?" I asked, smiling back at him.

He leaned toward me and gave me a bubblegum scented kiss on the cheek. Before I could react, he whispered, "I love you," and ran toward Patty's house.

"Very cute," Ethan murmured, watching him go.

I sat in awed silence, touched to the core as I realized that the most powerful kiss I'd *ever* received was courtesy of a five-year-old.

The amazing part was that I loved him, too.

In a bit of a daze, I led Ethan into the house so he could have a drink while I showered before heading to the airport. But just as I was about to climb the stairs, there was a frantic beating on the front door.

"What the hell?" I murmured, racing to answer.

I opened the door to find Thomas, wide-eyed and terrified.

"What's wrong?" I asked, dropping to my knees.

"Grandma," he choked. "She fell."

"Where is she?"

"In the kitchen," he sobbed.

I lifted him into my arms and ran to Patty's house, cutting across the lawn and taking out an azalea in the process, Ethan following close behind.

The front door was hanging open and as soon as I was through it, I placed Thomas on his feet and Ethan said to both of us, "Stay right here, okay?"

I nodded, and Thomas rubbed his runny nose with the sleeve of his hoodie. He looked so tiny, scared, and sad, my heart constricted and it was all I could do to speak.

"Everything's going to be okay, Thomas," I told him.

What the hell do you know?

BETWEEN THE SIRENS, flashing lights, and concerned neighbors, it was all a bit of a blur.

Ethan rode to the hospital in the ambulance with Thomas and Patty while I raced to the airport to pick up my parents. Despite the time difference and the long flight, they insisted that we go straight to the hospital as soon as we left baggage claim.

Dad looked tired but determined to help with the house, toting a suitcase packed with how-to books and his illustrious tool belt.

When we arrived at the hospital, Ethan met us in the waiting area, Thomas utterly exhausted and asleep in his arms. After a brief introduction to my parents, he said, "It doesn't look good, Laur. Massive coronary."

"Oh my god," I whispered, glancing at the limp form of an already orphaned boy.

"I know," he sighed. "I'm going to take him back to your place and put him to bed, okay?"

"Thank you." I leaned over to kiss his cheek, and he gave my shoulder a quick squeeze before leaving.

I watched him go, then turned to see Mom smiling.

"I met someone," I said, with a shrug that belied all Ethan meant to me.

"Someone very special," Mom said, not fooled for an instant.

Mom, Dad, and I caught up in hushed voices for a little while, and when I confessed to my fight with Tim, they both looked distinctly uncomfortable.

"We weren't going to say anything until it's all taken care of," Mom said.

"Until *what's* taken care of?" I asked, suspiciously.

She looked to Dad, who nodded. "Your brother's been in a little bit of trouble."

"What kind of trouble?"

"He's racked up some heavy gambling debts," Dad finished for her.

"Tim?" I asked, incredulous.

"He wasn't just using the Internet for dating," Mom said, wincing slightly.

So that's why he wanted me to sell the house.

"We're helping him take care of it," Dad said, quietly.

"It's been quite a year," Mom said, stifling a yawn as the day caught up with her. "Quite a year."

She eventually fell asleep on the couch, so I sat and watched my father scan the index of his plumbing book, running his fingertip down the column until he hit his target and flipped to the correct page.

As he read, I thought about some of the phone conversations we'd had in the past few months, when I'd called in an emotional state over Daniel and he'd gone into problem-solving mode, trying to fix everything.

I thought of all the times I'd cried into the receiver while he was on the kitchen phone, awkward and pragmatic, while Mom murmured her support on the bedroom extension.

I recalled the many times I'd called and after the initial greeting, Dad had hurried to say, "Your Mom's not here," as though warning me against an emotional outburst he was afraid he couldn't comfort properly, or the times when he was alone on the other end and kept repeating phrases like, "You sound good, Laur. Just terrific. Should I have Mom call when she gets back?", and I sensed he was crossing his fingers to end the call before the tears started.

He wasn't an overly emotional man, but he'd done his best, and I loved him for it.

"Hey, Dad?" I said, leaning toward him. "Thanks for everything you've already done, and all that you're willing to do at the house this week."

He looked at me for a moment, eyebrows slightly furrowed. "Well, I'm your dad."

"I know, but first all the Daniel stuff, and now this." I pointed to his stack of books. "Not all dads do *this*."

"I want to," he said, almost defensively.

"I *know*, Dad. That's the whole point. I'm trying to thank you."

"Well, you're welcome." He awkwardly cleared his throat.

"Lauren?"

"Yes?"

"You're a really good kid."

A sudden stinging behind the eyes threatened tears, so I nodded abruptly, and bit my lip.

After nearly an hour, a doctor entered the room.

"Ms. Peterson?"

"Yes," I said, rising from the bench.

"I'm sorry."

"Oh," I whispered, heart sinking. "*Oh.*" I sat down again, stunned.

We woke Mom, and let her know that it was time to go home, and on the way out to the car, she asked the crucial question that I knew was in both of their minds.

"So, what do you think will happen to that dear little Thomas?"

I already knew the answer.

"He's mine," I told them.

"What?" Mom gasped, stopping in her tracks.

I took a deep breath. "While we were waiting for the ambulance, Patty was still conscious, and she asked me to take him."

"And you said *yes?*" Dad said, shocked.

"I did."

"Lauren," Mom said, "That's a huge decision, an *enormous* undertaking." She looked to my father for help. "My god."

"It can't be legally binding," he said, shaking his head.

"I hope it is," I said, quietly. "And if it isn't, I'll fight for him."

"What?" Mom gasped again. "*Why?*"

I thought of the little boy with the missing tooth, the boundless curiosity, and the ability to make me laugh.

"Because when I told Patty yes, it was the one time in my life I blurted something I really *meant.*"

Epilogue

RACHEL AND STEVEN are getting married in a couple of months, and gearing up for the celebration of the century. I'm doing my bit to support her, which means making an olive green dress with puffy shoulders and an empire waist, which I'll actually have to *wear* on the big day, god help me. The communication lines are open between us, and the friendship is stronger than ever.

Gavin and Lucy have moved in together, and their relationship seems to be moving along beautifully. She still works at Knutsen, and he continues to freelance at home, which means he has dinner on the table when she walks through the front door every evening. The romantic sparks are flying fast and furiously, so dinner usually has to be reheated.

For reasons unknown, Candace is no longer eating foods with names that begin with *T* or *P.*

When ordered by the court, my brother joined Gambler's Anonymous and he has paid back nearly half of his gambling debt, but lost his Internet girlfriend to cyberspace. Our bond is tenuous, but with the help of regular e-mail and phone calls, it's getting a bit stronger by the day.

Dad ran into a bit of trouble with the tub upstairs, which left him in the care of a physician and my house in the care of a licensed plumber (who was willing to take Visa). He and Mom safely returned to Florida and are still enjoying the retired life, learning how to salsa and routinely sweeping each other off their feet, on and off the dance floor.

The craft fair was a tremendous success and I am now the proud owner of a part-time business, called Scraps, complete with a fabulous logo, designed by my very best *male* friend, Gavin. I still work for Knutsen Insurance, but if my business keeps building the way it has been, I won't be for long.

Ethan moved into Ida's place with me, along with *his* stuffed menagerie, which has joined the raccoon on the upstairs landing. He's still at JT's taxidermy shop, where he's making all kinds of great contacts for the future. As far as personal contact goes, he's romantic, sweet, and more than I ever hoped for.

And as for Thomas? He's doing much better than anyone expected, under the circumstances. His bedroom, next to mine, is packed with books, models, and unbridled enthusiasm. He's about to enter first grade, so we're off to buy school supplies this afternoon.

I'm twenty-six years old and I've been full of a lot of things in my life.

Full of spunk.

Full of loneliness.

Full of bravado.

Full of crap.

But when I look into the eyes of that little boy, *my* little boy, for the first time in my life I'm truly full of love.

Just full of it.